I0561866

TWISTED JOURNEYS

Albert Trajstman spent half a biblical lifespan working in science. He is the author of numerous publications that have appeared in learned scientific journals. Following a number of life changing events he ceased exercising his brain's left side to give his right side a go. Initially he tried his hand at performance poetry and he published a book of poetry. More recently he has appeared as an extra in numerous local and international TV miniseries and some movies.

In 2018 his first collection of novellas *Faraway Places* was published by Hybrid Publishers.

Also by Albert Trajstman

Faraway Places (2018)

TWISTED JOURNEYS

Three Novellas

Albert Trajstman

HYBRID
PUBLISHERS

Published by Hybrid Publishers

Melbourne Victoria Australia

© Albert Trajstman 2022

This publication is copyright. Apart from any use
as permitted under the Copyright Act 1968, no part may be reproduced
by any process without prior written permission from the publisher.
Requests and inquiries concerning reproduction should be addressed to
the Publisher, Hybrid Publishers,
PO Box 52, Ormond, Victoria, Australia 3204.

www.hybridpublishers.com.au

First published 2022

 A catalogue record for this
book is available from the
National Library of Australia

ISBN: 9781925736878 (p)
9781925736885 (e)

Cover design: Marchese Design
Typeset in Minion Pro

In Memory
of
Adam Trajstman and Renia (Hochrad) Trajstman

Contents

Journeys of a Prodigal Son

The pre-history of Niccolò Umberto

In which it is told of the rise and eventual fall of the Umbertos from the Year 1190 until 1552 when one Niccolò Umberto is banished from the family keep, once part of a now ruined castle, by his brother Frederick subsequent to the death of their father.

On the tenth of June in the year 1190 the Holy Roman Emperor, Frederick Barbarossa, died. While engaged in the Third Crusade, he died in the Saleph River in what is now Turkey but was then the Armenian Kingdom of Cilicia. There is, however, dispute about the circumstances of his death. Was he thrown from his horse and drowned, weighed down by his armour? Did he suffer a heart attack in the river while bathing? Was the current too strong for a man in his sixties cooling down on a hot day? All this is in dispute. So little is known of the circumstances of his death. What is also little known is that the one who risked his own life to retrieve Barbarossa's body was a very minor noble called Oddo Umberto. In some circles of the time, Oddo Umberto was known as Umberto the Insignificant.

There is much we don't know. For example, the fact that Oddo Umberto had not been as selfless as chroniclers of the time would have you believe. You see, Oddo Umberto, in a slimy attempt to ingratiate himself with the great leader or perhaps promote himself, had, earlier that day, given Barbarossa a rather large gold signet ring. Umberto had had the ring made up at great expense; an expense he could little afford. His plan was to give the ring to the emperor in the hope of currying future favours. He had waited and waited throughout the crusade for just the right moment to present the emperor with the ring.

On the face of the signet ring there was an oversized *U*. It is telling that when Oddo Umberto had given the ring to Frederick Barbarossa, he made much of the *U*. Umberto claimed that it signified Barbarossa's superiority over all men as the *U* stood for the Germanic word *Über*; *über* meaning superior. It is not without irony that the *U* also stood for Oddo's family name. By giving Barbarossa the ring with its giant *U*, it is possible that Oddo was claiming affiliation with, rather than honouring, the emperor. We'll never know.

No one knows when on that hot June day Oddo Umberto presented Barbarossa with the ring but it is a fact that he did so, and it is a universally unknown fact the emperor was wearing that ring when he hit the water and subsequently, one way or another, died. Umberto was one of the few who had seen the emperor enter the water yet there were certainly many witnesses who saw Umberto rush to retrieve the emperor's body from the water. What was not known to those onlookers was that Oddo Umberto had rushed to Barbarossa's body to surreptitiously retrieve the signet ring he had given the emperor earlier that day. All that was visible to those onshore was Oddo Umberto retrieving the emperor's body; this was sufficient to label Oddo Umberto as a selfless hero. He had entered the water as Umberto the Insignificant and emerged carrying Barbarossa's body as Umberto the Selfless.

Selfless heroes who risk their lives to save an emperor should be rewarded, and so it was that Oddo Umberto was rewarded. He was rewarded immediately by Barbarossa's son Henry the next Holy Roman Emperor. And he was eventually rewarded by Pope Celestine III.

In a show of honouring the deceased, Holy Roman Emperor Oddo vowed to the next Holy Roman Emperor that from now until the end of days, any firstborn Umberto son would be given the name Frederick. On hearing this the next Holy Roman Emperor glared at Oddo and said, 'That's all very well, but what if any one of these future Fredericks of yours has no sons or, worse still, no offspring – then what?'

Obviously Oddo had not thought out his offer of naming rights and rashly replied, 'High One, there'll be no worry over this as there will always be sons.' And whether by miracle or by some genetic quirk, future Umbertos were to produce at least one son per senior Frederick.

Rewards for Oddo came in the form of an elevated title status and acquisition of confiscated lands in the Piedmont region. The titles gave Umberto entrée into portions of society to which he had been previously denied. Such access led to opportunities for increased wealth but, more importantly, it led to his profitable marriage to Beatrice, the daughter of a prince from the Kingdom of Sicily. With that marriage came more land which, coupled with the lands he had been given in Piedmont, generated wealth from tenants and profitable agriculture.

The Umbertos were now on their way up and subsequent generations of Fredericks were astute enough to increase the family's wealth and prestige. Wealth and prestige came not only from firstborn sons but also from other birth order children. Amongst lower birth order sons there were cardinals, including one who was a close run second for the papacy; there were military leaders who almost always fought on the winning side; there were entrepreneurs who financed great projects from which they were the ones who profited most. As for the daughters, beautiful or not, the family's rising fortunes were more than enough to secure favourable marriages for each of them – except for those who, for reasons best known to themselves, became nuns.

The trajectory of the Umberto family's fortunes and influences was, for three centuries, unstoppable and ever upwards, but like all things a downward turn was inevitable. Anything that goes up must eventually come down, for such is the law of family providence.

So by the early 1500s things had already soured for the Umbertos. By that time, too many Fredericks had made too many bad choices – ranging from backing losing sides in wars or making the wrong wagers at the tables to aggravating those more powerful than themselves. But all their misfortunes could not be attributed to wars, gambling or getting on the wrong side of the very powerful. Plague and dwindling returns from agricultural products from Umberto lands also played a part. And there was plague often. Plague reduced the pool of peasants – peasants whom the Umbertos had exploited to work Umberto land. Diminishing peasant numbers made it more difficult to turn a profit from their labours.

Plague should know no class, but for some reason it sought out the Umbertos and hit them with a ferocity it had not meted out to other folk. Perhaps the genetic quirk that had assured a supply of sons in each generation was responsible for an extraordinary susceptibility to plague. In sweeps of the plague's scythe, too many of the Umbertos' brightest and youngest were eliminated – leaving only the dullards and the very old. Dullards and the very old are not great material to maintain family fortunes, let alone rebuild it.

By the mid-1500s, all that was left of the Umbertos was an old man, Frederick the elder, and his two sons, Frederick the younger and Niccolò; Frederick the elder's wife had died in childbirth during the delivery of Niccolò. As for the Umberto fortunes all had, by this time, been lost, other than a fraction of land in Piedmont that Oddo Umberto had been rewarded with in the twelfth century. That fraction of land that remained in the mid-1500s contained a small number of tenant farmers and a ramshackle castle tower which the last of the Umbertos used as their home. The Umbertos were now once again where it all began in 1190 – insignificant.

Frederick the younger was the favourite son and Niccolò was merely tolerated by both Fredericks. Frederick the elder never ceased blaming Niccolò for causing the difficult birth that had led to the death of his wife. He saw no value in this son and thanked God that Niccolò had not been his firstborn. On the other hand, the elder Frederick was besotted by his namesake and this son, Frederick the younger, could do no wrong. In all he did, Frederick the younger excelled – a sharp mind, an accomplished horseman and pious to a fault. Frederick the elder was sure that when he died he would be passing on what was left of the estate to a worthy inheritor. He was comforted by the thought that this son might be the one who would rebuild the Umberto reputation and fortune.

There was no love lost between the brothers and they despised each other. Each saw in his brother all that was bad in the world and so when Frederick the elder died Frederick the younger banished his brother from the household and all their lands in Piedmont. To tell the truth, Niccolò didn't see it as a banishment rather it was fraternal permission to strike out and be his own man unencumbered by the shadow of his sanctimonious brother.

Frederick had, of course, inherited all whereas Niccolò inherited nought except for a gold signet ring with an outsized U – the same ring that Oddo Umberto had given to and retrieved from Barbarossa on the tenth of June 1190.

Niccolò Umberto meets Lorenzo Delmare in Florence

In which Niccolò Umberto makes the acquaintance of the Venetian merchant Lorenzo Delmare and of the disagreement with a renowned artist over the price of a commissioned portrait. Promising to arrange a better and cheaper artist in Venice to paint the said portrait Niccolò Umberto accompanies Lorenzo Delmare to Venice.

Being what in those days was considered a handsome young man, being gifted with an easygoing nature and most of all, free of the overbearing piety of his brother, Niccolò Umberto sowed more than his allotted share of wild oats on his journey from Piedmont. As long as he was making his way away from Piedmont, he cared little of where he was heading. Surviving on his luck, charm and the generosity of strangers, he eventually made it to Florence.

In a Florence monastery for the night he made the acquaintance of a Venetian, Lorenzo Delmare. Lorenzo Delmare was in his late fifties, short, rotund and bald. What he lacked in physical attributes he more than compensated for with verbosity. He had a keen eye for quality and did not fail to notice Niccolò's gold signet ring. Lorenzo Delmare was quick to laugh at any joke – his or those of others. He found it impossible to deliver a joke without laughing during the telling of it. And as for listening to a joke, he could not help but laugh throughout its telling in anticipation of the punchline.

Lorenzo Delmare was a businessman who made more than a comfortable living by importing goods from the East and exporting whatever he could from northern Italy back to the East. Overall he would have been happy to be described as a prosperous, bald, jolly, stout man who loved his wife Rosetta, loved his daughter Cherubina, and loved his mistress the Duchessa di Palma. The order of those loves, however, was debateable and open to alteration, dependent on the direction of the winds.

After their evening meal and after too much wine, Lorenzo admitted he was in Florence to commission a painting of himself to present as a gift to his wife on account of their forthcoming thirtieth wedding anniversary.

'Tomorrow I go to the studio of the distinguished artist Ridolfo Ghirlandaio to commission my portrait. I've heard his skills at creating one's likeness are unparalleled. I suppose while I'm there, he'll scrutinise my visage and demeanour. Perhaps he will make some sketches and from there, after a time, he will commit my likeness in oils onto a canvas.'

Delmare was warming to this pleasant young man, so he added, 'Please come with me as it would do me a great honour if you would accompany me tomorrow.'

'I am available. So yes, I'll go with you. But there is something I could suggest and please forgive my directness. Given you say this Ridolfo Ghirlandaio is such a distinguished artist, I assume that his skill doesn't come cheaply, but can you be sure your money will be spent the way it is intended? It is possible that the great artist will take your money but arrange for an apprentice of lesser skills to do the work.'

Delmare was impressed by the young man's canniness. 'Well put. Very well put.'

Niccolò continued, 'And on another matter, you say the portrait is a gift for your good wife. A portrait is an excellent choice, if you have the money, and no doubt it is obvious you do.'

Delmare was pleased that the young man had concluded that he, Lorenzo Delmare, importer and exporter of Venice, was a man of substantial financial standing.

'And I'm sure you love your wife, but a greater show of love would be if you arranged for a portrait of your wife rather than one of yourself. Believe me, though I am not of your maturity and worldliness, I know how the female mind operates.'

'Yes, yes. Yes, I follow your line of thinking. A portrait of myself might be viewed as an act of conceit whereas a portrait of my dearest Rosetta would be viewed as an act of love. You are indeed a canny young man.'

The next morning the two newly bonded friends went to Ridolfo Ghirlandaio's studio where, rather than discuss the commission of Delmare's portrait, they discussed the commission of his wife's portrait. What seemed last night as simply a change of a portrait's subject turned out to be an impasse. Lorenzo's wife was in Venice and the artist was in Florence. The artist offered to send an apprentice to Venice to do the initial sketches and then the work would be completed by the master in Florence. To Delmare's surprise, his young companion took charge in dealing with the master. 'If you intend to use an apprentice then my friend here, the much respected Lorenzo Delmare, would require a reduced charge for the portrait.'

The artist responded, 'No, no, no. Definitely not at a reduced fee. I will have to send my best apprentice away from here so as to do the sketches. There is a cost to me if he is not in my studio. I lose his services in Florence and then there is a cost to me for his travel, food and lodgings. No, in fact the cost must be higher.'

Delmare was anxious not to lose the services of the great Ridolfo Ghirlandaio. If it meant an apprentice would do the sketches at a higher cost then so be it, after all he didn't want to be thought of as penny-pinching. He wanted to ask how much more it would cost if an apprentice travelled to Venice to do the preliminary sketches. Before he could say anything Umberto, in responding to Ghirlandaio's justification of the higher fee, said, 'That is true, but surely the skills of any your apprentices, even the most talented of your apprentices, would not equal those of their master. Those sketches would not be equal to those a great master like you would produce. After all you, the great Ridolfo Ghirlandaio, *supposedly* have the reputation for capturing facial likeness and character. So if an apprentice does the sketches, then a reduced charge is definitely appropriate.'

'There can be no reduced fee. I have already told you, the cost will be higher if the portrait's subject is in Venice and my studio is in Florence. On the other hand, Signor Delmare could allow his wife to sit before me in Florence.'

For Delmare that proposition was out of the question – out of the question, regardless of whether his wife travelled to Florence with or without him. Florence was no place for a virtuous woman like his Rosetta.

The meeting with the great master was not going well. It ended abruptly with Umberto slapping the bench so hard that the brushes rattled in their jars. 'This is extortion!' Then grabbing Delmare's arm, he stood and directed him out of the studio, saying to the artist, 'We will arrange a better deal in Venice – and with a better artist!'

Delmare was confused. What had started as a perfectly simple plan to present his wife with a wedding anniversary portrait had been scuttled by a young man he hardly knew. Though the end result was that there would be no Ghirlandaio portrait of him or his wife, he had to admire Umberto's boldness and he thought such a spirited young man could be an asset in his business ventures.

As Niccolò had no particular plans, he said to Delmare that he would be happy to travel with him to Venice, and if Delmare could put him up, he would seek out a cheaper and better artist in Venice to produce Rosetta's portrait. A grateful Delmare replied, 'Of course. I implore you to come to Venice with me as my guest.'

Niccolò Umberto's offer to procure a cheaper and better artist in Venice was an empty offer, for he knew no artists in Venice or elsewhere; in fact, he neither cared for nor knew much about art. All things considered, it had been a good morning's work for him as he had secured, for himself, a sojourn in Venice with food and lodgings included. He now looked forward to the company of an amiable and wealthy man. He looked forward to Venice and meeting Delmare's wife and daughter – especially the daughter.

Venetian escapades

In which Niccolò Umberto comes to live in the Delmare household and makes the acquaintance of Cherubina, Rosetta and the Duchessa di Palma. Niccolò Umberto assists Lorenzo Delmare in two successful commercial ventures but fails to search for a suitable portrait artist. Niccolò enjoys the carnal pleasures of the women of Delmare's household and of Delmare's mistress. He enjoys the distractions of the three women and of Venice to excess. Consequences of his pleasures force him to decamp for Bologna.

Eager to get Rosetta's portrait underway, Delmare asked Umberto how he would get him a better artist at a better price. 'You've been here one week and so far you have not even left the house, let alone come up with a suggested artist.'

'Quite right about that but I've been giving the matter of the portrait a great deal of thought.'

'So what have you come up with?'

'So far nothing, as I don't know Venice well. I need time to research the possibilities.'

'Very well, explore Venice. Take your time, but remember the wedding anniversary date approaches.'

There was something about women and in particular the female form that had always fascinated Niccolò. Maybe it started with a wet nurse's breasts; breasts that were not his mother's. Initiation to the softness of women's bodies came perhaps from stolen glimpses of his careless custodians naked at their ablutions – women of pendulous breasts or dimpled thighs or fulsome bottoms, and sometimes women possessing all three attributes. Initiation to the warmth of women's bodies came perhaps from an innocent soul who allowed an already not so innocent but cold child to snuggle up to her in bed. Later there came the housemaids, so many housemaids, who saw the possibility of personal advancement by succumbing to the advances of the master's son.

So it is no wonder that the adult Niccolò's fancies of women were of soft feminine roundness, were of the caress of feminine curves and were of the mysterious region between thighs and bottom; especially that. Then there was the heady mind spin triggered by their almost imperceptible musty animal scent, so faint that he believed that he was the only man gifted with the ability to discern it.

Umberto knew that reducing women to just these attributes was shallow; as he matured he added to their desirability the ways in which they differed from him. The conquest of their bodies was for him straightforward but the conquest of their spirit was not.

High up under the rafters in his room in Delmare's house and looking at the canal below, it seemed to Niccolò that if cities had genders then Venice was a woman. In masculine cities you travelled on solid ground. Stamp on any road, street or alley and a leg jolt followed. In masculine cities you knew where you were. You were in a solid and straightforward world. In Venice the canals' soft and pliable watery surfaces offered no resistance to a stamping foot. Not even a hint of a leg jolt; rather, the surfaces could part to engulf you, maybe drown you. Away from the canals the damp alleys followed no masculine sensibility. Instead, their logic was unknowable. The alleys were written in a code that would take someone like him more than one lifetime to decipher. Like women's hearts, the alleys were unreadable to Niccolò. The allure of women lay in their mystery.

In Venice mystery and its allure wafted from the Adriatic carried by salty breezes; mystery hid in fog-bound alleys; mystery wrapped the morning bodies fished from the canals. Undecipherable riddles and enigmas – Venice was secrets. Secrets whispered by unseen muffled voices that carried on a canal or came from behind a courtyard's wall. Venice was the woman who put her best face to the world while much more was hidden beneath the satin, lace and velvet. And what was hidden was more desirable.

From the mossy walls of the canal houses and their stained high-water marks, from the perpetual puddles in the piazzas to the dark dead ends of mouldy alleys, Venice was damp. Venice was a moist city smelling of ripeness, and for Niccolò Umberto Venice was feminine and he reckoned it was for the best that it was so.

Venice was a woman, yes, but there would be three women in particular. There was Cherubina, Delmare's daughter. Sweet Cherubina. Cherubina of the pretty face she had not inherited from her father. Cherubina of the slight, delicate form she had not inherited from her mother. There was Delmare's wife, the buxom Rosetta – ripe and juicy – and not far away, smouldering in a palazzo on the Grand Canal, there was the widowed lusty Duchessa Di Palma, *la stupenda*, the finest cut of a woman there ever was.

After Niccolò Umberto had spent much more than one week enjoying Delmare's hospitality and exploring Venice, Delmare broached the question of the wedding anniversary portrait again. 'Venice is a fine place, isn't it, and I'm sure you know it better now. So tell me, Niccolò, have you made any progress on the portrait? Time is of the essence.'

'Venice is a wonderful place, the canals, San Marco's and all that.'

'Yes. Yes. Indeed Yes. But the portrait? Have your meanderings taken you any closer to a suitable artist or even a suitable studio?'

'Well no – but I'm working on it. These things take time.'

And so Delmare allowed Umberto more time.

Another week passed and Delmare, now unable to stand the waiting, asked, 'How's it going with the portrait?' During that week Umberto had played *Primero* and *Gilet* in a tavern suitably far away from Delmare's house. He had spent time sitting in the sun by a particular backwater canal that had taken his fancy; there he fantasised about Cherubina – yet another fancy. And then when the sea breezes stiffened enough so as to whip up ripples on the canal, he made his way back to the Delmares. In truth, during that entire week he had neither tried to find an artist nor even thought of his promise to Delmare. Nevertheless, he answered Delmare's question with: 'Unfortunately still no progress, Lorenzo. No progress at all. Please understand that setting up these things takes time. You've got to find the right studio, find the right artist and find the right price. That's a lot of finding.

'In the meantime I'd be only too happy to help with your business enterprises – at no cost to you, as I'm grateful that you've given me food and lodgings. Now, not on the topic of the portrait but on the topic of money, allow me to put this plan to you. I have an idea how I could help you make a handsome profit.'

Always on the lookout for a business opportunity, Delmare asked, 'You have a plan that can turn me a profit? How so?'

Early in his stay at the Delmare's, Lorenzo had taken Niccolò to the storeroom where he kept his stock. Proudly Lorenzo had shown him the spices from the East, carpets from Persia and beaten copper trays from India, amber from northern countries and even lapis lazuli beads from Egypt. Merchandise from all points of the compass – aromas of the spicy East, warm glows of the amber from the cold North, glittering jewellery from the dazzling South and fabrics from the mysterious Orient.

Lorenzo explained that he had to clear stock to make room for ivory tusks that were already on the way from Africa. His biggest problem was to clear the finest silk damask without incurring a financial loss; he had over-purchased and now the fabric was stacked on pallets along one wall, from floor to ceiling. Lorenzo explained, 'As you can see, there's too much damask! I am stuck with the blasted fabric. Once it was all the rage and now no one wants to buy. If I can only clear the damask then the ivory can be stored. The problem is I can store neither the ivory nor the damask in someone else's storehouse. I don't trust any of the other storehouse owners. They're too much like me – shifty. So I've got to do something with all that damask. Otherwise? Well I don't want to think of an otherwise.'

Now Niccolò returned to Delmare's over-supply of damask. 'That damask you showed me in your storeroom, I reckon I can get it moved at a profit to you.'

'I'm listening.'

'I've an idea how we can create a demand for it. A demand such that furniture upholsterers, curtain suppliers and even tailors will be screaming for it. In other words, make it all the rage again. I tell you it can be done.'

'I'm still listening.'

'No one in Venice knows me, do they?' Niccolò omitted to add '... apart from a few scruffy players and drinkers in an obscure tavern.' He continued, 'My plan is for me, an outsider to Venetians, a complete unknown, to visit all the appropriate businesses where that cloth should be of interest. Upholsterers, tailors, curtain makers and the like. If they have damask in their workshops they might want to sell it. I'll ask if they have any damask. Not just a small amount but a warehouse full of the stuff. They'll wonder why I would want damask in such volume. I'll be a bit evasive and then let them in on a secret: *I'll tell you something, but whatever you do don't tell anyone.* I'll say damask has become all the rage from Padua to Rome and the people down there just can't get enough of it: *They're using it in all sorts of ways. If they could eat it they would! The problem is that south, all the way down from Venice, damask is virtually unobtainable.* I'll also say, in confidence with a wink and a low voice, that a group of wealthy manufacturers from Rome sent me north on a damask-buying mission. I'll say they told me: *Buy every skerrick of damask you can get your hands on and arrange for shipment to us.* Then I'll add: *And judging by what these manufacturers said, they would pay me for my effort. I'd say they would be willing to pay a very good price for the damask I find. Like I said, it's all the fashion and very rare – I reckon my masters would be happy to pay up to three times the previous going rate!* Then I'll ask again: *So, no piddling amount. I want to know if you have damask in volume? Volume!* I'll finish by saying something like: *It's not just a fabric. In today's world it's become gold!'* The next part is where you fit in, Lorenzo. You go to all the businesses I visited and tell them you've got a lot of damask but quote a price that is twice the going rate. They'll jump at the opportunity to get the better of you. In the end you'll have unloaded all your damask *and* made a profit.'

'You sneaky devil ... I think your plan might work. Whatever happens, I'll be in the clear as I'm not identified with you. You, on the other hand, might be in trouble once it is found that you lied to all of them.'

'Not at all. I will only have to say that my so-called masters cheated me as well. The bastards in Rome lied to me about the demand for damask. And in fact, they robbed me because I had to fund my trip north out of my own resources on the promise of reimbursement. I will then cry some tears. Say my wife and child are in Rome with no means of support while I'm stuck in filthy Venice without money.'

'But surely if it's known you are in my house they will tie the two of us together.'

'Well, we'll have to carry out our *trick* in parts of Venice we don't frequent. And as I said, whatever happens we will have to make it look as if we have both been cheated. Me, like I've said. And you. You will have to make out you sold the damask at a great financial loss. Willing to give it a try?'

'I sold at a financial loss? I guess I could make it look like a loss. Why not? What if I can show I paid more for the damask than I sold it for? I could say that I was willing to sell at a loss to make way for the ivory. I have a trusted notary friend who could, for a small fee, falsely verify I stupidly paid four times the going rate. Maybe I could have been cheated by the same people who cheated you, who knows?'

'So what do you think?'

Delmare replied enthusiastically, 'Let's do it!'

⇌

And so the great Venice Damask Scam was born. And so it was that Lorenzo Delmare cleared space for the tusks and in the process made a hefty profit from the sale of all his damask. And so it was that Delmare, now suitably impressed by Niccolò Umberto's business shrewdness, regretted that he had already promised Cherubina to another. As for the fear that the victims of the scam would seek revenge on Delmare and Umberto? Well, that was not to pass because all those scammed preferred to carry their financial losses in secret rather than admit to the shame of being identified as having been foolish. Mind you, the success of the scam did not quell Delmare's anxiety regarding the portrait, and after the tusks had been delivered and stored he asked Umberto, 'By the way, Niccolò, any progress on the portrait?'

He replied, 'I'm still working on it.'

One day not long after the damask scam, Delmare was lamenting to Niccolò that he wished he had pink salt to sell. 'Oh, Niccolò, if only I could put my hands on some pink salt.'

At that time in Venice, for those who could afford it, pink salt had become very popular. To serve pink salt at your table was a mark of affluence; it was extremely expensive and it was the current fad. Pink salt came from the Himalayas. It was carried down treacherous mountains in heavy sacks on the backs of strange little people, loaded onto the backs of camels, carried across the deserts then, by a circuitous route involving many hands and many lands, loaded on boats bound for Venice. Quite a process for merchants to acquire the pink salt – even Delmare couldn't source it.

For effect Delmare repeated, 'Oh, Niccolò, if only I could lay my hands on some of that pink salt.'

Niccolò replied, 'I've been thinking about that pink salt and I reckon we can do something about it. What if we had salt that is better than pink salt? What if we had blue salt, green salt or red salt?'

'But there's only white or pink salt, and pink salt is what sells well.'

'True, but what if we had, say, red salt? What if it was made known that red salt was better than pink salt? What if it was said that it came from the deepest canyons far beyond the the mountains that harbour pink salt? What if it was made known how difficult it is to obtain? What if it was said that it tastes better than pink salt and is better for you than pink salt? And finally, what if it cost more than pink salt because of all the other what ifs? Then we would make a killing.'

'But we don't have red salt. No one has red salt because there's no such thing as red salt.'

'True, Lorenzo, but we can turn ordinary and readily available cheap white salt into immensely desirable, expensive, very rare red salt. As we'll be the only ones who have the red salt, the entire market is ours.'

'So what are you suggesting?'

'I'm suggesting we create a desire for red salt in Venice, then we create red salt and then we sell it exclusively. That's what I'm suggesting.'

Delmare was amazed by the young man's imagination; an imagination that had translated to another potentially profitable business venture. Umberto was a man after Delmare's own heart – a man who was prepared to cross the line of honest business transactions in the pursuit of a financial advantage. Yet again Delmare regretted Cherubina was already promised to the young Albanese brat.

For this new scam (for that's what Umberto was proposing), Delmare figured that if someone was gullible to fall for a red salt ruse then they deserved to lose their money. After all, he reasoned that ultimately no harm was done because pink salt was in itself just a sham in that it only differed from ordinary salt in colour and subsequent price. So what was the harm in pushing red salt?

Delmare then said, 'I see how your mind works. This red salt venture has an identical structure as our damask venture. You see, we create a desire for the product, albeit by subterfuge, and then become the only ones who can fulfil that desire.'

Niccolò replied, 'Exactly, Lorenzo!' and added with a cheeky grin, 'Just like the transaction of passions between the sexes – and that's just as Nature has ordained it.'

'Yes, that's right. I now feel at ease that we will be acting in accordance with the laws of Nature. After all, Nature's laws are greater than the laws of Man.'

First the two had to work out how to dye ordinary salt red; dye it in such a way that it did not poison anyone. For that, after some experimentation, they found that a concoction of chilled beetroot juice worked best. By experimentation the pair discovered the saturation point of chilled beetroot juice and were soon able to produce any quantity of blood-red salt. So now they had the means of manufacturing as much red salt from cheap white salt. The next step was to create a market for the red salt or what Delmare had called a *desire* for the product. This was Niccolò's job.

Niccolò set about spreading rumours about the beneficial and weird red salt from beyond China: *From a place so far away that it is yet to be named.* At every inn Niccolò asked for the marvellous red salt. Anywhere men congregated he told them that red salt aided sexual performance. How Umberto managed it is not certain, but he managed to convince Rosetta of the properties of a fantastic red salt: *Consumed daily and rubbed on the face it improves the complexion. Not only that, it increases a woman's attractiveness and delays ageing.* Despite that it would have been an advantage for Rosetta to be the only woman in Venice with knowledge of the red salt's properties, Rosetta, ever the gossip, shared the information with all women in her circle, women who subsequently shared the information with other women and so on. In taverns Umberto told their owners that red salt in meals would increase the thirst of patrons and therefore increase the sale of beverages. At market stalls he asked if they would sell him red salt. Of course no stall had it: *What! no red salt? What a pity. In places where it is sold it walks out the door as soon as it goes on sale. You can name your price.* Any place that served or prepared food, he mentioned the red salt and how patrons would find the dishes prepared incomparably delicious. In the kitchens of the households, grand and modest, he spoke to the cooks about the red salt and how it would improve the demeanour of their masters and mistresses: *They'll think you're an indispensable household member. Probably treat you like family. Your position will be secure for a lifetime. Red salt? Mark my words, they'll love you for it.*

In time word got around about the red salt. Everyone was eager to get their hands on this miraculous red salt. The time had arrived to flood the market with Delmare's red salt. This they did and, to compete with the pink salt, they decided to set the price slightly lower than pink salt. By turning cheap white salt into expensive red salt, Delmare made quite a profit. This time he shared some of the profit with Umberto, all the time thinking what a wonderful son-in-law he would have made.

There came a day when Delmare told Umberto that he would need to be away for three days. A grand old house in Vicenza had fallen on hard times and was selling off much of its chattels, and it seemed to Delmare that there might be items there that he could acquire for resale. For Umberto these were to be three very strange, carnally loaded days.

'From tomorrow I'll be away for three days. It will take me one day's travel to get to the estate, one day to examine its valuables and one day's return journey. While I'm gone there is nothing you need do for me save deliver this letter.' Then as an afterthought he added, 'And I beg you to make some progress on that portrait.'

With that he handed Umberto a letter addressed to Duchessa di Palma and an address on the Grand Canal. 'Please deliver it tomorrow around noon and under no circumstances read its content.'

Delmare left early next morning for his three days away, and about half an hour before noon Umberto set off to deliver Delmare's letter. After having been told to not read the letter, it was impossible for Niccolò not to read it. He stopped by a wall that had warmed in the morning sun. Resting his back against the warm wall he carefully unfolded the letter in such a way that it could be returned to the state it had been given to him. No one would know that he had read the content of the letter.

The letter to the Duchessa di Palma read:

> My dearest Isabetta,
>
> I have entrusted this boy to deliver this message that I, your ever eager stallion, am unfortunately unable to attend our prearranged tryst. It pains me, mia stupenda, mia Betta, to be absent from your amorous heart, your warmest and deepest parts. I promise that we will ride lustfully together at the earliest moment upon my return and then we will once more be conjoined in ecstasy.
>
> Yours and ever available,
> Renzo

Niccolò Umberto smiled and muttered to no one in particular, *Renzo? Betta? Mia stupenda? Renzo the stallion? Ass more likely. Sly bastard!* Armed with this revelation the day was panning out to be more interesting.

On being ushered to the duchessa's rooms, Niccolò saw an imposingly regal woman; a very presentable woman in her early forties. She was seated before a food-laden table that had already been set for two – Delamare and the duchessa. After dismissing her servants, she eyed Umberto from head to toe before she beckoned for him to come forward. At this point he handed her the letter. 'This is from my master Lorenzo Delmare and he has commanded I give it to you.'

She read the letter to herself, scrunched it up and dropped the ball into a jug of wine. 'Has your master told you of the letter's content?'

'No.'

'Have you instead read the letter behind his back?'

'No. Why do you ask, madam?'

'Oh, it's just that you strike me as one who would not have delivered a letter from Lorenzo without reading it.'

'As I said, madam, I have delivered his letter to you and that's as far as it goes.'

'Pity. But I do like the look of you. Are you hungry?'

'Yes.'

'I was expecting Lorenzo for this meal after which I was expecting him to stay with me for the rest of the afternoon. He's not here but you are, and that's no pity, so rather than waste this fine meal, I ask that you dine in Lorenzo's stead. Please sit yourself by me and let's dine.'

Niccolò sat as close to her as decorum with a stranger would allow but the duchessa insisted he pull his chair closer to her.

'Do you like oysters?' Before he could say one way or another she took the plate before him and said, 'Of course you do! Every man likes oysters so allow me to load your plate. Please pour us some wine. I am sure it has been improved by the infusion of Lorenzo's letter.'

They sat closer that would be accepted for strangers of the opposite sex. During the meal the duchessa would from time to time stroke his thigh, all the while explaining the intricacies of Venetian cooking. There were even times when she would let her hand linger on his crotch. He had in all his time never encountered a woman so forward. For Umberto this was new behaviour from a woman, and he wondered if such feminine behaviour was the norm in Venice.

After they had finished the carafe but not all the food the duchessa said, 'Enough of the meal. I was expecting Lorenzo today but he is not here. Pity. At least the table I had had prepared for that gluttonous little fellow has not been wasted thanks to you. I was expecting him to stay here for the afternoon with me but he is not here. In truth I have been primed with anticipation for the afternoon since this morning. Now that you've eaten in his stead, you should spend the afternoon with me in his stead also. So let's not waste the afternoon.'

The duchessa stood up from the table extended her hand to Umberto. He knew where matters were heading and he was eager for this post-meal experience. He took the duchessa's hand and she led him to her bedchamber where an afternoon of earthly delight was enjoyed by the pair.

When the afternoon and their passions had begun to wane the duchessa said, 'It's time you left. You have sufficiently exhausted me and, what's more, an old girl like me needs her rest.' In a reversal of their journey of several hours earlier, she took him by the hand and retraced their path back from her room and past the table that still bore the remnants of their noonday meal. As they passed the table she retrieved the scrunched up letter that now rested at the bottom of an empty wine jug. She gently unfolded it on the table and flattened it to press out the creases. 'Look, poor Renzo's letter is dry. Well, well, well, the ink hasn't run. The letter's still legible.' She reread the letter and then passed it over to Niccolò. 'Here, you take it. You never know – it might be of use to you one day.'

That evening Umberto replayed the events of the day, feeling no remorse for his dalliance with the duchessa; it had been most enjoyable. After all, he was a free agent able to engage in such affairs without harm to anyone. Delmare, on the other hand, was not a free agent, and his betrayal of poor Rosetta was another thing. How would Niccolò handle his knowledge of Delmare's infidelity? Though it was not his business, he resolved that he would tell Rosetta in the morning.

He knew that after dropping such a bombshell, his stay in the Delmare household would be obviously at an end. By telling Rosetta he would lose the friendship of Delmare and it would be apparent that he had not only read the letter but also divulged its content to Rosetta. It left him wondering from where his concern for the feelings of Rosetta had come; they had had not much in the way of conversations with each other. After all, his interactions with Rosetta were no more than those required for the sake of politeness. This contrasted with his relationship with Delmare which lay somewhere between friend and master–tutor. It was not like Niccolò Umberto to care one way or another about anyone other than himself, so he was at a loss to explain from where his new-found sense of morality had come. There was no way that exposing Delmare's infidelity would be of any benefit to Umberto; in fact it could come at a cost. The only explanation Niccolò could provide for his impending revelation to Rosetta is that he was going to enjoy the disruption it would cause in the Delmare household.

In the morning after his escapade with the duchessa, Niccolò found Rosetta alone in the kitchen. She was pounding a ball of dough with a vengeance. Every so often she would erotically massage the dough, then extend it before rolling it up into a ball again. Not knowing how to start, Umberto placed Lorenzo's letter on the table and just said, 'Read this.'

Rosetta wiped her hands on her hips, blew away some hair that had fallen across her flour-dusted face and picked up the letter. The result was nothing that Umberto had expected. She looked at the ceiling for a while before speaking. 'This explains a lot between Lorenzo and me. The best way I can put it is that for this past year we've been wife and husband in name only. Certainly not a couple as far as matrimonial obligations, if you know what I mean.'

Niccolò knew what she meant. Rosetta continued, 'Yes I'm angry and hurt, but that can keep for now. What I want is revenge. Revenge against Lorenzo, not his lover. I couldn't care less about that woman. It's Lorenzo I'd like to hurt. If I could cuckold him it would be sweet revenge. And for me, the sweetest revenge would be if I could do so behind his back without him ever knowing.'

'What is the point of that?'

'The point would be that I would know and forever be warmed by that knowledge. It would be something I had done that Lorenzo had not the slightest inkling of. I would look at his face and I would know something that would rend him if only he knew. That, my dear Niccolò, would be my power. It would be the sweetest revenge and one I could savour all my life!

'I have an idea that I should strike while my spirit is so inflamed. Would you do me the honour of taking me now? In this kitchen. On this table. Surrounded by the dough that I was preparing for his favourite dish.'

Events were unfolding in a way Umberto's wildest imaginings would not have considered possible. At Rosetta's mention of the dough he recalled her caressing and fondling of the dough, so how could he refuse her? He could only manage the questions, 'Here? Now?'

To which Rosetta answered, 'Yes, yes, yes. A thousand times yes!' And so it was that on the kitchen table, Niccolò Umberto obliged Lorenzo Delmare's wife.

Events that had happened over the past two days were unexpected. The women of Venice were certainly different from those of his previous experience; there was a forwardness that was at the same time disconcerting and yet appealing to Umberto. Having been prepared to risk his standing with Delmare over the disclosure of the letter's content, it was a relief that nothing would come of it. The irony was that after Rosetta's knowledge of the letter's content, her pleasure would be in not telling Lorenzo about her kitchen table frolic. Delmare would know neither that Rosetta knew of his infidelity nor of her revenge.

Events still had some further twists. The morning after Rosetta had wreaked her revenge and Umberto was descending the stairs, Umberto heard sobbing coming from Cherubina's room. For a moment he wondered if Cherubina had witnessed her mother's table top performance with him the day before. It was possible ... Rosetta and he would not have noticed an onlooker. In Umberto's experience, in the heat of passion awareness of the rest of the universe vanishes – only the two actors expand to fill the entire universe and there is nothing else.

As in the stories of chivalrous knights and maidens in distress, there had to be a maiden sobbing first and then a knight in shining armour to save her. Now here was a maiden in distress who might need rescuing. He entered her room and asked why she was crying. After some coaxing, Cherubina revealed the true source of her unhappiness.

'All the time I burn with desire. Eros will most surely send me mad! Everywhere I look I see the carnal. I see the curve of a man's calf and I burn. I imagine his manhood and I burn. Even the shape of certain fruit torment me. Even as I speak to you, I am sure there are couplings under every roof in Venice, behind every locked door and on every bed. The whole world is one lascivious throbbing organ and I long to be part of it. It seems that there is a great feast that everyone is enjoying yet I am excluded. All around me there is erotic throbbing, throbbing and throbbing of couplings. I can't remain virginal a moment longer. There is no end to my unrequited desire. My promised marriage is years and years away and ...' Here she broke off, thought for a moment and then with big cow-eyes looked directly at Niccolò Umberto. She begged, 'Please help me. Release me from this torment.'

After she had told him of her distress, she closed the door and they sat on her bed. Niccolò could have said no but here was an opportunity where he could take advantage. So he took the lead. The oddest thing then followed. Cherubina took out a carnival mask from the trunk at the foot of the bed. 'I saved it from last year's Carnival. Do you mind if I wear it when we ...' Here she broke off for a moment and then tried to add more but only got as far as saying, '... when you ...?'

'Of course I don't mind. But why the mask?'

Cherubina could have told him the true reason but only said that it seemed that their love-making would be more enjoyable for her that way. The real reason lay in the fact that she felt that to not wear the mask, she would be forever be embarrassed to face Umberto. With the mask she was someone else and not Cherubina. What's more, by wearing a mask Cherubina was being true to her Venetian roots, as the wearing of a mask liberated the wearer to engage in carnal delights with apparent freedom. Umberto still had an opportunity to act honourably and refuse but instead he said, 'Come here.' So with her skirts pulled up, bunched around her waist and wearing the mask she came to him.

For the third time in three days Umberto had obliged a woman of Venice. He mused that if cities had genders then Venice was certainly a woman; perhaps three women.

When Delmare returned from his three days' absence he asked, 'Did you deliver that letter?'

Umberto answered, 'Of course.'

Then Delmare asked, 'Much happen while I was away?'

'No, very quiet. Hardly anything at all. How was your visit? Buy anything?'

'No, there was just rubbish.'

For five weeks after he returned, Delmare took to bed with a chill he had picked up during his three days away. Then for the next three weeks after that he continued to feel poorly and he certainly never visited the duchessa over that time. Life for Niccolò Umberto in the Delmare household continued as before, but now with both Rosetta and Cherubina avoiding him.

Until one day during Delmare's illness Rosetta stopped him on his way out the door and said, 'I am pregnant. And it is without doubt you are the father.'

'Me?'

'Yes, you. I've not been with anyone else.'

'Lorenzo?'

'Certainly not him. Not with him for a very long time. It's definitely you.'

Wondering how he could extract himself from this dilemma, he was surprise when Rosetta added, 'I felt I should tell you but you need not worry about it. Pardon me if I speak frankly here but I can make Lorenzo the father. I will offer myself to him for as many times as I can. He will have me just as he has had that other woman. With daily rubbing of the red salt, my complexion will be fairer than his lover's. He will have me because I know the little pig will never overlook an opening if it is offered. He'll believe the child is his, such is his vanity. So vain that he would never believe that my pregnancy could happen without his doing.'

Rosetta's revelation and her solution to the matter deserved a drink, so Niccolò made his way to his usual tavern. He had only gone a few paces out of the Delmare house when two men who had been waiting for his appearance sidled up to him and demanded that he go with them.

'Why?'

'Because the duchessa has so requested. That's why.'

After the man spoke, Niccolò recalled seeing these men before when he had delivered Delmare's letter. One man had manned the street entrance to the duchessa's house and the other had ushered him to the duchessa.

As soon as her servants had left the room the duchessa told Niccolò that she was pregnant.

'Wonderful but why tell me?'

'Tell you? You're the father, dear boy. That's why.'

'Me? Why me and not someone else? Why not Delmare? You're lovers so it could have been Delmare. Someone else and not me?'

'Dear boy, it's you and only you and I'll tell you why. First, there are no others. Only Lorenzo – and of course, once with you the afternoon Lorenzo couldn't come.'

'So it still could be him.'

'It's not him. Have you heard of the hollowed lemon? I suppose not. Why should you, you're not a woman. Men! What do they know?' Answering her own question she loudly said, 'Nothing!'

The duchessa then went on to explain that on the afternoon she had spent with Niccolò she failed to insert her usual hollowed out half a lemon – the half a lemon that became a cervical cap. She said she never forgot to insert the hollowed lemon when an assignation with Lorenzo occurred. She would excuse herself from Lorenzo for a few minutes – in order to freshen up of course. Lorenzo was never aware of her trick. The time Lorenzo sent his message that he would have to cancel their lover's tryst she was angry. On the other hand, she was taken by the fresh handsomeness of the young messenger Lorenzo had sent. Already inflamed with the anticipation of an afternoon of passion, she surrendered herself to the young buck, forgetting her hollowed half lemon trick.

'So you see, dear boy, you are responsible for my condition. But don't let it disturb you, sweet boy. I'm well satisfied with the time we spent that day. But like that meal we shared, it was consumed, it is over, finished and now it is a thing not to be dwelt upon. More to the point now is my subsequent situation and what I will do for you.

'That I should bear a child in my widowed state is no impediment to a woman like me. Especially in a town such as Venice. No problem whatsoever. My haughtiness and my indifference and contempt to what gossipers will say is perhaps one of the many privileges the title of duchessa allows me. At least the duke left me that benefit. I could sail naked down the Grand Canal singing *Ave Mari Stella* or lift my skirts and empty my bowels in the middle of Piazza San Marco and not an eyebrow would be raised. The most that would be made of it would be a comment like: *Duchessa di Palma is quite a character, isn't she!* After all, Venice is neither fusty Florence nor prissy Pisa, and thank God not slumbering Siena. No need to fret as I can assure you my confinement will only add to my allure. Gullible Lorenzo will suspect nothing other than the child is his. Given that he has managed only one child in all these years of marriage, I am certain he will relish the idea that he has gained a new-found fertility. It is something, puffed with pride, he will brag when with his friends, such is his conceit. He is bound to say something like: *I didn't know my own potency*. And as for you? I suggest you leave Venice. Leave it for a place suitably removed from here.

'Now let me return you a favour. As you are currently employed by Delmare, I will arrange for you to be employed elsewhere. That elsewhere is Bologna. It is suitably far away. I know a Jew, Mordechai Levi, in Bologna. He is the head librarian within the university. You might not know it but that library is one of the finest in all Europe. It holds many, many marvellous collections of books. There are works of great antiquity, there are rare editions and there are books of much interest to a curious mind. The head librarian Mordechai Levi has a great interest that it should become Europe's best library.

'I will write a letter of introduction to Mordechai for you. I will write well of you and perhaps exaggerate your intellect. I will ask that he provides you employment in the library. By the way, don't be disturbed that he is a Jew – that is no impediment to his eruditeness. Among the Jews there are the good and the wicked; the intelligent and the stupid; the beautiful and the ugly. Jews are like any other people. The Jew Levi is a pleasant and learned soul; somewhat bookish but that befits his status as a university's librarian.'

The duchessa went to the writing desk to prepare the materials for Niccolò's letter of introduction and recommendation. As she was about to start writing, she looked over her shoulder and asked, 'Now please tell me your full name and I will write it in my letter now.' After she had finished she folded the letter neatly, dripped heated wax on the fold and with a flourish that ended with a loud thump she stamped it her seal. Niccolò's only thought was: *Damn the bitch! I won't be able read what she wrote.*

Shaken by the duchessa's news but pleased with her solution, Niccolò Umberto headed back the Delmare house, but not before stopping at a tavern: *Celebration! Celebration! Celebration!* By the time he left the tavern the world was looking rosy and he would survive the dual pregnancies intact. He had landed an introduction to a new job and a new adventure. He was safe: *Oh, the world is a wonderful place for me.*

Somewhat tipsy, Niccolò had wanted to sneak into the house and go up to his room for a rest: *Too much news for one day. I need a rest.* Just as he had heard Cherubina sobbing when he had passed her room on the day she wore the carnival mask, he heard her sobbing again. Just as before, he entered her room. As before, he saw her sitting on her bed – distressed as before. As he was about to ask what the matter was, she looked up at him and said, 'Niccolò, I'm pregnant by you. What are *we* going to do?' After a day of announcements of three pregnancies the added *we* came as a further shock.

The next week followed uneventfully for Niccolò, apart from Cherubina daily taking him aside, imploring whether he had come up with a solution to *their* predicament: *Ask, ask and ask. She's just like her father asking about that portrait, but it's about her predicament and not the portrait.* Each time she asked, he'd fob her off with a variation of, 'Don't worry, my sweet Cherubina. I'll find a way out of this mess. I promise.'

∼

With the duchessa's letter to the Jewish librarian in hand, Niccolò saw that flight from Venice was going to be the best solution to the dilemma of his impending fatherhood. The duchessa had paved the way and now what remained was to extract himself from the Delmare household with as little scathing as possible.

Rosetta's situation was obviously in hand, owing to her feminine wiles. In all the time spent in his garret room above the Delmares' bedchamber, Umberto had heard nothing at night from Delmare's room below other than arguments between Lorenzo and Rosetta, Lorenzo's snoring and the occasional fart from one or the other. Now, at least once nightly over this past week, and now this morning, it was clear that Rosetta's feminine wiles were operational. She wasn't going to take Lorenzo's slow recovery from his illness as an impediment, and apparently neither was Delmare himself. From the Delmare bedchamber he could hear a rhythmic creaking bed, moaning and then a quickening of the creak's rhythm followed by Rosetta gasping: *Oh! Oh! Lorenzo again please! Don't stop, you virile wild beast! Again and again and yet again!* In fact, over the past nights he had listened to Rosetta's exultations of Lorenzo's performances with relief. Lorenzo's effort and Rosetta's artifice meant he would soon be off the hook as far as Rosetta's predicament was concerned. Even Lorenzo would have something to boast about when he would be the one attributed with the pregnancies of both Rosetta *and* the duchessa. His friends would say: *Lorenzo, you sly old devil. Your arrows hit the mark!*

The only one to suffer from all this would be Cherubina – poor, sweet Cherubina. Without a plausible explanation other than immaculate conception, her situation seemed hopeless. Niccolò had suggested she could say that her betrothed, the Albanese boy, had placed her in her condition. *Are you mad? He is but eleven years of age and I was a virgin before you had me.* So Niccolò told her to have faith as he would solve the problem. Cherubina asked, 'Honourably?'

And he answered, 'Yes of course honourably, my little dove. Leave it to me.' But with the duchessa's letter safely tucked away and Bologna calling, Niccolò had no need to solve this problem pregnancy. Cherubina would have to explain this inconvenient pregnancy on her own. Niccolò rationalised that though Cherubina's situation was regrettable, it was, after all, the way laws of Nature sometimes worked.

Two days after he had said to Cherubina, 'Leave it to me,' Umberto snuck out of the Delmare household.

As the carriage rocked and jolted, and with Venice well behind him, Niccolò Umberto thought about his adventures there. He had gone to Venice promising to organise a portrait for Lorenzo Delmare and he had made no effort to that end. Instead, he had sponged free board and lodgings in a comfortable environment. Despite his failure to deliver on his portrait promise, Delmare had trusted him enough to engage with him in a couple of business ventures – business ventures of Umberto's making, business ventures which were in truth scams. On the positive side, those scams had been very profitable. Delmare had also trusted him to deliver a letter to the duchessa and to deliver it to her unread. *Well,* he thought, *more's the fool Delmare on that.* As for sneaking out on generous Delmare and trusting Cherubina, Umberto felt not the slightest twinge of discomfort.

Then there were the three women. In particular he felt self-satisfaction with his sexual exploits in Venice. *Three women!* Three women and ultimately he was safely away from the responsibilities of his actions with them. Not only away but, thanks to the duchessa, headed to something interesting.

Mordechai Levi, the Bolognese University Library and a missing book

In which Niccolò travels to Bologna and enters in the service of the Jew Mordechai Levi in the university's library. Umberto and Levi discover that at least one volume from the series God's Agreement with Man *is missing from the library's collection. There is an exhaustive search to find whether the library ever had such a volume. Levi considers it a slight on him as head librarian that the series is incomplete; he considers it a threat to his people.*

Venice the moist. Venice the slippery. Venice the sultry. Venice was a woman – for Umberto it had been three women. In contrast, Bologna was the smell of knowledge. The musty smell of knowledge and learning borne on parchment, on old paper, on leather and ink. It lay in books that rested on Bologna's libraries' shelves. Listen and you will hear knowledge in student throngs, in street corner arguments between learned scholars and in Bologna's university where every mother's student son is a genius.

Knowledge wafted from lecture halls to settle on the shoulders of passers-by; motes of knowledge settled like dust on unsuspecting shoulders. In the libraries of Bologna, spirits of the greats who had contributed to the books rose from the written words and mingled with the smell of knowledge, knowledge waiting to be liberated from pages shared with reminders of the not so greats. The not so greats who had thumbed the books in their struggles to understand had left behind their signs on the pages. Signs such as greasy splodges from fingers licked to turn a page; signs such as snot plops from dripping noses; signs such as obscene sketches hidden under folded corners and profanities written in the margins – *For the best fuck in Bologna visit Adeleta* and underneath some joker had written – *Go at your own peril. Adeleta has the pox* and beneath that yet another hand had scrawled, *Best fuck in Bologna? Your sister of course.*

The university's library, Mordechai Levi's library and its books were physical manifestations of knowledge, but this was lost on Niccolò Umberto. For Umberto, Bologna's air and Levi's library, unlike Venice's fecund humid air and exciting slippery passageways, were dry and smelt only of dust. For Niccolò Umberto, dry and dusty Bologna could only be genderless and boring.

Mordechai Levi was not a young man. His wore his white hair long at the sides, so long that it flowed below his shoulders. The top of his head was bald save for a few cobwebby wisps. On his bald pate he wore a black velvet skull cap as was the custom of the Jews. His beard was full, long and white and still carried some flecked traces of the red hair of his youth. His forehead was domed and below it were bushy eyebrows over pale blue eyes set in deep eye sockets. Poor eyesight had given Levi an intense stare when he looked at someone and a squint when he read. His nose was straight and well-proportioned; it was an elegant nose that contradicted stereotypes regarding a Jewish nose. The totality of his facial features gave him the appearance of a scholarly and wise old lion. Mordechai Levi was, in fact, not only as scholarly and wise as he appeared but also highly intelligent. Niccolò Umberto, who had never knowingly met a Jew, thought: *The Jew looks just like a Christian.*

Niccolò Umberto handed Mordechai Levi the duchessa's letter. Recognising the seal, Mordechai Levi said to the young man, 'How interesting. The duchessa writes to me, a mere humble university librarian.' He commenced to read the letter. He muttered, 'Strange woman.' He read on. To no one he said, 'She's avaricious like many men, especially men from Venice.' Then addressing the young man, he added, 'She hasn't changed at all – she still thinks and writes like a man.'

Mordechai Levi then placed the letter on his desk and said to the young man, 'Do you know what is in this letter?'

Niccolò Umberto said he only knew that the duchessa had written him an introduction to the librarian. He also added, 'Apart from that, how should I know what's in the letter? I don't read other people's letters,' but then he thought: *How the hell could I know without leaving the seal untampered?*

Mordechai Levi stared at the young man longer than was polite and then said, 'I must say the duchessa writes well of you. You must have pleased her in some way. As a favour to her, I will take you on. Can you come here tomorrow? Do you have accommodation? If not, I will arrange something for you at a student hostel.' Then, pointing to a jumble of books on the floor, Levi added, 'You can start tomorrow by helping me with those.'

Not being a bookish person, the librarian's request left Niccolò wondering what he was getting into. As far as he was concerned, books were things either the well-off used to furnished empty wall spaces or things stored in libraries. And libraries he believed were for the hiding, from those who could read, of dangerous ideas that lurked in books. But more importantly, he failed to see how anything in books could lure women to his bed.

Displeasure at tomorrow's task was obvious in Niccolò's face, so Levi added, 'No need to look so. This is important work. Knowledge must be stored in such a way that it is accessible to those who seek it. You see a jumbled pile over there but it's much more. In those books there are people who now continue to live on – the ancients, the poets, the philosophers. Not only people but also histories and stories. Knowledge is power and those books contain it. It's all there.

'As long as there are books, the people and ideas in them will always be alive. People of a book survive forever. One way or another, their stories are told long after their physical presence has gone from this earth. And the library is where you find them. That's why libraries are so important and that is why that pile is important.'

Thinking only about himself, as usual, Niccolò Umberto asked,

'What about me? Where's my story?'

Levi looked directly at him and thought: *Impertinent idiot. What was the duchessa thinking sending me him,* but replied, 'Your story? Ah, I believe your story will be written one day but its author is yet to be born. Now here is the address of your hostel and remember to tell them Mordechai Levi the librarian sent you. Be back here early tomorrow as there's a lot you've got to learn.'

❖

There was a lot for Niccolò Umberto to learn and for the next half year Levi taught him the workings of the library. Niccolò learnt that books were stored according their date of acquisition. Levi taught him tricks for finding shelved books; and they both wondered whether a better method could be devised for the cataloguing of book acquisitions. Surely with better cataloguing, there would be a more efficient way of retrieval of shelved books.

In the absence of female distraction and with the help of Levi, there was time for Umberto to improve his Latin. A propos the lack of female distraction, it must be admitted that Umberto found his way to the proverbial Adeleta – the whore specialising in university clientele and who, contrary to an inscription written in the gutter of an obscure book, was at that time pox-free. It was not that Niccolò found his times with Adeleta not sexually pleasant and it was not that she was a communal university institution, but there was no excitement to their sex-making. How unlike his time with Adeleta was the illicit pleasure he had experienced with the duchessa or the satisfactory appropriation of Delmare's Rosetta, or even his gratifying initiation of Cherubina. These three coital events in Venice had been ego-boosting, whereas post intimacy with Adeleta he was crestfallen not only by member deflation but also by ego deflation.

Less time with Adeleta gave Niccolò Umberto more time for Latin, which led to Levi being impressed by his helper's progress, which in turn led to Levi giving Umberto a six-volume set of Latin texts for his further education. 'These six books are very special. They form a complete set and they are extremely valuable. Read the series from cover to cover or just dip into sections. It's one way for you to improve your Latin. Who knows, their content might lead you down the path of spirituality. Enjoy the journey.' Levi neatly stacked the six volumes on Niccolò's table.

Niccolò Umberto picked up the topmost book and carefully turned the pages. He then said, 'To me they look like any other books in the library.'

'Perhaps, but these six books have quite a history. You see books here but when they first came to light they were in fact scrolls – scrolls were the manner my people traditionally kept written information. The original scrolls were written sometime between the falls of the two temples. One author or more? I'm not sure, but judging from the breadth of subject matter I would say that a series of books with the title *God's Agreement with Man* must have had many authors. Though whether one author or one thousand authors is not important. What is important is they exist. It is a miracle that they have come down the centuries – first from scrolls, then to books.

'And as for their relatively more recent history? As far as I have researched I know that in 1099 a Jew, Aaron Ben Yoshua, traded the scrolls to a Bernhardt of Albi, a knight in the service of Raymond IV Count of Toulouse. The scrolls were traded by Ben Yoshua in return for safe passage out of Jerusalem during its siege. Certainly it was by the intervention of the Divine that the scrolls made their way safely to France where they were translated into the Latin volumes you have before you. The translations were made early in the 1100s at the request of Bernhardt of Albi. After the scrolls were transcribed to book form, the original scrolls were either lost or destroyed. And that is a great pity. I can only hope that the translation into Latin has maintained the original Hebrew intent.

'How many copies of the series were made? I'm not sure and it could very well be that the library's set is the only one ever in existence. But we what we know is that a series was in the hands of a descendant of Bernhardt of Albi. That is the series the library acquired in 1376 – almost two hundred years ago. Quite a journey from their start as scrolls in the Holy Land so long ago to the Latin translation books in your hands here. Please take care with these volumes.'

Then, because Mordechai Levi had been aware of his young assistant's visits to Adeleta, he added, 'Instead of spending your time and money on Adeleta's transient and communal affections, why don't you immerse yourself in these substantial volumes.'

⌒☙⌒

The weather in Bologna had turned cold and wet, making it easier for Niccolò to spend time with the books. As a consequence, over time, his command of Latin improved further, but the spirituality the books were supposed to impart eluded him.

If, as Levi had implied, the subject matter of the six books was significant, then in their physical appearance the books were unremarkable – Niccolò had already commented to Levi that they appeared no different from the library's thousands of other books. The six books were leather bound, with embossed titles on the front board, and whatever gilt had been in the embossing appeared quite fresh. Unfortunately, for two of the books the leather was starting to split along the spine. Centuries ago scribes had carefully provided the Latin translations in an attractive script, and an unknown person or several unknown people had skilfully painted the colourful illustrations. Apart from that, to Niccolò these books were just uninteresting books which Levi had asked him to read. If anything was cryptic about them, then it was the symbols at the bottom of each book's spine. He had lined the books upright on his desk and it was apparent that each book's spine had a different gold embossed symbol. The symbols were the Latin letters A, F, VI, C, I, VII. What could they have meant? Did the letters spell out something important? Was there a specific order in which they should have been ordered to spell something important? And if that was so, then in what language was it? Could an important revelation be found in the spine? On the other hand I, VI, VII and C were Roman numerals. Surely if two thirds of the symbols were numerals then that had to be significant.

The next time Niccolò saw Levi he asked him if he had any idea what the lettering on the spine of the books of *God's Agreement with Man* meant.

'I've not thought very much about it. I have always thought it related to a cataloguing system used a long time ago by Bernhardt of Albi's librarian. The numerals I, VI, VII and C hint at a cataloguing system but the letters A and F don't seem to fit. If the Roman numerals relate to the series itself, then in all probability the numbers VII and C are wrong as we believe that the six volumes form the complete set. I have to admit if it is a cataloguing system then it makes no sense to me.'

Umberto said, 'I'll play around with the order of the letters to see if anything comes up in any recognisable language that uses Latin script.'

Levi asked, 'Using the six symbols – A, F, VI, C, I, VII – have you any idea how many words you could make?'

'I consulted with the mathematician Lodovico Ferrari.'

'Lodovico Ferrari? I suppose you mean *our* Lodovico Ferrari here in Bologna?'

'Yes.'

'He visits our library from time to time. It's said he'll go far here in Bologna. So what was his verdict?'

'He said using the six letterings on the books' spines there would be seven hundred and twenty words.'

'Seven hundred and twenty! And how long do you think that would take you?'

'Not too long.' Then with a cheeky wink Niccolò added, 'It's that or Adeleta.'

⤌

Contrary to what he had told Levi, it took Niccolò Umberto longer to work through the seven hundred and twenty permutations, and each time the six letterings gave him nonsense words.

'All I've got is meaningless rubbish.'

'That's the nature of research. You often follow a path that leads nowhere but not all is lost. At least we can safely reject that the spine symbols form a word recognisable by us.'

'So where do we go from here?'

'Perhaps I, VI, VII and C stand for volumes 1, 6, 7 and 100 but I find this to be both unacceptable and unpalatable. Unacceptable because C would then stand for Volume 100 and it seems beyond reason that *God's Agreement with Man* would require at least one hundred volumes. The Lord's message should be concise and not require one hundred volumes or more.

'Our great sage Rabbi Hillel was once asked by someone to teach him the entire Torah while standing on one leg, to which Hillel replied: *That which is hateful unto you do not do to your neighbour.* So you see, God is not a spendthrift with His message. Similarly, a series with one hundred volumes to get His message across would be a wasteful extravagance. So I'd say a series of one hundred or more volumes seems impossible.'

'And why unpalatable?'

'Unpalatable because if I, VI, VII and C if are volume numbers, then it would mean we have at least ninety-four missing volumes! So I am disinclined to believe that I, VI, VII and C are volume numbers. And also, what numbering do we assign to the spine letterings A and F?'

Levi thought for a while and suggested the title *God's Agreement with Man* might be a clue. 'If you have read the series, as I've asked, then you'll know the subject matter of each volume deals with Divine promises made to man but that's about it ... The title? Does the title give anything away? The words *God's* and *Man* are easy, for there can only be one God. That's unambiguous.'

'And so is *Man*,' added Umberto.

'So that leaves us *Agreement*. So what do we make of the word *Agreement*?'

'It is … a settlement, an understanding, a concord, a covenant. I suppose there are other words, but that's the best I can come up with at the moment.'

At this point Levi became excited. 'Covenant! The Great Flood! Of course it's His covenant. The volumes are of a holy nature and cover aspects of God's agreement with man. In other words, we could replace the word *Agreement* with the word *Covenant*! Any half literate knows that following the Great Flood the Lord made known His covenant with man with a rainbow. The rainbow is the clue to solving the riddle of those spine symbols.'

'So how does that help us?'

'The symbols on the spines are A, F, VI, C, I and VII. Young man, if you had ever taken note of the colours of a rainbow and improved your Latin, then you'd know that in Latin the colours are Rubei, Aurei, Flavi, Viridis, Cæruleus, Indicus and Violaceus; that's Red, Orange, Yellow, Green, Blue, Indigo and Violet. We get the A and F from the first letter of the words Aurei and Flavi. As for Cæruleus and Indicus – C and I? Well, in this case they're not Roman numbers but the first letters of the words Cæruleus and Indicus! Similarly VI and VII are not numbers but proxies for the first letters of Viridis and Violaceus. A bit more complex here, as what we have are two words starting with the letter V, and to make matters more difficult both words have the same second letter. Apparently to get over this, they have been distinguished, this time using the Roman numeral I for the first and the Roman numeral II for the second. Now, employing Occam's razor, one should keep it simple and it is simple to keep to the order of the colours of the rainbow, and so VI is Viridis and VII is Violaceus. What is good about this theory is that it puts to rest the idea that there are many more volumes in the series.'

'Very good, but Levi, I think you are in for an unpalatable surprise. The library's *God's Agreement with Man* has six volumes and the rainbow has seven colours. The library has no volume with

R for Rubei on its spine. If our rainbow colours explanation for the symbols on the spine of each book is to be correct, then either the Red, Rubei, volume is missing from the library or the library's collection of *God's Agreement with Man* is incomplete and has always been incomplete since 1376. For the rainbow theory to work, there must be a Volume R.'

Faced with this, Levi replied, 'Well, then, there has to be a Volume R somewhere in the library. Surely the library would not have knowingly purchased an incomplete set in 1376? Perhaps the Volume R has been misplaced or, worse still, stolen. We must start a search for that volume.'

Other library work was put on hold while the two men searched for the missing volume. It is easy to gloss over the first month it took Levi and Umberto searching the library for the volume of *God's Agreement with Man* with R on its spine.

First Levi suggested, 'Let's check whether the library ever received a Volume R when it purchased the set in 1376. Then let's see if at any other time the library acquired a copy.'

The search, however, was tedious. They searched over a month in a grimy basement, an ill-lit and poorly ventilated basement where the library's records were stored. The two men worked long every day reading acquisition records – centuries of acquisition records stored in boxes and trunks; boxes and trunks stacked against the walls; centuries of acquisition records in rolled dusty scrolls placed, without an obvious sense of order, on the shelves. The jumble motivated Levi to say, 'These shelves are a disgrace. What an abominable mess. The entire basement is a disgrace. Above ground the library presents to the world order and rationality but down here in the basement it's chaos and disarray.'

Niccolò Umberto replied, 'Somewhat like life. The part of us we present to the world is more acceptable than what lurks beneath our façade.'

'Perhaps. One day I must get some semblance of order down here, but as always, there's never sufficient staff.'

Niccolò said a silent prayer to hope he wasn't going to be the person who Levi would request to bring order to the basement.

Now to the stacked boxes and trunks. In the main they were labelled, but nevertheless Levi insisted they be checked lest what they sought had been put away where it shouldn't have. The search finished when Niccolò found an unlabelled box behind another unlabelled box. In that box at the rear they found a rolled scroll that described the acquisition of six volumes of *God's Agreement with Man* from the library of the Albis. The relevant section had the sentence: *On July 30th 1376 the library has acquired six volumes* (A, F, VI, C, I and VII) *of the works* God's Agreement with Man *from Anton of Albi.*

'At last!' shouted Levi, 'See – the 1376 acquisition makes no mention of a Volume R. No Volume R!'

'But there are still two questions.'

'And what may they be?'

'The first question is, did the library at any time and independently of the 1376 purchase or acquire a Volume R?

'And your second question?'

'Has such a Volume R ever existed? We don't know. Its existence could be a fabrication of our deductive reasoning. After all, it could be something we've assumed exists because it fits our rainbow colours theory.'

'Your second question will require research beyond the library. Your first question can be resolved if we continue our search through these shelves, boxes and trunks. There's much yet to do. Unfortunately for you, my work upstairs never ends so I need you to camp down here and continue until the search is completed. I'll make sure your requirements are met and I'll send someone to help with the task.'

Niccolò wished he'd never raised the first question because it meant staying the basement until all the remaining scrolls, boxes and trunks had been checked.

Three weeks passed in the basement where Niccolò Umberto slept, ate and attended to his bodily functions. His search through the remaining scrolls, boxes and trunks continued with the help of a number of different library assistants. In the past he had looked down at these assistants. He considered none of them his equal but now he envied them, for at the end of the day they could leave the basement. Sometime towards the end of the second week he sent a message up to Levi: *If I'm to stay down here then the least you can do is send for Adeleta.*

Levi replied with the message: *She is an illiterate whereas the assistants I send you are not.*

Finally after yet another week everything had been looked into – scrolls, boxes and trunks. The exhaustive search of the library's acquisition records had answered Niccolò Umberto's first question – if a Volume R ever existed, then a copy of it had never been held by the library.

And only when the search had been completed did a pale and exhausted Niccolò Umberto emerge from the basement to announce, 'It's finished! There's nothing down there. I'm off to see Adeleta.'

Mordechai Levi replied, 'So that leaves the question whether a Volume R exists and if it does, then where. As for Adeleta? I'd advise you rest and clean yourself before you see anyone.'

❧

Did a Volume R really exist and if so how many copies? Levi secretly hoped Volume R did not exist. It might seem surprising that Mordechai Levi, the lover of books, would wish the nonexistence of a book. The way he saw it was if that book did not exist, then as far as the series of *God's Agreement with Man* was concerned his beloved library was not deficient, for without that volume's existence it followed that the library held the complete series. If Volume R did not exist, then he was not deficient as a librarian. Odd, but that's the way he saw it. But there was also another dimension to the existence or otherwise of a Volume R.

Because Mordechai Levi was a Jew, there were many in the university who resented his elevation to the position of head librarian of the University of Bologna. *For Christ's sake, he's not the man for the job. Why? Because he's a Jew and you know what those people are like.* The way Levi saw it was because he was a Jew he had to be not just a head librarian or even a good head librarian, but the best head librarian possible; he carried the burden of being a Jew and that meant nothing he did should reflect negatively on the Jews of Bologna and for that matter all Jews anywhere.

It hadn't escaped Niccolò that for weeks after the discovery that the library didn't have a Volume R, Levi had been in a deep depression. Finally Niccolò approached the librarian and said, 'It's more than likely a Volume R has never existed. And if it does and the library doesn't have a copy, so what?'

'So what? You ask so what? I believe so very much hangs on the library not having the volume.'

'Well, what if the library lacks one volume of *God's Agreement with Man*? Is it really so important to you? It's only a book after all.'

'Let me explain why it's so important not only to me but to my people. Horrific events have occurred to us.' And here Levi meant the Jews. 'Over the centuries and in many lands, from Barcelona to Vienna to Prague and elsewhere, Jews have been hunted and killed. Hunted and killed by sanctioned packs of supposedly gentle people. Gentile people, yes. Gentle people not always. Jews have been killed for no other reason than they are Jews. And you don't have to be a great scholar to know that as long as there are Jews, these abominations will happen to them. It has happened and it will happen in other places and in other times. Over and over again, with any excuse. It is not beyond the realm of possibilities that, even here in civilised Bologna, a library's incomplete series of a book like *God's Agreement with Man* could be the spark that lights the fire for the burning of Jews. Persecution because the library's head librarian – Mordechai

Levi, the Jew – was perceived to be derelict in his duties.'

'Persecutions? What is it with you people? Why do you see persecutions as your unique domain? Persecution is the way of the world, and many others, apart from Jews, have suffered it. Have you considered that you are so much on the lookout for persecution that you see it when there is none?'

'Yes, there is an element of truth in what you say, but history cannot deny that we seem to have been singled out through the ages. Of course, we try to avoid it in many ways. Whether we try to blend into a community and adopt its ways, or we strive to be worthy of the society where we live, or whether we keep to ourselves at a safe distance, we are eventually attacked for being who we are.

'It's my opinion that our best hope is by doing deeds that are to the benefit of all people – all people and not just *our* people. Finding that book, if it exists, procuring and delivering it to this library, would be of benefit not only to my people, but to Bologna itself. The book would be of benefit to all.'

'A book of benefit to all? Of benefit only to those who care to read it.'

To which Levi replied, 'Yes, that's the way of books.'

Levi thought for a while and then added, 'Perhaps you'll understand why books are so important to me if I tell you that I owe my existence to books. I have alluded to the horrific events that have befallen my people – degradations, humiliations and most dreadful … massacres. And as I've said, these have occurred to Jews for no other reason than they are Jews and thereby not the same as those who are not. Being different and a minority has throughout history made Jews an obvious and easy target. They have been convenient scapegoats. They are easy people to be blamed for whatever catastrophes occur, catastrophes in communities where Jews may have lived and contributed. And bizarrely, in these catastrophes the Jew himself has also been a victim. You see, plague knows no race, no religion. All men are its meal. Acts of Nature such as earthquakes or floods make no distinction between Jew and Christian. All are equally victims, but it is the Jew who is blamed. If a Christian child disappears, then immediately the cry goes out that it must have been the work of a Jew. No. The work of all Jews. And as I have said, it has been thus for a long time and certainly will continue to be thus. I know of the slaughter of the Jews in Spain. Slaughter sanctioned by your church and Spanish rulers. But wait.'

Levi went to one of the shelves and came back with a book. 'It's described in this book. You may read of it later.' Then he added, 'If your stomach can tolerate the details.' Flicking through the book, he stopped and with emphasis said, 'Here! This section chronicles the killing of Jews in Spain throughout the 1300s.' Flicking some more pages, '... and here's something about the killing of the Jews of Barcelona in 1391. The details are horrible. But they are only words, and can words ever possibly convey the terror of the victims as they tried to survive one more breath? Facts, yes, but the actual feelings? How can a writer convey the fear of a woman stripped of her clothes being chased by a mob bearing staves and swords? She is running for her life and the braying mob is closing on her: *Kill the Jewish bitch! Kill her!* How can words make you feel what she felt? It's impossible. Can words convey the terror of a child seeing his mother beaten to death by that mob and then seeing her dismembered? Or the terror that child experiences before the mob turns on him. Describe the feeling that a father experiences when he sees his child thrown onto the pyre. You can't. It's impossible. Words, words, words – only words. There are no words that can convey the reality, but at least the words in books allow us to know that such events happened. And why did such events happen?' Pausing between each word for effect he answered his own question, 'It – happened – because – they – were – Jews. They were Jews, that's why.

'All this brings me back to me owing my very existence to books. Do you know of the slaughter of the Jews of Lisbon in the Easter of 1506?'

'Should I?'

'I suppose not. In 1506 my grandfather, also a Mordechai Levi, was a bookseller in Lisbon. His only son, Shimon, my father, assisted him in that business. In 1506 my late father was a young man who had grudgingly entered his father's business. My namesake had sold a chest of books to a fellow dealer, a Jew from Porto, and it was my father's task to deliver the books to the purchaser.

'Although it was a Friday, my father set off on the first day after the Passover of that year, Passover being our seven days of observance of the Jews' deliverance from slavery and exodus from Egypt. The day he set off was the 23rd of Nisan in the year 5780 which to Christians equates to the 17th of April in 1506, and as it happened it was the Good Friday of that year. For my father it was fortunate that he was well out of the environs of Lisbon by Easter Sunday. For on that Easter Sunday began the Lisbon massacre of Jews and New Christians. You know of Jews but what of New Christians? New Christians? They were Jews who had converted to Christianity. What a bitter joke was played on them! It did them no good when the massacres happened. I suppose it stands that a Jew by any other name is still a Jew, and a Jew is a Jew is a Jew ad infinitum. But I digress unnecessarily. Suffice to tell you that on that Easter Sunday there began the slaughtering of Jews – men, women and children, young or old, it made no difference. The rampaging through Lisbon was horrible. The burnings in the squares, the deadly beatings and all manner of horrid killings. The streets ran with the blood of murdered Jews and the banks of the Targa glowed with burning Jews.

'The killings had started because a New Christian had questioned whether a supposed sighting of Christ's face illuminated on a church's altar that Easter Sunday was perhaps only an aberration of candlelight. From this simple query, the killing started and continued for days. In those dreadful few days, my father's entire family was murdered along with many, many of the Jews of Lisbon.

'Fortunately for my father, he was well out of Lisbon and understandably he never returned. Why should he have done so? There was nothing there for him except memories and the necessity to live alongside brutal Jew-hating murderers. Why go back and wait for the next disgruntlement to escalate to another massacre?'

Niccolò asked, 'So did your father deliver the books to this other place?'

'Porto. It was Porto in Portugal.'

'But you are in Bologna. Were you from Porto?'

'Yes, Porto and Bologna are the only two towns I know, however I consider myself Bolognese.'

'But you've always spoken of the world as if you know so much of it.'

'Books. My knowledge has come from books. They are my life. The acquisition of the knowledge contained in those books is my life. Without a doubt I owe my existence to books – a trunk-load of them taken from Lisbon and delivered in Porto! My father used to say if it wasn't for that trunk-load of books, he would not have survived the Lisbon massacres and consequently I would not have been born.

'To complete the story, my father stayed in Porto and was offered work with the bookseller who had taken the consignment. In time, my father married that bookseller's daughter who was to become my mother. I was born shortly after my parents married – of course, a respectful time after they wed.

'From my very beginning I was surrounded by books. Books of all sorts were my constant companions. Nothing delighted me more than a book and my father fostered my love of books. Old books, new books it didn't matter. So long as it was the written word, I was happy. At a very young age I showed a precocious aptitude with the written word. By the age of nine I had mastered several languages and I read in those languages. I had an ability to crack the code behind the syntax of languages. I must have been an impressive child. After attaining thirteen years, a passing rabbi from Bologna suggested I join him to further my education in the university town that Bologna is. My parents agreed to this and that is how I came to Bologna.

'In Bologna it was only natural that my life would orbit books and, though being a Jew and still quite young, I was able to be apprenticed to the librarian in charge of this library. I must have been more than adequate to the task because when that librarian died, I was appointed to his position, a position I have held ever since then.'

'Life unfolds in strange ways, don't you think?' said Niccolò. 'Despite what you have said about your love of books, perhaps if your father had been a milliner it might have been different. If your father had been a milliner required to deliver a consignment of hats to Porto that fateful Easter Sunday, and if your father had instilled in you that a trunk-load of hats had saved his life and so eventually it led to your existence, would you be a milliner today?'

'A very interesting thought. You are a more interesting person than I had first thought you to be, Niccolò.'

'All I'm saying is, are we not objects created by events over which we have no control?'

Levi replied, 'How far do you want to take it? For if there had been no massacre then my father the bookseller – not the milliner – would have returned to Lisbon and seen nothing lifesaving about books. What then? As far as it relates to me, he would not have met my mother and I would not have been born. But irrefutably, here I am in charge of this library so let me suggest we should not waste time on what might have been.

'Enough of that for now. Our pressing task is whether a Volume R exists, and if it does, then how, where and when can we acquire a copy. In the meantime, we'd better attend to what we know exists and catalogue that pile of books.'

The missing volume from the series *God's Agreement with Man* exists

In which the Council of Jews of Bologna instigates a search throughout the world to find a copy of the missing volume. A chance encounter establishes the volume's existence.

Whether a Volume R existed was the new problem. For the next year, Levi sent letters to his network of librarians throughout Europe and as far afield as the libraries of Oxford and Cambridge. The search via the libraries proved fruitless. In each case, no library had heard of the series *God's Agreement with Man*, let alone its Volume R. On the other hand, Levi received congratulatory letters from the libraries regarding Bologna's good fortune in having such an apparently rare series. Levi's query to the world of libraries generated much interest, so much so that the Vatican's Bibliotheca Apostolica commanded Levi grant Vatican scholars' immediate and unfettered access to the series. In an atypical lapse of humility, Levi said, 'Well, well. The Vatican commands and we happily obey. So it appears, whether our series is complete or otherwise, we are the only library that has *God's Agreement with Man*. At least that's something.'

Only to be brought down when Niccolò Umberto added, 'Yes, but it is possible our series is incomplete.' And for Levi, other than the nagging worry the Volume R might really exist, the matter rested there; for Niccolò, at least for the time being, it meant a continuation of dusty and boring work in the library.

A year had passed since the fruitless search for the Volume R and Levi was now certain that it did not exist: we've been so stupid, he thought. Our rainbow colours explanation for the spine coding must have been wrong! It sent us off on a useless hunt. And what's been the outcome? Now I'm stuck with nosey Vatican idiots coming here regularly expecting to be treated with reverence.

~

It was the time the Ottomans had conquered Hungary; they went on to rule it for the next 150 years or so. Invasions and conquest of one's homeland often drive one to flee. Now it should be remembered that Bologna, being a university town, had its share of passing academics, with reputation of its library not being the least of the university's drawcards. It was the case that the philosopher Tibor Csorba, seeing no future for himself in a Hungary under the Ottomans, was one of many who had fled Hungary.

One of the consequences of the Ottoman take-over of Hungary was the demise of its fabulous Bibliotheca Corvinia, established by King Matthias Corvinus. An outcome of the Ottoman's conquest was that over time, the library's manuscripts were dispersed; the library's stocks had been taken for well-meaning safekeeping, stolen or taken away to Turkey by the conquerors. By the time Csorba made it to Bologna, the great library in Buda Castle was a shell of its former glory.

Csorba's initial experiences in Bologna were much the same as that of the many refugee academics who had gravitated to the city. Like the other lost souls without letters of introduction, Csorba's prospects were bleak. In common with other vagabond or refugee academics, he lived a hand-to-mouth existence. For these academics, their lives centred around scrounging what they could or prostituting their academic skills to noble, but less gifted, Italian students of the university. For a fee these refugee scholars attended classes, provided written materials and did research for lazy, rich or dumb students who would rather spend their time carousing in the taverns or gambling dens. It was an agreeable arrangement for both parties; students satisfied requirements of their patrons and the university while the refugee scholars not only survived another day but occasionally found themselves involved in academic challenges of their liking.

Cosimo Sforza, perhaps one of Bologna's most useless students, was the illegitimate son of an equally useless illegitimate son. Although only distantly related to an obscure branch of the Sforza dynasty, Cosimo styled himself a Sforza. Cosimo was what you would call a party boy. For him Bologna was not its university but a place for debauchery. He figured that when one would rather partake in what the bible says one shouldn't, then to hell with the bible. Instead, you pay some refugee scholar to do your bidding at the university. In Cosimo Sforza's case, Tibor Csorba was that person. It was in the performance of such an arrangement that Tibor Csorba found himself in Levi's library.

A stranger with a strange accent asked Umberto, 'I'm looking for the series *God's Agreement with Man*. Have you got it?'

'Has the Vatican sent you?'

'No, I'm here for Cosimo Szf…', and here Csorba, in the interest of maintaining Cosimo Sforza's dignity as well as his own, cut-off what he was about to say and said, 'I'm here because I'm interested in the series.'

'You're sure you're not from the Vatican?'

'Definitely not. So have you got the series? Yes, or no?'

'Oh yes, we have it. And it's the complete series.' What a surprise. None of libraries that Levi had contacted knew of the series and yet here was a stranger who did. 'Follow me. We keep it in the basement. Sure you're not from the Vatican?'

'Do I look as if I'm from the Vatican?'

Niccolò stopped and looked the stranger over. 'No, they're better dressed.'

As they entered the basement, Niccolò asked, 'How did you hear of *God's Agreement with Man*?' He had expected the stranger to say he had heard from one of the libraries Levi had written to.

Niccolò was stunned to hear the stranger say, 'Our library had the complete series.'

'What library was that? We wrote to almost all major libraries and none had heard of the series.'

'I don't know anything about that, but the Bibliotheca Corvinia used to have the complete series until the Turks sacked the library. That was about thirty years ago. The Turks took whatever they pleased and the library is nothing now as nought of interest remains.'

'That must explain why my master Mordechai Levi never sent a letter to the Bibliotheca Corvinia. But how do you know about the series if the Bibliotheca Corvinia was destroyed so long ago?'

'My father was an assistant in the library and he taught me to read using that series.'

'Heavy reading for a child?'

'Not really – if you knew my father you'd understand.'

Niccolò Umberto got the library's complete series and placed them on a table in front of Csorba. 'Wait here and I'll bring our head librarian to meet you.'

Soon Niccolò returned with Levi, but before he could make the introduction the stranger said, 'This isn't the complete series. Where is the volume with R on its spine?'

In unison Levi and Niccolò asked, 'The Volume R exists?'

'Most certainly! Why do you think my father called *God's Agreement with Man* the rainbow series? On the series you've presented me the spines are A, F, VI, C, I and VII. It doesn't take too much brain power to see that the letterings are proxies for Aurei, Flavi, Viridis, Cæruleus, Indicus – Latin for Orange, Yellow, Green, Blue, Indigo and Violet. It's so simple it doesn't qualify as a code. Even less use of your brain in the abstract and more use of your eyes in the observation of the natural world will tell you these are the colours of the rainbow. In order no less! Observation of the natural world again will tell you that a colour of the rainbow is missing and *ipso facto* a volume is missing.' Turning to Levi and Niccolò, Tibor

Csorba asked, as a lecturer would, 'And that my friends is …?'

Levi replied, 'Volume R.'

'Yes, the volume with the letter R on its spine. The letter R for Rubei – the red band of the rainbow. It might interest you that when my father used *God's Agreement with Man* as my reader, we named the volumes by the colour for which the spine referred. My favourite was the Volume R, the red volume, and I see your library doesn't have it. Pity.'

Ignoring Csorba and turning to Niccolò, Levi said, 'So the red volume, Volume R is a reality.'

To which Csorba said to Levi and Niccolò, 'Yes it is, and your library's series *God's Agreement with Man* is incomplete without it.'

The Devil had come to roost on the old librarian's shoulders to mock him. The Devil dug his claws deeply and rasped: *Your library is deficient. You are deficient. You are a Jew. Therefore all Jews are deficient.*

In taking the position of head librarian, it had been Levi's goal to make the library equal to, if not better than, the best of all libraries. He had told the selection panel that had chosen him that he was capable of achieving his goal. In this matter he tried to turn his religion, which some of in the panel had viewed as a deficit, into a positive: *We are a learned people. Some even call us the People of the Book. We value learning and scholarly pursuits. We are also a people with connections, a network that can be called on for favours not only of a monetary kind but for matters of the mind. So trust in me to elevate the status of the library.*

Levi knew that this was dangerous talk on a number of levels. He had used stereotypical generalities to characterise his people, generalisations that either applied to all religions or were patently wrong of all religions. Also if, as it seemed, he was willing to take the credit for the rain, then surely he would eventually have to be willing to take the blame for either the drought or the flood. He knew all this but he was ambitious enough to want the position of head librarian of Bologna's university.

The Jewish community of Bologna was not large and though it may have wanted to keep a low profile, it was not possible when there were obvious signs of their presence. Obvious signs such as the eleven synagogues; more than in all of Rome. There were Jewish Hebrew printing presses producing learned works catering to Jewish intellectuals. The Jews were to be found in many places; in too many places as far as some Bolognese were concerned: *Just look at them! Who the hell do they think they are? They're everywhere. They're in loan banking, commerce and medicine. They're everywhere!*

Although their numbers were small, most walks of life in Bologna felt the presence of the Jews and even the university had its share of Jewish academics. No, they did not have a low profile – rather, they were low fruit to pick when it came to loathing. If something went wrong with your banking activities, whose fault was it? The Jewish bankers of course. If a commercial deal went sour whose fault was it? The Jewish merchants without a doubt. If your ancient grandmother died one day before her hundred and third birthday whose fault was it? Of course it had to be the Jewish doctor who had treated her with great attentiveness and skill and had kept her alive until the day she inevitably died. And as for culture? Anything that was depraved was the work of a Jewish creative.

Levi had grown up with the story of the slaughter of the Jews of Lisbon so he was well aware how vulnerable his people were. Whether Jews of Bologna had a high or low profile would make no difference when it came to averting something like what had happened in Lisbon. The hatred and distrust of the Jews was ingrained and even the slightest comment, even more innocent than the one posed one Easter by a New Christian in Lisbon, could trigger horrific consequences. Levi was well aware of this and he wondered whether his library's missing Volume R could be such a trigger. He would have to gather Bologna's two Jewish fraternal societies, the *Hevrat ha-Nizharim* and *Hevrat Rahamim* and see how they could avert a disaster because of something as small as the missing Volume R.

'My fellow society members, the situation is grave and it has the potential to become catastrophic.'

'Come, come now. How can something as trivial as a library's incomplete series pose a threat to our wellbeing here in Bologna? We are Jews, yes, but we're Bolognese as well. This town is our home and we are part of its fabric. The missing book, after all, is your problem and not our community's.'

'I take your point that a missing book might seem a trivial issue, but I assure you that something as trivial as that can change not just my fortune but all our fortunes. Remember we have our enemies in Bologna. We are not liked and at best we are merely tolerated.'

'You exaggerate.'

'Haven't you heard people say things like: *Jews are untrustworthy; Jews are all liars and thieves; Jews would steal the coins off a dead man's eyes*. And soon it becomes: *Jews control the banks. Jews are the hidden hand behind the Vatican. Jews kill Christian babies and drink their blood.* You should know that if even one Jew should do wrong, then all Jews are deemed to have done that wrong. In the eyes of most non-Jews, no Jew is blameless.'

'If we accept your warning then what do we do?'

'We must find the missing volume. We must do so for whatever it costs, monetarily and effort. When we find the missing volume, we should make a big noise about it and then we must ceremoniously donate it to the university. A gift from the Jews to Bologna. That's what we must do.'

'Isn't there a risk in what you suggest?'

'Why would there be a risk?'

'What if we have promised to deliver the book to the university but we fail to find the book, or if we find the book but it is not for sale? Don't we create yet another arrow that can be fired at us?'

'What arrow?'

'A broken promise.'

'Yes, but I suppose we could make no promise and announce what we have done only when we have the book. We could do that, but that would diminish the esteem we would have gained otherwise. And that's not all. The way things work for Jews anywhere, it wouldn't be long before there are whispers and then shouts: *Those deceitful Jews stole that book from the library in the first place just to make themselves look good when they returned it!* No. I suggest the best way forward is to announce the book is missing and the Jews of Bologna will search everywhere for it to donate to the university's library.'

'Well, if that's what you suggest we do, then we will vote on it. At the outset let me tell you, Mordechai Levi, you have my vote.' A vote was taken and Levi's plan was carried.

After a year's hiatus the search for the missing book recommenced. Of all the disparaging criticisms that could be levelled at the Jews of Bologna, their ability to network was just another one: *They're everywhere and the bastards always stick together helping each other.*

Everyone in the Jewish community knew someone who knew someone who was related to someone who had a friend who could find something you needed. It was the case where a nephew in Pisa had an uncle in Pescara who had an old friend in Padua who had connections in Parma who could find someone in Perugia who could do something for you. The system worked like banking but where the transactions were not with money but with favours – favours were lent as credit to be repaid later with interest. Consequently the Societies decided to call for the repayment of many favours and the message was sent: *Find the missing volume of* God's Agreement with Man *that has the letter R on its spine.*

Taking a gamble and true to his word, Levi informed the university's authorities that its library had never had, the apparently rare, Volume R of *God's Agreement with Man*. He further announced that the incomplete series was a slight on the university's standard of scholarship but fear not because, whatever the cost, the Jews of Bologna would find the missing volume and donate it to the library. Unfortunately, there was something about the network for which Levi had not accounted. You may very well have a nephew in Pisa with an uncle in Pescara who has an old friend in Padua with connections in Parma, and no matter how hard a certain someone in Perugia tries, you may still not find what you search for.

And so it was that after many months, the world's best network came back with: *No book* and *Nothing found* and *Are you sure such a book exists?* Levi's gamble had not paid off; the university knew of the library's deficit and that now there was no book in the offing. To them, Bologna's Jews had made a hollow offering and it was not too much of a stretch for them to think about terminating Mordechai Levi's appointment.

Niccolò Umberto was surprised that the Jewish network had not been successful. If he was to believe Tibor Csorba, the Hungarian scholar, then Volume R certainly existed. Csorba had seen it, he had held it and he had read it. It had once been in the Bibliotheca Corvinia until the Turks came. And it was with that in mind that he went with the suggestion to Levi that the search for the missing volume should have been elsewhere.

'Start with the Turks! They're the ones who sacked the Bibliotheca Corvinia and they're the ones who in all likelihood have the book.'

Levi was annoyed that his upstart assistant should have come up with something he hadn't. It was, after all, the most straightforward place to start.

'Well done, Niccolò. The Turks, of course. So tell me, how do we look for a book that was taken – no, stolen, so many years ago?'

'Just as you did before. Set your network to the task again but this time they're to look to the east.'

'Back to Turkey itself?'

'Of course, and perhaps all the way to Constantinople.'

This time it wasn't long before a cousin from Cotrone heard from an aunt in Capua who had a friend in Calabria who had heard a Jewish sailor from Cairo headed to Crete say that someone had heard of a Pasha Mukhtar in Constantinople who might have the much desired book for sale should the price be right. And as if this new search had been his idea all along, Levi proudly said to Niccolò, 'See! Our network is like a well-oiled machine. It is very effective.'

What followed were exchanges of letters between Levi and the Pasha. After some toing and froing, a price was agreed with the Pasha stipulating the provenance of the volume once in the hands of the library would be never divulged.

'Why must the provenance of the volume not be divulged?' asked Niccolò.

Levi replied, 'Our guess is the Pasha obtained the volume by ignoble means.'

'Then can he be trusted?'

'We currently have no alternative but to trust him.' And now Levi sprung Niccolò a surprise, 'But can you be trusted? The Societies have raised money for the volume and for the journey to Constantinople and back. I nominated you, Niccolò, to be the man to carry out the task. We want you to go to Constantinople to purchase the book and return with it to Bologna. The Jews of Bologna have promised to provide Volume R of *God's Agreement with Man* so, under all circumstances, you must come back to Bologna from Constantinople with that book. It's so important that you do return with the book, for to do otherwise would make our life in Bologna far less comfortable, if not impossible. So we are trusting you with this mission.'

Niccolò in Constantinople

In which Niccolò Umberto travels to Constantinople to purchase the missing Volume R but becomes seduced by the wonders of that city. Exercising a blatant lack of application to the task with which he has been entrusted, he spirals into wanton decadence.

If Niccolò Umberto found Venice to be a woman and Bologna genderless, then Constantinople was most surely a hermaphrodite. Just like a hermaphrodite, it was a blended body; it was the fusion of Europe and Asia; it was the union of man's highest ideals and his basest depravities. But seeing Constantinople as a hermaphrodite was not enough and it would be more accurate to say it was multi-gendered – it was male, it was female and of genders not yet to be named. It was awash with colours, sounds and flavours.

Then there was hashish. Hashish for the buying. Hashish for the asking. Hashish for the taking: *Come get from me your hashish! Merhaba! Merhaba! Stranger want hashish? I gots! I gots! I gots best hashish in all world. Come get from me you hashish!* You must understand that Constantinople catered for all pleasures so it satisfied every carnal desire and any intellectual pursuit, and like its hashish, once tasted it was difficult to give up.

Of course, Niccolò Umberto had every intention of seeking out Pasha Mukhtar and purchasing the missing volume. He had promised the Jews of Bologna that he would return with the book; they had, after all, trusted him. It was the honourable thing to do, and if that wasn't sufficient, then around his neck the weighty purse chaffing against his skin was a constant reminder of his task in Constantinople.

In Bologna Levi and his fellow Jews had calculated how much money would be required for Niccolò's personal needs, so the purse contained enough to cover the book's purchase and then some. Niccolò argued to himself therefore as some of the money was his for his personal needs, he could spend it in whatever way he chose. After all, it was for his needs and he alone knew what his needs were. And if he should overspend, then he was confident he was skilful enough to bargain down any pasha, be he the one named Mukhtar or otherwise. And what's more, with Constantinople calling him, the book, Pasha Mukhtar and the Jews of Bologna would have to wait.

There were many things Niccolò had heard about Constantinople, but hearing of them paled when contrasted with seeing and experiencing them. He wandered the Grand Bazaar clutching the skin-irritating purse to his chest. He sniffed spices he'd never smelled before, he rubbed beautiful fabrics between his thumb and forefinger, he sampled meats on skewers and he saw races of people he had never seen before attired in the strangest of costumes. He had heard of the eunuchs of Constantinople and as he pushed through the crowds he wondered which of them were eunuchs: *Is that one? Maybe that one? Or that one?* – and he winced at the very thought of how they came to be so. On the forecourt of a pavilion he saw that whirling dervishes were real and he watched in fascination.

He wandered the docks where he had arrived earlier and saw it with renewed excitement. Boats from all over were unloading and reloading. He had not seen such industry since he had left Venice and he wondered whether some of loadings would eventually find their way to Delmare's storeroom. And as the day was ending and lights and braziers were lit throughout this city of the East, he concluded that Constantinople was providing the heartbeat of the whole world.

That night in the tavern where he stayed he fell in with a group of fellow travellers, and it was there around the fire that Spiros the Greek taught him the wonders of hashish. Later that night Emel, whose name meant desire, came to his room above the tavern to teach him that not all women are the same. By cock's crow he was certain that had he been born here, in Constantinople, then surely fire would flow through his veins in place of the northern ice of indifference. And as the sun shone warmly onto his face to wake him, he mumbled to himself that at heart he was a man of the East.

In the morning he left with Spiros who showed him other sights. This time it was the crowded narrow alleyways with their colourful shops, shouting street vendors and fortune tellers. But most importantly, of all the Turkish delights to warm the heart, he was shown where the hashish and the girls were the best. There were alleyways that, unshackled from the Earth, wound lazily up around hills on their way to the heavenly heights. And from those heights above the city Niccolò Umberto saw the Horn and the comings and goings of every vessel conceivable; all were clear and sharply defined under that brilliant sun. Constantinople sparkled. Constantinople was a diamond. Niccolò told Spiros that if paradise exists, then Constantinople was undoubtedly modelled on it. Spiros agreed, saying, 'There can only be one real paradise and my brother, this is it.'

Back at the tavern that night after the ingestion of hashish, Niccolò fell through a tunnel of altered perception of time where what had passed before Constantinople was yet to happen. And as if in a dervish's dance, the tunnel swirled and swayed until it became a funnel through which he continued to fall. He fell until by some unknown process wings sprouted from his shoulders and carried him up to the sky. He heard the angels singing and God spoke to him in a language he didn't understand. Though he didn't understand the words of God, for no man ever could, he knew it meant paradise was to be found everywhere. There was paradise in every colour and every sound. There was paradise in the cry of a new born baby and the moan of a pleasured woman. Paradise was everywhere and all things were paradise. Then God spoke again and Umberto, though he didn't understand His words, understood God's message that entry to paradise was available to all – kings and beggars, wise men and fools – if they'd only knock on its door. Niccolò Umberto tried to thank God for the hashish but his tongue refused to move and when it did, God had gone. And in the morning when the sun shone warmly onto his face to wake him he mumbled to himself, as he had the morning before, that at heart he was a man of the East.

Days passed in the hunt for new sensations and nights passed with his friends – Spiros, Emel and hashish. God had become more elusive and rarely heard. Instead He was replaced by a three-headed woman with the head of the duchessa, Rosetta and Cherubina. And out of each of the three mouths was spewed a three-headed child with each child's head being that of Niccolò Umberto.

More days passed in sensual pleasures and more nights passed in the thrall of hashish reveries until one day, although the morning the sun shone warmly onto his face, he woke in panic and confusion. The skin-irritating purse was not against his chest and it was nowhere in his room. Even his gold signet ring with its oversized *U* was not on his finger. Surely Spiros would know about these disappearances, but when he asked around the tavern, he was told that Spiros had left during the night. Niccolò no longer had money for the delights of hashish, for the magic body of Emel, for his tavern accommodation, let alone for completing his mission in Constantinople.

To clear his mind, he wandered the alleyways he had wandered with Spiros. Had it been days ago or was it weeks ago or was it years ago? With reborn eyes he saw crowded narrow alleyways where poverty reeked from every humble dirty shop, where street vendors cheated customers and fortune tellers only dealt out lies. And of the so-called Turkish delights he heard the sellers of hashish whisper their false realities and he saw the clinging harpies who posed as women. He heaved and puffed up alleyways that rose steeply upwards and twisted to strangle the hills and every step he took reminded him he was shackled to the Earth. And beneath a searing sun from the heights above the city, Niccolò saw it was not a diamond but just another shit pile. He recalled that the deceitful Greek Spiros had told him there can only be one real paradise and my brother this is it.

Many times during what was left of the day, he thought he had seen Spiros in the crowd just ahead; in the forecourt of the Hagia Sophia, at the foot of the Galata Tower and even near the walls of the Topkapi Palace. Each time he hurried to confront the man he found him to be not the right Greek, not his Greek but just another Greek. As he could not return to the tavern where he owed money, that night he slept behind a warehouse at the docks. Worse than not returning to the tavern was that he could not return to Bologna without the book; if not with the book then at least with the skin-irritating purse less his expenses. And for the first time since he had entered Constantinople, he longed to be sheltered in his ancestral home or protected within the cool depths of a northern pine forest.

In the morning no sun shone warmly on his face and under the leaden sky of that morning he shivered. He had failed Mordechai Levi, who in turn had failed the Jews of Bologna who in turn had failed the Christians of Bologna. For the Jew haters of Bologna, and there were many, the failure of the venture might be twisted to demonstrate Jewish deceit.

As the morning progressed and Niccolò thought on the matter, he too reasoned that the failure was not his after all, it was the Jews who had foolishly entrusted the task to him – foolish Jews. Furthermore, were it not for a bookish Jew's desire to have the complete set of volumes, then Niccolò would never have found himself in this predicament. After all, what harm had he done? If Mordechai's library didn't have the complete set of books, then so what! Weren't there enough books in Bologna to drown any reader? No harm could occur if that one book of all the thousands upon thousands of books in Bologna was not in the university library. Surely not and therefore no harm was done. If it should reflect poorly on the Jews, then it wouldn't be on Umberto's head. If it should happen that the Jews of Bologna suffered, he would not. And what did it matter, after all, they were only Jews and suffering had always become them.

Niccolò leaves Constantinople

In which Niccolò Umberto leaves Constantinople and sails into rough seas. He is washed ashore on a strange island where he meets the refined Turk Yilmaz and his daughters.

The wind behind Niccolò Umberto pushed the little boat through the Dardanelles but it could not blow away the paradox of Constantinople. The further into deeper waters the boat sailed, the deeper became the paradox. How could a place that had in the beginning offered him so much end up giving him so little? In Constantinople he had glimpsed paradise and now the wind driving him away from Constantinople taunted him. It whispered that paradise had only been his version of paradise. Just a dreamer's paradise. And then on the wind's breath he thought he heard it say: *There is only one paradise and you've not even seen its shadow but trust me, there are many hells.*

The little boat was headed for Chania on the island of Crete. So what if the boat's master had taken a carnal liking to him. Free passage on the boat was better than wandering the docks like a spent ghost. And as for the amorous captain? Well, Niccolò was certain that he could fend off the old sheep-fucker. What Niccolò could not fend off, however, was the storm the Chania-bound boat ran into two days out from Constantinople.

The sky blackened, waves were stirred till they rose against the sides of the boat and washed over the deck. A malevolent wind shrieked in his ears the same refrain he had heard before: *There is only one paradise and you've not even seen its shadow but trust me, there are many hells.* And now the boat was tossed in a whirlpool.

Timbers creaked, splintered and finally snapped. The little boat was broken, and as in his hashish reverie, Niccolò fell through the whirlpool's funnel until wings carried him high. He heard angels singing. He saw the three-headed woman again – duchessa! Rosetta! Cherubina! – and as before, each woman's head spewed out a three-headed Umberto child. Then each child's head called him Father! Father! Father! After which he heard and felt no more.

Bad men drown. Good men drown. Men of indifferent nature drown. Men such as Niccolò Umberto rarely drown. So it was the case that, except for Niccolò Umberto, all on that boat who had left Constantinople perished in the storm; so long sheep-fucker and your crew – I don't need you anymore. Welcome to your own hell, young Niccolò.

⤛

The sea takes and the sea gives. It took the ship and its crew, but it also gave up Niccolò Umberto to an island. Did you know that in its giving, the sea washes up all manner of treasures and in its giving, the sea spews up all manner of garbage? So, depending on your bent – one man's meat is another man's poison – what did an island's old crone collecting driftwood make of her find? Her find? A naked young man, unconscious and baking under the sun on the blazing white sands of the shore. Treasure or garbage? The answer was neither. Here was just another thing the Turks in the garrison on the bluff would have to be told about. So the withered old woman, with skin like tree bark, shuffled her way to the garrison to tell them of her find. *Maybe they'll reward me?* And so it was that the garrison was told of a young man washed up on the sands; and so it was that Niccolò Umberto was placed across a donkey's back and taken by the Turks to their garrison.

In the whole of that crone's life, there'd been a Turkish garrison on the bluff. In fact, there'd been a Turkish garrison on the bluff for at least a century and a half. That garrison? Though the locals referred to the three houses that stood alone on the bluff as the Turkish garrison, it was just three common-looking white sugar cube houses just like others on the island. Granted that one house, the commandant's, was larger than the other two and was better appointed, but the three houses hardly made it a military garrison. But there it was – a garrison with only three men because someone in the Ottoman bureaucracy had figured that three was the optimum number for a show of force on that particular island. Granted that there were only three Turks up there, well, five if you included the commandant's identical twin daughters. Granted that the three men up there were Turkish military; the whole thing was not a proper garrison but just a show of Ottoman presence. And as for calling the male occupants of the garrison Turkish military, well, yes, it was a military posting of sorts, but you must understand that aside from the three houses, the male occupants of those houses hardly had a military appearance. For starters, they rarely wore military-style garb; they favoured the simple fashions of the locals. But being Turks and not Greeks, they believed being Turkish was enough to distinguish them from the local peasantry. You see, the so-called garrison existed to intimidate and remind the locals to whom they owed their allegiance.

One, the commandant, was an educated, refined man and the father of the twin girls. Twin girls? More to the truth, they were identical young women. If a name must be given to the commandant, then it would be correct to call him Boluk-bashi Berat Yilmaz, boluk-bashi being the Ottoman equivalent to the rank of captain. Perhaps, for clarity, he could be formally called Captain Berat Yilmaz, but as titles were not of interest to him, he preferred Berat Yilmaz unless addressed by his subordinates. As for the two subordinates, they were good for obeying orders and carrying out the distasteful duties of the garrison. But beyond that they were, after all, only crass men of uneducated peasant stock. As far as Yilmaz was concerned their destiny was pre-ordained, written in the heavens as he was disposed to say. Surely they existed only for the time being to be in his service and one day, God willing, they would fall as cannon fodder for the empire on foreign soil. You could say Yilmaz saw them as mule-like men, just beasts of burden and no more, though he thought it odd that one sang with the purest angelic voice and the other played the çeng as if inspired by God Himself. Certainly these men had names, but for Yilmaz their names were unnecessary and of no interest. But if you are curious then for the record, the singing angel was Mustafa and the God-inspired çeng player was Kulu. As for Yilmaz's identical twins, their names were Phoebe and Hilaeira – and if you were observant enough, you would have noticed Phoebe was the girl with a mole on the left side of her neck, whereas Hilaeira had her mole on the right side of her neck.

The twins looked down at the naked man sprawled on the floor of the room their father used as his office. On father's prayer mat! What had father been thinking to allow this? The stranger was beautiful. Fair but not too fair; dark enough to reveal the white annulus on a finger where a large ring must have been. How unlike he was to the unappealing beetle men of the island, those gnarled islander peasants who started swarthy and ugly and disintegrated as they aged. How unlike he was to father's two helper beasts – father's mule-like men of angelic voice and Allah-inspired hands.

The girls moved closer to the sprawled body. Was it alive? Closer to it, they saw the man's chest rise and until the lungs filled and then they remained full for an eternity. The man whimpered and then his chest sank. *Ugh. It's alive!* yes, ugh, but nevertheless their eyes were drawn to his member; small and vulnerable – a shrivelled worm that could not have been the source of everything. Surely no power resided in this unattractive and comical appendage. How could a thing of beauty such as this man be blighted by such a maggot? And what of the scrotum, that wrinkled purse; full but not of coins? Yet this is a man. If this man was so, then so must it be for all men, whether they were of beauty or otherwise. God had played a discordant note here, first with Adam, and thereafter with all men. And maybe that was His purpose, for the twins knew true beauty required a suggestion of imperfection. It was the same logic espoused in one of their father's books where it had been written that to be truly alive, one must also know that there is death. *Yes, yes, we know all this, but tell us, God, how does this male blemish fit in with all the beauty in love poems?* Their question was asked but God did not answer. The only sound in that room came from the wheezing breath of the unconscious man. Then, as if he had read the twins' minds, and as if driven by modesty, the unconscious man covered his genitals with his hands. *Yes, that's better. Look how beautiful he is now.*

Yilmaz had entered his office unnoticed. He observed his daughters' interest in the naked and unconscious man. He observed their curiosity, especially with the young man's genitals and he knew his daughters had lived in isolation too long.

⤛

For the next two weeks, the twins took turns nursing Niccolò. In his state he did not know that it was two girls and not just one who nursed him. In fact, there were not many lucid moments for him until one day when a soft breeze gently billowed the curtains of the room, and through the lace it caressed his cheeks, soft as the hands that had nursed him. There had been strange music and an angel singing but that had stopped. Now he heard song birds in the lemon tree outside. Somewhere, not too far away, there was the sound of waves on a beach. The pillows were soft and the sheets smelled ever so faintly of lavender.

In the darkness of that evening when all was still, he tried to remember.

Father died. I left with the ring.

He felt for the ring and found nothing. Was there ever a ring? But certainly there was Venice and the Delmares. Venice and the Delmares. Think! Think! Was there a woman of status? A duchessa? yes, there was. And the other women? The two women. The Delmare women. Well, one woman and a girl. Somewhere there were books and dust. The dust of boredom! Boring books of Bologna and its library. Books, books and more books. And a Jew. Who cares about the Jews of Bologna or Jews of anywhere? I don't. But books? No, not all books but one book in particular. A book that was important? A book? There was a book and then there was Constantinople. What's a book got to do with Constantinople?

Venice. Bologna. Constantinople. Venice. Bologna. Constantinople. Venice. Bologna. Constantinople. So tired. I'll sleep just a few moments more. Sleep until the pretty girl comes back. The pretty girl with magic fingers that touch me ever so lightly; her touch as soft as the gentlest of butterfly kisses. That girl who tends to me in dreams will come again. Sleep now.

In his sleep Umberto heard the honeyed music again and knew that it was a tune yet to be written played on an instrument yet to be created. *All this for me, Niccolò Umberto.*

The young man's condition had improved. Days recuperating were now spent resting under the lemon tree at the front of the house. In the shade of that tree, high on the bluff, he saw below him a beach and waves, the waves that had dumped him on the island and the beach where he had been found.

He now remembered Venice and its three women. He remembered Bologna and its dry books and the old Jew Mordechai Levi. He remembered Constantinople and in equal measures he remembered its hashish-drenched beauty and terrors. He even remembered what his mission there had been and he knew he had failed. He shrugged off that failure as unimportant because now he knew that the one pretty girl was two girls identical in all their beauty. And he fantasised.

Niccolò Umberto had never seen such beauty and he wondered, just as he had wondered with Cherubina, how men such as Delmare and the Turk, who he now knew as Yilmaz, could father such beauty. And in his dreamy state, he speculated on beauty. If the hand of the Creator was perversely contrary so as to allow such inversion of the quotient of beauty, then it must follow that the fathers of Yilmaz's subordinates must have been exceedingly handsome for their sons to be so repellently ugly.

How superficial was Niccolò Umberto's assessment of beauty. Yes, Mustafa was bent. His head sat not on a neck but instead jutted strangely from his chest. His shoulders seemed to be higher than his head, giving him the profile of a vulture – the carrion eater. His face was pocked. His lips were thick and his teeth were rotted and few. But from his misplaced head's throat, into his foul mouth and through his mouth's fat flaps had come the angelic singing that had comforted Niccolò Umberto in his delirium. And in truth, had Mustafa's features had been that of an angel, his singing would not have been more beautiful or sweeter.

And when the squat and fat Kulu, Kulu of the shortened limbs and deformed fingers, played the çeng, it was with God's perfect hands. There was beauty in his music and it was not just in his skill but also in the perfection of its tune. Deformed Kulu was an idiot who created tunes of beauty from the disorder around him; melodies that lifted the listener to a plane above the earth. And it was this deformed idiot Kulu who had played and created the honeyed music heard by Umberto in his sick man's dreams.

Had Niccolò Umberto remembered the God of hashish's words about paradise being everywhere and in all things, then a slight adjustment to the concept would have made it clear that the same could be true of beauty. But as it has been already written, Niccolò Umberto's assessment of beauty was superficial.

When the worst of his ordeal was over, Niccolò Umberto remembered all that had happened – in Venice, in Bologna and in Constantinople – and he figured that whatever had happened he had gained. For either he had gone down with the small boat out of Constantinople and if that was so then this island must be paradise, a paradise, where unlike the Muslim martyr's paradise with his seventy-two virgins of unspecified desirability, he had been rewarded paradise with two virgins of exquisite beauty. On the other hand, if he had actually survived the sinking, he had landed on an island that was as good as paradise and he muttered: *Niccolò Umberto, you lucky bastard!*

The island and the ruined temple
on the plateau

In which Niccolò Umberto is acquainted with the island's topography, its inhabitants and its stories. He is taken on a journey to the ruined temple on the plateau and learns of the properties of the temple's environs.

In the village, or few scrabbly block houses that made it a village, the old crone who had found Niccolò had become a person of interest. It's not often that a stranger instead of driftwood was found on the sands.

Two old women sitting in the sun with their swollen legs splayed observed the crone shuffle past. 'That's Elena who found the man.'

The other old crone responded, 'Pish tish! What do I care? He's not the first man she's said she's found in her time. On the beach, the fields and in the forest. There are more than a few juicy things I could tell you about her and men.'

The first replied, 'You're jealous it wasn't you on the beach and for what it's worth, in the fields or in the forest. You're just jealous.'

'Me jealous? Rubbish. She's never been a beauty like me, she's just been lucky.'

Three young men returning from the olives and the vines saw Elena. One whistled and then called to her, 'Your love life is going to get better again. I saw the stranger's out and about.'

Another man nudged his friend. 'I hope her heart can take it.'

And a third man sniggered, 'Her heart take it? In her day, every hole in her body could take it!'

All three laughed.

And as the young men passed a house, a young woman sweeping at her door thought: *Our men are not like the driftwood man; our men are extremely ugly and coarse beasts.*

In the beginning, Niccolò never wandered far from the garrison, just to the village. As far as Yilmaz was concerned, the young man could come to no harm if he went to the village: *It might do him good.* And on the first day in the village, the crone who had found Niccolò claimed him as her own boy. She yelled so that all around her could hear: *My son! Here he is. It's Tasso, my son, he's come back to his old ma.* She took him by the hand and led him to her small house: *Son, I've made some nice fish just the way you like it. You must try.*

And why shouldn't she call him her son, she had every right to do so. After so many barren years where an angry sea had taken so much from her and given only driftwood in return, her patience had been rewarded. The revenant was hers. The sea had returned something of substance to her. He was her child delivered by the midwife sea.

And for those around who heard her receive Niccolò as her son, each one thought the same. One said, 'Are you mad or blind or both? He's nothing like your Tasso!'

'He does and he is.'

Another, so spiteful that she was known as The Bitch, yelled, 'You old cow, the sea took your Tasso away. Years ago. You must remember or have you gotten so old that you've forgotten?'

'Yes, I remember, and now the sea has given him back to me.' Pointing at Niccolò she added, 'Here he is back from the dead. Back to his old ma where he belongs!'

The Bitch retorted with, 'He doesn't look anything like your ugly Tasso. Your sight must be going or have you forgotten what Tasso looked like? What do you say about that, you old cow? What's more, he doesn't understand a word we're saying. You're a stranger to him just as he is to everyone here. I tell you, he's someone else from somewhere else! So what have you got to say about that?'

'He *is* my boy!'

'Rubbish. I'll tell you again your boy was ugly. Just like you. And his father – whoever he was – must have been ugly also.'

'He's my boy made better by the sea. Yes, he looks different and yes, he's forgotten much of our language. Maybe death at sea does that.'

'Rubbish! None of our others taken by the sea came back. Neither better nor worse. They never came back. What do you say about that?'

'See! It just proves that my boy is special. He's special ... that's what I say.'

Taking Niccolò by his hand, she led him to her house. 'And now for some of that fish you used to love.'

⁓

One day Yilmaz asked Niccolò Umberto about the village. 'How do you find the folk of the village? My girls ask why you go there and not stay here. I've an excellent library and you are welcome to visit its shelves.'

'The village? It passes time and I've picked up a smattering of their language. A bastard Greek. But still Greek. As for your library, I thank you but for the time being I've had my fill of libraries and their books.'

That evening after their meal Yilmaz and Niccolò Umberto sat on the terrace overlooking the sea. Perhaps it was the star-spangled purple sky or the lemon-scented warm balmy breeze or just the effects of the hookah that emboldened him to tell his story to Yilmaz. He told Yilmaz of his homeland's forests of the North; of an unloving father and a straight-laced brother. Banishment. After banishment followed Venice and the merchant Delmare; the three women of Venice, each different. And as Yilmaz was the father of two daughters, Niccolò gave a sanitised reason for his flight from Venice. From Venice on to Bologna and its library where an old Jew Mordechai Levi was the librarian. In Bologna there was the discovery of an incomplete set of books which led to his mission to

Constantinople. He told Yilmaz of Constantinople, its two faces and the temptations of that city.

Yilmaz heard everything, said nothing and understood beyond the words spoken. He knew that even unloving fathers and straight-laced brothers are not always so. If they are so, then there are reasons, reasons that would elude a young man like Niccolò Umberto. As for banishment? Well, more often than not banishment is a blessing. It gives the chance to wipe the page clean and start writing a new story of oneself. And the three women of Venice? Three women – one the mistress of his employer, one the wife of his employer and one the daughter of his employer – and a young man like Niccolò Umberto? Although Umberto did not tell the full story of his involvement with the three women, Yilmaz was sufficiently worldly to guess what had happened in Venice. He felt that whatever had happened on the part of the women it was understandable, for such is the nature of many women when tempted, but where was this young man's faithfulness to his employer? And so Yilmaz guessed that Niccolò's reasons for leaving Venice were of course much less noble than in his telling.

What about the library, its librarian, and Umberto's failure to secure the missing volume? As far as Yilmaz was concerned all Jews—past, present or future—find ways to survive persecution. Such is their nature for they are God's chosen ones. But the missing volume? Well, that was more than interesting because Yilmaz's library housed a copy of that book. His own copy! And Yilmaz thought: *How strangely the world unfolds. The boy travelled from Bologna to Constantinople in search of that book, failed, and yet a copy of it rests wedged between other books on a shelf less than fifteen paces from where the young man now sits.*

What about Niccolò's lack of discipline in Constantinople? On this dereliction, Yilmaz pardoned the boy as Niccolò was young and not of the East, and the delights of Constantinople are never easy to keep in check for any young Westerner.

Apart from the occasional gurgle from the hookah, they sat in silence until Yilmaz said, 'The Niccolò Umberto whose journey you have described tonight, is he the person you seek to be? That person is a person in whom others have put their trust only to see it abused. Think on it. Your father and brother, surely they expected some return for the privileges birth into their family gave you. I would say that banishment was not an act of malice but a gift to improve yourself. The ring you described as your paltry inheritance should have been not just a gold trinket to you but a potent reminder to respect from where you came. In my opinion, it was your talisman, and a unique talisman at that. You lost it to a Greek thief in Constantinople. A Greek who led you to hashish but, as they have said since the fall of Troy: *Beware of Greeks bearing gifts.'*

As he didn't want to embarrass Niccolò about the three Venetian women, Yilmaz didn't mention them but said, 'In Venice, you left a kind employer, that merchant Delmare. Surely you had a responsibility to the one who had provided you food, board and employment? To leave him without a word was not only ungrateful but also unkind.'

The hookah gurgled some more while they sat in silence until Yilmaz couldn't resist it, and just before he rose to leave he said, 'In Venice. Those three women. Yes, I know the duchessa arranged your employment in Bologna so she was complicit in your departure. I wonder what gratitude you gave her. Yes, yes, the dalliance with Delmare's wife was a mutual transaction but you must admit that you took advantage of the poor woman's situation. Finally and perhaps the gravest of your Venetian escapades was the callous treatment of the young Cherubina. She was the youngest and the most vulnerable of the three and yet you abandoned her.'

As he said this to Niccolò, Yilmaz transposed Cherubina for his twin daughters.

'A true gentleman would have remained in Venice to support Cherubina. I would say your conduct was disgraceful to all who dwelt in the Delmare household. And though you haven't yet told me the full truth – though it is easy to deduce – I'll tell you, man to man, you had no right to behave the way you did. Your departure from Venice was far from gallant. It was worthy not of a noble man but of a thief. You were no more than a thief slinking into the night with his sack of stolen goods.'

Then on cue, and as if to emphasise what Yilmaz had just said, the night sky was streaked by the trails of a spectacular meteor shower. After it had finished, the two men sat in silence for a while until Niccolò Umberto stood to go inside. As he left, Yilmaz said, 'Think on what I've said. Goodnight.'

Later in his room Niccolò thought on what Yilmaz had said and settled on: *Old fool! What would an old Turk living on an island like this know about the world?*

⤫

Niccolò Umberto's putative mother watched as he finished off his second beaker of the local sweet wine, then asked; 'So, Tasso, do you like it?'

Putative Tasso nodded and held his beaker up to for more.

'Strange, son, you used to hate this.'

Niccolò knew where this could be heading: an admission of the truth to her that he was not her Tasso. To placate the old woman's doubt, he explained, 'Death does strange things to one … mother.'

To which the old woman replied, 'Apparently.' Then, not as an afterthought but to convince herself she added, 'My son.'

But why had her reborn Tasso forgotten so much? Yes, he knew one could walk the island's coastline and beaches in two or three days. Niccolò Umberto had seen the island's white sands and he had seen the sea a clear turquoise. Putative mother added that it had been always so – the sun reflected off the sandy beach transforming it to a dazzling mirror at midday and then at sunset and sunrise the sand was a soft pink like a new-born baby's tongue. She wondered whether original Tasso had in death trapped some of the midday sun and what she now saw was original Tasso's dazzling reflection.

New Tasso had told her that when he had turned his gaze inland, the land shimmered as it baked. Further inland he had seen that there were fields with long grasses where shepherds guarded their sheep. In a particular field there were stunted gnarled olive trees and straggling grapevines. The old woman told him the trees of that field produced the olives he had enjoyed so much on his visits to her. And as for the field's grapevines? Well, they were the grapevines that produced a particular type of grape from which the island's intoxicating sweet wine was made. 'Ambrosia, the nectar of the gods', she added.

And though he had not wandered that far afield she wondered, if he was really Tasso returned, then why did she have to tell him that beyond the fields there was a forest and a mountain, streams and waterfalls? Why did she have to remind him that here and there the forest's darkness was banished by shafts of light sent from the heavens? Did he not know these heavenly shafts were the carriageways by which the old gods descended to earth? Magic happened in such places. Much to the displeasure of the priest, it was to such places in the forest, pierced by shafts of light, that village folk went to make their requests to the old gods. These were places where whispered or merely unsaid phrases, such as: *May my sheep be spared of pestilence* or *Please this year ensure I do not carry yet another child* or *Make Mano fall in love with me*, were sent on their way along the shafts. Sent in the hope that they were heard by the gods. And only if the request was heartfelt and only if the gods were pleased was there a remote possibility that the gods would be kind. Though she didn't tell new Tasso this, she had visited such places in the forest and made requests for her son to be returned from the dead. She knew her pleas had been heartfelt and the gods must have listened – wasn't the young man in her home at this very moment proof of that?

But still, why did she have to remind him of the sweet summertime smell of the forest pines where she had taken him to play when he was a child? He must have remembered that. Could death have robbed him of the sweet memories of the honey bees in her hives, or the dance of the grasses on the breezes or the distant mountain? And of that distant dangerous mountain? Why had he asked whether the mountain was ever visited? Every villager knew the mountain of the island was not to be visited. It was there the evil spirits of malevolent ancients still dwelt in the ruins of the mountaintop temple. Though the villagers didn't know it, the temple was already a ruin the day, eighteen centuries earlier, Alexander the Great had visited the island to supply his warships with island mutton, oil, wine and honey.

Most perplexing to the old woman was that new Tasso knew nothing of the island's ancients. She had to tell him, 'In youth the ancients were full of vigour and lusty. The men were like gods and the women like goddesses; each man an Adonis and each maiden an Aphrodite. The ancients, both male and female, were overly energetic with acts of fornication and they were most skilful in such pastimes. This being so, the island might have been considered to be a lecher's paradise but the gods had made sure there was a price to pay for such wanton frolicking. Bizarrely, it was an unhappy fact that the gods had deemed that as these people aged, they began to look like gnarled trees. It was their fate to shrink in stature, their fate for their skin become as bark and their limbs to become twisted. The gods had decreed this fate for both genders.

'If age is supposed to bring wisdom then it was not so for these people. In age they had little to say, and they did naught but stare. Toothless and gap-mouthed they stared. The old men stared to the mountain top where their temple sat and the old women stared to the sea. No one knew what visions these stunted geriatrics saw in the mountain or the sea; it was unknown to all but themselves. The young could have asked but, as it has ever been, the young were not interested in what their elderly had to say. Perhaps the young feared the answer might distract them from their lascivious gambols.

'When the blessed end came to the decrepit elderly, they were laid to rest in the field just beyond this village. Laid to rest, yes, but not as you might think. There were no graves as we might know. A grave to them was not a rectangular trench dug to certain depth, instead it was a hole dug just as you would to plant a tree. The corpse was then placed feet first. Can you imagine – feet first! And corpse's trunk? That was now upright and mostly above the level of the ground. The gods had planned it well, for in time male corpses transformed into the island's much prized olive trees. For females the procedure was the same except they became the grapevines and in time produced the grapes from which the island's peculiar wine is manufactured.'

The old woman's eyes narrowed and she passed on the warning. 'But take care how you scrape the bark or break even the smallest twig of the olive trees and grapevines. For the plant's wound will bleed and if that blood should touch your skin, then beware. It is said, and who am I to deny its truth, that the visions it induces will surely drive you insane with melancholia.'

Niccolò, so as to further convince her he was her Tasso returned, lied and said, 'Yes, yes, yes, mother I remember all that now. I remember you told me.' And with that the old woman knew that this was not her Tasso returned; she had never told the original Tasso of the wanton lechery of the island's original inhabitants for he had been just a child when she told him of the ancients. Then again, she could have been wrong and her Tasso may have learned about all this from others. So she held that as long as she believed he was her son, then he was without a doubt her Tasso returned from the dead.

⤳

The weather was changing; hookah smoking outdoors in the evening after dinner no longer happened. One evening as they sat by the hearth, Yilmaz told Niccolò about the ancient temple on a plateau on the mountain.

'I've heard of the temple from an old village crone – the one who believes I'm her son.'

Yilmaz replied, 'The village fools don't venture there. But I have. The temple is built in the style of the Athenian Parthenon and like the Parthenon it is also in ruins. Despite its ruinous state, such as decayed columns and fallen masonry, it is still a building of great beauty. More important to me, it is a place of profound spirituality.

When there, I find my mind given over to calming thoughts. In its environs I found peace conducive to inner searching. From the windy plateau one sees, as an angel might see, over the forest with its supposedly magic glades, over the field known to the villages as the field of the dead and beyond to the coast and the sea. Though you might think it not possible when at the ruined temple, I've seen beyond the horizon's lip to Gallipoli in my homeland and to my childhood home and into the room that was once mine. Such is the magic of the windswept plateau. It is beyond reason, but while there I have seen into the past and into the future. Not just one past or one future but every possible past and every possible future. In one future and one past I even saw your arrival on this island. The temple, ruined or otherwise, is truly a place of great spirituality. The ancient people of this island chose the site of their temple well.

'You might think it was the result of a hashish-induced fantasy but no such substance was involved the night while sitting on the temple's ruined steps I was able to see – to truly see. I saw beyond the furthest star to many strange corners of the universe, corners where the physical laws of our world did not apply. I saw celestial systems being born and dying over countless millennia, all seen in less time than a heartbeat of a gnat borne over the islands by the Meltemi winds. And at the same time as I voyaged the infinity of the universe, I stared deeply into the heart of a blade of grass growing from a cracked block of temple stone. All its constituents became known to me as if I had known them forever. Then those constituents revealed more universes within themselves. Such is the magic of that place. It is a place of deep spirituality.

'On the other hand, and perhaps of great disappointment to the locals, I can assert there is no magic in the forest glades; that's just primitive talk, but there is magic on the plateau around the temple. As I have said, the ancients, whoever they were, chose well when they built their temple on that windswept plateau. I must take you there one day.'

A day arrived when Yilmaz determined Niccolò had returned to full strength. It was the day he caught Niccolò stealing lustful glances at Phoebe and Hilaeira and he thought: *The young man needs other distractions.* And so he decided it was time they should all go to the plateau and its temple.

~≈~

Before dawn they set off in single file on donkeys. Yilmaz at its head, delighted in equal measure at being both in charge and a gracious host; Niccolò followed next, for after all he was the guest; in the rear and sharing a beast, for they were light, were Phoebe and Hilaeira. Yilmaz's subordinates had left the day before with heavily laden donkeys to prepare a campsite beside the ancient ruined temple.

In the early morning light, when the grasses were still moist and limp with dew, the little column reached the olive groves and vineyards of the dead. There they continued in reverential silence, picking their way through the closely planted stands and rows of olive trees and grapevines. Once clear of those parts, Yilmaz spoke for the first time: 'Soon we'll enter the pine forests; the so-called glades of magic are there. But before we reach the forests we will rest by a pool. It is an exquisite rocky basin fed by tumbling pure waters of a mountain waterfall.'

They reached the pool by midmorning. There they rested and ate goat's cheese embedded in Turkish bread; Yilmaz offered Niccolò some island wine, adding that he could not participate as his beliefs exclude the pleasures of alcohol.

Perhaps it was Yilmaz's test of Niccolò, then again it may have been an act of innocence, but it came to pass that the twins removed the entirety of their clothing; not a stich was left on their identical and perfect feminine forms. Once disrobed, they ran lightly to the basin to frolic in its waters and brave the showers of the waterfall. They were more than most desirable and if it happened to be a test, then in truth Niccolò found it very difficult to feign a lack of interest. Niccolò Umberto had been tempted and he had succumbed to furtive side glances on many more than a handful of occasions. And now by the pool, the temptation was such that he struggled to limit himself to even those furtive glances at the splashing nymphs. It was for him a great ordeal.

Finally, in an effort to be a worthy guest, he averted his gaze and resorted to an old trick of counting in groups of seven from one hundred down to two. He did not know what he would do when he reached two. Before he reached two he was rescued by Yilmaz who suggested he close his eyes and attempt sleep. After the wine sleep and dreams came quickly.

The sun was no longer high when Yilmaz gently roused Niccolò and commanded that they be on their way again. The twins were neither in the water nor were they around the pool's edge. They had gone.

Yilmaz had sent Phoebe and Hilaeira ahead to be sure they arrived at the temple before nightfall. Niccolò asked whether Yilmaz had any fear of his daughters travelling alone through the forest.

Yilmaz replied, 'No. They know the way and no harm will come to them. We are rational men and therefore we know there is no truth in the native tales of the forest's dangers.' Then, pausing for effect, Yilmaz looked at Niccolò and added, 'Any harm that could ever come to them would be from more earthly sources.'

Niccolò found the journey through the pine forest somewhat dull. He had, despite Yilmaz's scepticism, imagined ethereal shady glades alive with magical creatures, but instead he found those shafts of light from the heavens alive with midges and dancing motes. After their journey through the forest, Yilmaz pointed to a mountain trail that would eventually lead to the plateau and its temple.

As it was getting dark, the subordinates had already placed lighted lanterns at the base of each of the temple's ruined columns. Nearing their destination, above them Niccolò Umberto and Yilmaz saw through the early evening mist the ruined temple floating on regularly spaced points of light.

A campsite had been set up alongside the temple. The sun had set and now the lanterns at the base of each column and a flickering campsite fire cast everything in an otherworldly glow. In this light the hook-nosed subordinates took on the look of birds of prey, the twins took on the look of angelic purity and Yilmaz seemed to have aged into a wrinkled sage.

After the meal they sat around the fire, Yilmaz staring into the fire as if to find meaning in it, Niccolò drinking more of the over-sweet wine, the twins humming strange melodies, while one subordinate provided accompaniment on a stringed instrument unknown to Umberto. The other subordinate dozed. Yilmaz poured Niccolò another wine and asked if he had heard of the great poet Rumi and his beautiful poems. Niccolò had not so Yilmaz added, 'Of all poets, he is without any doubt the greatest.'

The once gentle breeze had transformed to the usual rougher one of the plateau. Niccolò drew his blanket tighter and moved closer to the fire's warmth. Yilmaz noted that the young man had drained his tumbler so, leaning closer, he refilled it with more wine and as he did so he said, 'There is a poem I like and I think part of it goes like this:

> *The wind is pouring wine! Love*
> *used to hide behind images. No more!*
>
> *The orchard hangs out its lanterns.*
> *The dead come stumbling by in shrouds.*
>
> *Nothing can stay bound or be imprisoned.*
> *You say, 'End this poem here and*
>
> *wait for what's next.' I will. Poems*
> *are rough notations for the music we are.*[*]

When he had finished the poem Yilmaz asked, 'Do you think poems are rough notations for the music we are?' But Niccolò, his mind now befuddled by the wine, could only manage, 'It's a thought-provoking idea.'

Was it the magic of the setting or merely the wine that delivered to Niccolò Umberto a bizarre dream? He dreamed of the end of a universe that was only the island and all on it. For no reason other than what was found in the logic of dreams, assembled in the field of

---

[*] Part of the poem 'The Music We Are' by Rumi, taken from *Rumi the Book of Love*, translations and commentary by Coleman Barks (HarperCollins, 2003).

the dead were Yilmaz, the twins, the subordinates, the villagers and, in the form of a goat, the island itself.

In the dream, for his failure to deliver the missing volume of *God's Agreement with Man* to Mordechai Levi, Niccolò had been forced to take on the role of a Papal Inquisitor. With the power invested in him by the Pope, he interrogated Yilmaz's subordinates and asked them how this island-bound universe should end. The subordinates conferred for a while and then agreed that the universe should end in any way the Almighty pleased with one condition, the condition being their coupling with the twins. They then added that knowing their luck in the draw of lots, they'd have more chance coupling with their donkeys. The dream Inquisitor Umberto replied that in the main, the subordinates had chosen well. He added that he supposed any ending that had the non-dreaming Niccolò Umberto having his way with a twin was more likely. Better still was any ending that had the non-dreaming Niccolò Umberto coupling with both girls, preferably both at the same time, as such an ending would be in keeping with his licentious nature.

Next Inquisitor Umberto picked up a burning stick from the campfire, held it to Yilmaz's chest and asked how the end should be. Unfazed by the burning stick at his chest, Yilmaz said that unlike his subordinates and Niccolò Umberto, who were cheats and liars, any ending would do so long as somewhere it was recorded that Yilmaz possessed charity, intelligence, sophistication and superior breeding. With that Inquisitor plunged the burning stick, which had now become a spear, into Yilmaz's chest. Yilmaz's response was to call the Inquisitor a fool.

Then it was the twins' turn to be interrogated. In unison they said they'd be more than happy for the island universe to end. It made no difference to them as they'd had enough of their isolation. Their isolation was equivalent to non-existence so to end it all now made no difference. Then Phoebe, or was it Hilaeira – for even now Niccolò was never sure which was which – had an idea. She said Father had told them of the places Niccolò had visited – Venice, Bologna and

Constantinople. Of those places they had seen Constantinople so it held no attraction for them. In the sweetest voice possible, Phoebe, or was it Hilaeira, made a suggestion: *If it pleases the Inquisitor and of course the Almighty, though we're not sure He exists, we would fancy an ending where, irrespective of what happens to everyone else, including Father, we are spared and allowed to go to live in Bologna or Venice.* An argument followed between the twins whether it was to be Bologna or Venice. One wanted Bologna because at the university there were bound to be the handsomest of students. The other wanted Venice because it was a place of fashionable folk pursuing romantic escapades. For a solution, Inquisitor Umberto offered each twin their choice but they declined as they could never bear to be separated. As it goes in dreams, it was possible for Inquisitor Umberto to ask the opinion of the donkeys and the island in its embodiment as a one-eyed goat, a one-eyed goat with a tiny version of the ruined temple on its back, as it has been said such things are possible in dreams. The donkeys said to hell with everyone, except themselves. They would be happy if the island was spared and they were released to wander in peace forever in the shade of the olive groves and grapevines in the field of the dead. In dreams it is possible to converse with animals, and so because the island was represented in proxy by a one-eyed goat, the island itself was interrogated. The island said it would like an ending that allowed it to quake, as many of its sister and brother islands of the region had; to tremble violently until it had shaken every living thing off its back; then to be permitted to sink below the sea drowning the cursed temple – the temple that it failed to completely destroy more than two millennia earlier.

When Niccolò woke he remembered the dream and wondered why the villagers had not been interrogated. With the dream fresh in his mind, Niccolò said to Yilmaz, 'I had the strangest dream last night.'

'In this place we all do. I believe that the ancients chose this plateau to build their temple because of its special properties.'

'Special properties?'

'Yes, special. Special is a suitable description of this location's properties. Come, I'll show you something.'

Yilmaz led Niccolò away from the temple to a small depression surrounded by a jumble of masonry; either time or the island's earthquakes had destroyed whatever structure had once stood there. Perhaps it had been a small shrine. The jumble of stone blocks and small columns were in fact what was left of a small construction, similar to but much smaller than the main ruin on the plateau.

'This is what's left of a chamber. My guess is that it fell to ruin at the same time as the temple. It's up for debate whether the chamber had been a small shrine or a small temple. I've paced it out and it's about the size of my library room. What is interesting is the fissure into the earth at its centre. See there,' Yilmaz said, pointing to the crack about one pace in length. The crack was surrounded by bushy weeds.

'Yes, I see it. It looks like a woman's …' Niccolò stopped mid-sentence, as he realised that Yilmaz might have found what he was about to say crude and offensive. Instead he repeated, 'Yes, I see it.'

'I believe that this is the source of the mystery of this place.'

'How can that be?'

'The fissure must lead deep into the earth. For all we know it could go to the centre of the earth. That in itself is interesting, but more to the point it is from time to time that vapours from the deep are emitted through the vent.'

'So?'

'Well, it is my opinion those vapours contain the essence of the magic one experiences here. The gases come from the depths and are emitted through the fissure. Who knows who cooks up those gases way down there – angels, evil spirits or benevolent spirits or perhaps even the Devil himself. Then, depending on the winds, the magic vapours may reach the nostrils of anyone in the vicinity of the temple. The rest such as visions and wild dreams follow. It's all very similar to a hashish-laced hookah.' Then, looking Niccolò Umberto directly in the eye, Yilmaz added, 'Like Constantinople? Eh?'

'Have you shared your theory with others?'

'No. Before I do such I must know myself how I would feel about the elimination of the mysteries of this place to have it all explained by its mechanics. The knowledge of how something happens is like finding out how a magician has performed his magic. The wonder is gone. As a child I saw ghosts yet now I am certain they don't exist. I have many explanations for my childhood ghosts. My childhood ghosts may have been just the mist above a pond or the play of the light on a curtain or just my childish imagination. And in possession of those explanations, what has happened to my ghosts? They no longer reveal themselves to me. Knowledge increases understanding of the world, but for me knowledge also diminishes the wonder of the world. To make the world exciting we need the wonder of it.'

'Then surely that's a case of saying that ignorance is bliss?'

'Perhaps. But don't you think there are times when it is better not to know how something happens and instead experience that something? There are times when the *knowing* is the barrier to a full experience.'

Niccolò thought awhile and then said, 'I think you might be looking for enchantment in the wrong places. The librarian Mordechai Levi of Bologna found enchantment and wonder in knowledge. His thirst for knowledge was his driver. Mind you, Bologna is such a place. Though definitely not for me, Bologna fosters the acquisition of knowledge. Levi's mind was such that the knowing of the mechanics of things, as you called it, brought him joy. His world was not diminished by the knowing of its workings. For him, seeing through the smoke and mirrors of a magician's tricks would have surely resulted in the pleasure of saying: *Ah! So that's how it was done.*'

'Maybe you are right. People differ in their wants, and your Mordechai Levi appears to be a different man from me. I suppose there is the desire for mysticism and there is the desire for knowledge, and I have yet to master the blending of the two. Come let's return to the others.'

Niccolò Umberto makes a second visit to the ruined temple on the plateau

In which Niccolò Umberto makes a second trip with Yilmaz to the ruined temple. Under the influence of the plateau's vapours he lays bare and in greater detail much about his past. On the way back Niccolò Umberto suffers an accident. He is left alone while Yilmaz goes back to the garrison for assistance. Niccolò Umberto experiences strange visitations while waiting for Yilmaz to return.

There came a day when Yilmaz asked Niccolò if he would like to visit the ruined temple on the plateau again. 'This time let's make it just the two of us. We don't need my daughters nor my subordinates. How about it?'

Though this time Niccolò found the journey to be less interesting, he remembered what Elena had told him about the bark of the olive trees and the grapevine. Niccolò wondered: *How could it be that these plants bleed sadness and melancholia?*

Yilmaz knew what Niccolò was thinking and without any prompting, as if his answer was a random sentence, said, 'Do you think the things they say about this place are possible or are they just old wives' stories?'

How did he know what I was thinking?

Yilmaz continued, 'Don't worry, I didn't read your mind, I merely turned around and read your face as we passed the olive trees. You must remember there have always been seemingly strange things in this world, but once we have their explanations they no longer seem so strange. As I've said before, for me mysteries make life interesting. I very much doubt, however, that sap from the olive trees and grapevines can induce melancholia and sadness. I would argue an islander with the propensity for melancholia had once come in contact with that sap. The sap did not alter his condition but the poor islander associated it with his melancholia. That is the most likely explanation, for it has been my observation that the natives of this island have within them a natural inclination towards melancholia and sadness. So much for the charms of island life!

'And what of the so-called magical properties of the glades we will encounter? The natives claim the glades possess such properties but I have not seen any evidence for it. Again, perhaps an islander had made a wish in such a glade and that wish was by chance granted. What of the countless wishes made in the glades that were never granted? What's more, there must be a list of reasons why one would never hear of the ungranted wishes. Top of that list would be the embarrassment of being one who was unworthy of the hypothetical spirits granting your wish. More to the point, I would say that almost all wishes made by islanders are secret, thereby making it impossible to verify the efficacy of the granting.

'You see, for what at first appears to be unexplainable there are often rational explanations, explanations that do not require the spirit world. And as for the power of the plateau where we're headed? Well, I've already voiced my belief it is the gases emitted from the depths of the earth through a vent that account for the strange revelations experienced around the ruined temple. But don't get me wrong, the explanation as to how those revelations happen does not for one minute diminish the powerful value of those revelations.'

They reached the watery basin where the twins had frolicked in naked innocence. Niccolò wondered whether their behaviour had really been so innocent or had they decided or been instructed to tempt him: *Did old Yilmaz set them up to do that so as to test me?* And why had he fallen into such a deep, almost drugged, sleep the first time he had been by the basin? The last time he had slept as deeply was in Constantinople, courtesy of a hashish vendor. This time at the basin Yilmaz said that they would not stop. 'You've already experienced the charms of this place so there is no need to stop. We'll press on until we reach the plateau with its ruin.'

The pair then rode on in silence. When they reached the glades with their shafts of sunlight Yilmaz said, 'No spirits here. Just motes and a peaceful atmosphere.' And then as if to taunt Niccolò, 'Make a wish and see if it eventuates.'

Niccolò Umberto made a silent wish: *For Christ's sake, get me off this island; the sooner the better.*

⇌

Without the presence of Yilmaz's subordinates, they had to set up their camp by themselves. This time at Yilmaz's suggestion, the camp was set up as close as possible to the fissure. Both complained with their exertions setting up the camp. Looking at his hands, Yilmaz said, 'A man of my age and status shouldn't have to do this.'

Niccolò replied, 'It was easier last time because Mustafa and Kulu set up for us. I have to admit it's been a long time since I have done anything like this by myself. Honestly, not since after my father's death and my brother Frederick took me to the woods to enlighten me as to what he deemed was the path I should follow in life.'

'It seems to me that your brother's suggestions may have fallen on barren ground. Perhaps we might talk later on such matters.' Then looking at his hands again and examining his fingernails, Yilmaz added, 'But first please collect some firewood as I fear it will be a long and cold night.'

That's right, you old bastard with your clean hands, you've got me doing the dirty work.

The vapours from the fissure had not been apparent during daylight but as the skies were darkening the vapours became clearly visible. The wafts of luminous gases prompted Yilmaz to say, 'I think tonight will be profitable; very profitable.'

'How do you mean very profitable?'

Pointing to the vapours, Yilmaz said, 'Oh, profitable for my understanding of you and perhaps for your development.'

'Your understanding of me and my development?'

'Yes. From what you've already told me there's still much about you I'd like to understand. And as for development? Well, you must agree that for all of us there's the need for development.'

'I don't follow you.'

'Maybe I should have said your *improvement* rather than your development. A man's life should be a journey of self-improvement. That journey is God's gift to all men, though for some it perhaps is a burden. I suspect, even if you are unaware of it, you have much to improve within yourself. The vapours might help me in the understanding of you and provide you with insights to your development.' Here Yilmaz corrected himself, 'Sorry, I mean insights to your improvement.'

As far as Niccolò Umberto was concerned, Yilmaz was overstepping. *What the old man is proposing is a rape of my private thoughts.*

That evening as they sat around the fire, Yilmaz unrolled the hookah from the cloth it had been wrapped in. 'Let's partake. I will lace it with a little something I've kept aside for such a time as this. You, having been in Constantinople, are no doubt acquainted with Ottoman mind-expanding substances. Let me assure what I have here is not the run of the mill hashish such as you might pick up from a shady backstreet tout. This, my friend, is the king of kings of substances. Some call it the Persian inhalation of truth because it helps the user see truths that otherwise are hidden. So forget poor imitations such as alcohol or hashish, as they lead you nowhere. Alcohol dulls the mind, not to mention all other bodily sensations. And as for hashish? It promises paradise but more often than not delivers something very different; it provides illusions and not truth. But this Persian substance will, my young Christian, set you on the real road to the truth. Are you willing to take that journey to find the truth about yourself? With the vapours from the depths of the earth, truth inhalation and the hookah, tonight should be a night of enlightenment, don't you think?'

Ever eager to embark on new sensations, Niccolò Umberto greedily sucked on the hookah's mouthpiece and never noticed that Yilmaz did not partake. Whether the night had been one of enlightenment, Niccolò could never answer. His recollections in the morning before they set off from the plateau for the journey back were that he had done a lot of talking and Yilmaz had done a lot of listening. He remembered that during his time of listening, Yilmaz's eyes had glowed in the dark and from time to time he nodded sagely. But if one were to ask Niccolò Umberto what he had talked about, he would have been at a loss. All he could remember was that Yilmaz asked questions and he had answered. *What were those questions Yilmaz had asked? And what were my answers? I don't remember. I just don't remember.* He concluded that if the Persian substance lacing the hookah had been the road to enlightenment, then he would prefer a hashish dealer's product and alcohol every time.

In the beginning their descent was uneventful. When they reached the glades with their supposedly spiritually charged shafts of light Yilmaz asked, as if to mock the place, 'Do you see any spirits or sense anything special about this place? I certainly don't. No spirits here. Just motes that's all.' Then, as if to taunt Umberto as he had done the day before, he said, 'Go on, make a wish.' And again as before, Niccolò made a silent wish to be rid of the island and back with the world.

While crossing the field with its olive trees and grapevines, for a reason unknown to anyone, Niccolò's donkey stumbled and died. And as the donkey's front legs folded, Niccolò started to slide forward; without thinking he grabbed for the closest olive tree's branch. The branch snapped, and on his way down Niccolò's face grazed the tree's trunk. Just before his head hit a small boulder, he muttered: *Oh no, not the sap of melancholia.* He then passed out.

Unable to travel with him, Yilmaz left him at the base of the olive tree and rode to the garrison to get help and another donkey.

❧

Niccolò Umberto had no idea how long he had been sitting on the ground with his back against an olive tree's trunk. His head throbbed and his arm ached. He was not sure where he was. *I was at the ruin with Yilmaz but how did I get here?* He tried to get up but he did not have the strength. His head ached and his memory of some recent events had disappeared. He couldn't remember what had happened at the plateau, but he remembered the mysterious glades and Yilmaz's taunt to make a wish. He saw the donkey lying on its side and remembered that he had fallen from it.

Then a man spoke and he recognised the voice. Sitting opposite him, also with his back resting against the trunk of another tree, was the Venetian merchant Delmare. It was Delmare, but not as he had remembered him. This Delmare was a shadow of his old self; no longer the jovial fat man, this was a morose and thinner Delmare. His eyes had disappeared and the rims of their sockets were those of a man who had done much crying.

'You little Piedmont piece of turd,' he said. 'You've well and truly fucked me over. Broken me in so many ways. Did you think those scams you concocted would go unnoticed forever in Venice? We both should have known nothing remains unnoticed for long in Venice. Nothing! Neither scams nor indiscretions. Some say secrecy is the charm of Venice, But no, Venice seduces you to believe your secrets are secrets forever and held back by a secure wall, while all the time behind your back those secrets are leaking out drop by drop. Did you ever wonder what would happen once word got around of what your so-called business ventures really were? I bet not, you shit streak.

'Now no one wants to do business with me. My business was built on trust and now no one trusts me. I have no business and I'm financially ruined, but what would you care? If that was the only legacy you left me, then that would be bad enough. But no, your stench lingers on in all the corners of my life and it will remain with me until I die. You, the human cesspit, do you think I don't know about you and the duchessa? And you and Rosetta. And you and my little sweet Cherubina. I know all about that now. All of Venice knew before I knew. I've got three of your bastards in my care. Yes, yes, the duchessa can take care of her bastard but what of the other two? With my business gone, do you think I can afford to provide for Rosetta's and Cherubina's? Tell me how can I do that? Well, Rosetta's maybe. I'm left with the problems you created and you scurried away like a fetid canal rat. But I insult the poor rat for you're less than the filthiest canal rat. Do you know, not that you'd care, my former friends laugh not behind my back but directly at my face. Cherubina's child is definitely your responsibility! I hope you die a thousand times. Die, you maggot!'

Niccolò Umberto must have dozed off and when he awoke his head still throbbed. The Delmare who had spoken to him was gone. In Delmare's place leaning against the same tree where Delmare had been was Mordechai Levi. Levi's eyes blazed with the fire of multiple generations of persecution. Though Levi didn't speak to him, Niccolò understood everything conveyed by Levi's glare. He understood the before-death fear of facing a mob in Barcelona or Vienna or Prague who chanted *Kill-the-Jew*. He felt the heat of the night-time glow of Jews burning along the banks of Lisbon's Targa. He shivered when he thought of heaps of broken dead Jews, like broken and discarded dolls, piled high in the city squares of Barcelona. And for that moment, and only for that moment, he understood and felt the horror of it all. Levi then shook his head and pointed a trembling accusing finger at Niccolò Umberto, but before he said anything he burst into flame. Then Levi was consumed by fire as the Jews on along the banks of the Targa had been. Levi was reduced the same way as Umberto had once witnessed at the burning of heretics. And soon Levi was no more than ashes, ashes to be scattered on the freshening wind.

Once again he passed out and once again he woke to a throbbing head. No longer could he see the pile of ashes that had been Mordechai Levi. Though he could not see his father and brother, he heard their voices carried on the wind and wondered how that could be. Surely his father was dead and his brother was far away, administering Umberto lands. Then they appeared before him. His father spoke: 'Niccolò, you are the greatest disappointment of my life. You are without a doubt the lowest of the low to carry the name Umberto. You're a disgrace.' His father then asked, 'Where is the ring I left you? That ring has been handed down through the centuries but now where is it?'

Then his brother answered the father, 'Father, surely you must know that everything Niccolò touches is lost or wasted. He himself is a worthless, lost and wasted soul. I had hoped that by banishment he might have developed some redeeming qualities, but I see that he is as dissolute as ever he was.'

Niccolò Umberto's head ached more than ever and again he heard more voices on the wind. This time the voices were not those of his dead father and his older brother, but the voices of Yilmaz and his subordinates coming for him.

The Notes on Niccolò Umberto

In which Niccolò Umberto gradually recovers from his fall. He discovers a workbook titled Working Notes on Niccolò Umberto *lying on Yilmaz's desk. He reads the notes and is much disturbed.*

The garrison was empty. Yilmaz and his two mulish assistants had gone to conduct their survey of the forests. The twins were nowhere to be seen so Niccolò Umberto concluded they had also tagged along for the forest survey. They had left him here. Obviously they had thought after his fall he would be best left at the garrison.

After sitting on the terrace for a while, the sun drove him to the coolness of indoors. He wandered without any particular purpose from room to room. He noticed that there were thin patches on the pile of Yilmaz's prayer mat; the patches corresponded to the position of the prayer giver's knees. He noticed that the twins had not made their beds. He noticed a damp patch on a whitewashed wall of Yilmaz's library and wondered why he had not seen it before. How could it be rising damp when everything else was baked dry? He then gazed at Yilmaz's desk – a jumble of papers, writing implements and a workbook lying face down. Without giving it much thought, he picked up the workbook and turned it the right way up. With the book facing him he could read its title. Immediately a jolt of lightning hit his heart and from there it bifurcated upwards to his throat and downwards to his legs; from his mouth it stole saliva and to his knees it gave a tremble. He had to sit down until the book's title returned to focus. It was a book whose title read *Working Notes on*

Niccolò Umberto: A study of the self-centred male.

He opened the book. The contents page indicated that the workbook was divided in sections and subsections:

The subject – Niccolò Umberto

- *Subject is a self-obsessed young man (Niccolò Umberto from the north of the Italian peninsula). Having overcome a number of obstacles (banishment from his family home, flight from Venice, near drowning) he now views himself as invincible. He is completely immoral in his relationships with either gender. He sees women only as objects for his own sexual gratification; in my opinion he treats them shabbily. He feels no responsibility to those who have given to him succour and entrusted much to him (the Venetian merchant Delmare, the university librarian Levi and the Jews of Bologna).*

Lorenzo Delmare – Venetian Merchant

- *Umberto's duplicity with Lorenzo Delmare – no intention to help him out with getting a significant portrait done.*

- *With respect to Delmare's hospitality, Umberto is leechlike.*

- *Umberto's untoward* ~~prying into~~ *curiosity about Lorenzo Delmare's private life – it is to be noted that Delmare trusted Umberto to deliver a private letter to the duchessa unopened – Umberto broke that trust.*

- *The business ventures – From what I understand these ventures served in the main to benefit Umberto. As far as Umberto is concerned, he was clear of Venice while the unfortunate Lorenzo was left there to face whatever negative outcomes resulted from their salt and damask scams – if such outcomes should surface. If my knowledge of Venice serves me well, negative outcomes of the scams were bound to occur. As they say: 'Beware the Venetian who discovers he has been cheated in business.'*

- Umberto's ~~fucking of~~ sexual dalliance with Lorenzo's wife. No matter the circumstances this was unacceptable behaviour.

- Umberto's despicable dereliction of duty in Constantinople (See later notes).

Duchessa Di Palma - Delmare's Paramour

- Umberto and the duchessa in their lack of moral depth are ~~birds of a feather~~ very much alike. It seems to me both are self-centred, self-seeking and avaricious. In my opinion Umberto and the duchessa are cut from the same cloth - in a just paradise they deserve each other, and similarly in a vindictive hell they deserve each other.

- To them everyone is a plaything to be moved around life's board in such a way that it befits them. Even though it was to her advantage to have Umberto out of Venice, at least the duchessa arranged for Umberto to find employment in Bologna. Perhaps she is of a more generous spirit than Umberto?

- The solution to her pregnancy was not even of Umberto's doing - however, unlike Umberto, many men have taken responsibility for a child conceived by them as well as a child _NOT_ conceived by them.

Rosetta Delmare - Delmare's Wife

- Umberto took advantage of a very distressed woman - surely he could have 'talked' with her, helped her find a solution to Lorenzo's infidelity.

- Once again the solution to the 'unwanted' pregnancy was not of Umberto's doing.

Cherubina Delmare - Delmare's Daughter

- Once again Umberto took advantage of someone (her young lust - perhaps?) but worse still, he left Cherubina to sort out _THEIR_ problem - classical case of a rake's abandonment and not taking responsibility. Man should be better than that.

Mordechai Levi Librarian of Bologna AND the Jews of Bologna

- Umberto was entrusted with money raised by the Jewry of Bologna and sent on an important mission to bring back the book. He failed in that task due his partaking in the depravity of Constantinople – no one forced him – it was his weakness and selfishness. This was Umberto's betrayal of the faith decent people (Levi and the Jews of Bologna) had in him.

- Umberto's failure to deliver the book to the university library could well lead to serious ramifications and might have grim consequences for his Jewish patrons. His failure might very well hasten the expulsion of Jews from Bologna. Once they are gone, how many centuries will pass before they are permitted return? If they are not expelled then they might perhaps be confined to their own limited area of the town. [In the tongue of the Venetians they refer to such an enclave after their word for foundry, namely 'GHETTO'.] It mustn't be overlooked that Pope Julius has already instructed the destruction of the Talmud and many Jewish texts. The Jews having made a promise to return with the missing volume and then failing to fulfil that promise might be deemed as evidence of their lack of reliability – an argument might run along the lines that if they can't be relied to organise the purchase and return of the book, then what can they be relied on? The outcome might be that they are not worth having around – perhaps not the main reason for expulsion of Jews from Bologna, but certainly it would add 'fuel to the fire'.

Niccolò Umberto in Constantinople

- Some might posit that Umberto's behaviour in Constantinople is merely that of an inexperienced young man who succumbed to the temptations of that city.

Theories

The Nullus Theory:

- The young man is a complete innocent. Though his actions harm others, he means no harm. He is a simple fellow who is unaware of the consequences of his actions. He innocently follows the principle wherein his actions serve only his pleasure without thinking beyond his own enjoyment <u>AND</u> most importantly, truly believes he is blameless. I find it hard to support this theory as, by all accounts, <u>he is intelligent, well learned and world-wise.</u>

The Inherited Behaviour Trait Theory:

- Somehow the ~~curse~~ burden of an ancestor's lack of moral sensitivity (a trait) has emerged once again. Who knows, perhaps the seed of an ancestor has within it an essence that is transferred immutably through the ages to subsequent generations, only to ~~reappear~~ manifest if certain conditions are about. In the case of Umberto, could the lack of morality of an ancestor have been passed down through time only to ~~reappear~~ manifest in our era in him? To establish such a hypothesis I would need to know more about his forbearers. Incidentally, this theory absolves the young man from any intentions to harm others on the grounds that he is a victim of his heredity. Knowing what I know of him, this theory would meet with his approval as it absolves him of responsibility for his actions.

- Surely there are other theories yet to be developed! Perhaps after I've spoken with him other theories will declare themselves?

<u>Preliminary Assertions</u> (Gleaned from conversations with the young man)

• Regarding the Three Women of Venice:

Umberto may have left Venice thinking smugly about his carnal achievements but we know better. To this date I have decided to leave him thinking thus but let us unpack his encounters with these women. In his encounter with the duchessa, what was he? Let me tell you he was no more than an accoutrement to her lunch – a side-dish, if you will. She cared nought of him. And her act of generosity – the letter of introduction? Well, it was for her benefit as it was a genteel way of eliminating him from Venice; you see, the duchessa cared as little for Niccolò Umberto as he did for her – as I have written earlier they are cut from the same cloth. Even if he wrongly believed his encounter with the duchessa had been on his terms, then can he consider the tabletop antics with Rosetta an achievement? Again he would have been wrong. What was he here? As far as I see it, he was no more than a convenient way for a woman to salve her anger at an unfaithful husband. No more than that and, for all I know, perhaps even less. That now brings us to Cherubina – sweet and vulnerable Cherubina, the virginal Cherubina. Here he most certainly thought he was the one in control, the instigator of events, her one and only, her first. On these matters he was right in one attribute only. He was her first. You see, once again he was a means to an end. He was no more than a drink to slake Cherubina's thirst, a meal to fill her empty belly or a backscratcher to reach an itch. In my opinion, he was no more than that! What of the request that she hide her face behind a Venetian mask? Let's examine this closer. By her wearing the mask, Umberto was not having Cherubina; he was merely having some woman in a mask. You see, all the time the masked Cherubina could see his face and not vice versa. Surely one could say she was having Niccolò Umberto and not the other way around.

It would seem that Umberto was incidental to the three women. That all this is so is attested by the fact that the duchessa wanted him out of Venice. It also is significant that subsequent to his liaisons with Rosetta and Cherubina, stairway meetings or other chance meetings with them did not even elicit eye contact with him. The interactions that each engaged with him later was only to announce the forthcoming maternal predicaments they had found themselves. While the two more mature women, each in her own way, were able to solve the problem pregnancies without his help, he failed dismally when asked to solve Cherubina's predicament. In fact, both mature women were pleased to see him out of their lives and out of Venice. Maybe Cherubina would have wished he'd stayed around long enough to solve their problem.

All things considered, if my assertions above hold true, Umberto's behaviour toward the three women was detestable. No man of breeding (which I believe he is) should behave as he has. He must be cured of such conduct. But how?

- *Regarding the Jews of Bologna*

  The young man does not appear to ~~harbour~~ embrace any prejudices toward the Semites – though throughout ~~the ages~~ their history, for the Jews there have been many who have had such hatred. (Fortunately in my country the treatment of these people has ~~in the main~~ been benign.) The young man worked cooperatively under the Jew Levi. He must have been sufficiently ~~respected and~~ trusted to have been taken to the bosom of the Jews of Bologna – so much so as to have been tasked with going to Constantinople to fetch and return to Bologna with a book they highly prize. Keep in mind that though they are canny with money, the Jews nevertheless had sufficient trust in him to send him on his way to Constantinople with a heavy purse!

Keeping in mind the dire consequences that might befall the Bolognese Jews because of his failure, I find his lack of compassion dishonourable – an honourable man would have returned with the book. It is for his failure in this project that I find Umberto lacking in decency. Once again I say, he must be cured of such conduct. And once again I ask, how? Or is it even possible?

A fear of mine

What if this young man is incapable of insight and he functions purely at the level of an animal? It appears that he lacks an understanding of the connections between one's actions and the consequences of those actions. I have to caution myself against thinking of him as an idiot but at times it is difficult not to do so. Who knows? Perhaps another visit to the fissure on the plateau is needed.

When had Yilmaz gleaned all the information about Umberto? Niccolò Umberto recalled that one evening, the night of the meteor shower, when he had shared a hookah with Yilmaz under the lemon tree and he had told Yilmaz his story, perhaps it had been that night. It was the night Yilmaz had spoken his thoughts on Niccolò's account of his banishment, his time in Venice, Bologna and Constantinople. But now Yilmaz had transferred those thoughts into a study of him. Niccolò wondered if he had babbled too much when under the mystic influence of the plateau's vapours and the hookah's mysterious Persian ingredient during his second visit. Had he rambled when he had fallen with a dead donkey? On the other hand, and more embarrassing, had he prattled out more of his life's story when Yilmaz had come back with the sidekicks Mustafa and Kulu to collect him from where he had fallen? *Perhaps in one of those unguarded moments when I was vulnerable – if so those would have been times when I was less myself but revealed more of myself.*

Yilmaz's crossings out, rewritten words and unanswered questions showed that the workbook was a work still in progress. Yilmaz had done Niccolò Umberto's life the indignity of reducing it to an academic study. In Yilmaz's book he was no longer the man *Niccolò Umberto* but an object of scientific interest. He had been rendered an object of enquiry in what appeared to be a discipline he didn't know by a man who knew too much about him. *Yilmaz may think he knows a lot about me but he has written me not the way I see myself.* He put the workbook back as he had found it and decided he could never confront Yilmaz about it.

Departure

In which Yilmaz advises Niccolò Umberto to be a better man. Niccolò Umberto is given Yilmaz's copy of the much sought-after Volume R. He is given a number of instructions. Namely, return with the book to Mordechai Levi in Bologna, make amends with the women he has wronged in Venice and ask Delmare for his forgiveness. Niccolò Umberto leaves with the book on a supply vessel heading for Constantinople. On reaching Constantinople Niccolò Umberto must choose between two actions.

A few days after Niccolò Umberto had read Yilmaz's workbook, an Ottoman supply ship arrived at the island. Although he would have liked to study Niccolò Umberto more, Yilmaz suggested that Niccolò should leave the island on that ship for its return to Constantinople. As he had no desire to become further entrapped in Yilmaz's surreptitious study of him and as he had had enough of the island, Niccolò agreed with Yilmaz's suggestion.

The plan was that Niccolò, once arrived in Constantinople, would immediately retrace his original journey back to the Italian peninsula. Yilmaz told him that he could earn his passage back to Constantinople and in return the ship's captain would make arrangements for Niccolò to find work on a boat back to Italy. 'The physical exertions involved on the vessels and the bracing sea winds will do you good.'

The night before Niccolò's departure, Yilmaz took him into his library and took a book from the shelf. It was Mordechai Levi's much desired but missing volume – the Volume R. 'This is the book your librarian friend sent you to Constantinople to obtain. You failed miserably in that endeavour. And though this book is of great value to me, I am giving it to you so that you can make amends for your failure. If there is a lesson for you here, it is that sometimes a man must give up what he values in order to right a wrong. Though in this case it is I who is giving up something of value to me to right a wrong of your doing. Be that as it may, I ask that you take this book back to Bologna and become a better man.

'Become a better man by doing just deeds and behaving charitably. The Prophet would have asked that of you. Your own Saviour would have asked the same. Even in the sacred teachings so dear to the librarian Levi of Bologna, you will find exactly these directives. So please set your life to doing just deeds and behaving charitably.

'Doing just deeds and behaving charitably is what distinguishes man from the beasts and insects. Such proper behaviour is the price of admission to live in a civil world. Religions of all beliefs have recognised this, and that it is why all religions, albeit in different words, have held this view – it is a universal.'

Niccolò was lost for words. But Yilmaz was not and he continued, 'You have much for which to atone. After you have delivered the book to the librarian Mordechai Levi, it is mandatory you return to Venice. There are three wronged women you must somehow face. The two mature women have most likely resolved their problems in a manner that is satisfactory to each. But if you are to be a decent man, and as decency often comes with pain, then till your dying day you will carry the pain that you have children in Venice who, for the greater good, will never know you. Cherubina, however, is another matter and she must be faced. In that matter, unlike the book, I have no solution I can take from a shelf and give to you. This is a wrong you must right yourself. If it is of any comfort, there are legions of men who have been challenged by the same problem and many of them have found an honourable solution. I must leave it to you to find an honourable solution.

'Let us not forget the merchant Delmare. Surely you owe him much. In some fashion you must ask his forgiveness and find a way to correct the wrong you have done him. Do all these things and you will be an honourable human.'

❦

The entire village had gathered at the island's simple wharf to see him off. Most conspicuous of them all was Elena. She clung to him, wailing, 'Don't go, Tasso. I beg you don't leave me again. Do I have to lose you again? A mother can only bear so much from her son before her heart is broken.'

He lied, saying that he would soon return to her, but that did not placate her and now, wailing even louder, she fell to her knees and tore at her hair. For her sake, he helped her up and made a big show of hugging her before the assembled villagers. 'There, there, mother dearest,' and lying once again Niccolò turned to the villagers and shouted, 'Listen, everyone. Listen! This is a promise I make to my mother – I will return!' And though no one knew, other than Elena herself, Elena would live out the days she had left scouring the beaches of the island, not for driftwood, but in anticipation that a merciful sea would once again spew back her son.

❦

Yilmaz was a wise man but, unlike Niccolò Umberto, he had none of the Devil residing within him. As far as Niccolò Umberto was concerned, there was no point to the struggle to be an honourable man. He figured that an honourable man was bound for hell just the same as any dishonourable man; an honourable man would end in that place but without experiencing as much fun on his journey there. Therefore as soon as Niccolò Umberto reached Constantinople, he abandoned his obligation to sail back to the Italian peninsula and make amends. Instead he sold the much valued book in the old book market not far from the Grand Bazaar. After that he sought out the hashish dealers and then ran to the tavern where he had many times been overwhelmed by Emel, Emel whose name would forever mean desire. For you must understand, a dishonourable man such as the prodigal son Niccolò Umberto had many more journeys and adventures to experience.

Death always wins

In which it is told of the final days of the elderly Niccolò Umberto before he would eventually become dust.

Men who live long enough become old men. Niccolò Umberto was now an old man. He could work that out without knowing what year it was. His purple feet, swollen ankles and shortness of breath were always there to tell him he was old. And if these were not enough, then there was his bladder. *Oh what I wouldn't give for a night of uninterrupted sleep; uninterrupted by the need to piss every hour with the piss of fiery nails.*

Niccolò Umberto now had lived longer than his father had. He had lived longer than his older brother Frederick. That's Frederick Umberto the pious straight-laced brother; that's Frederick the beneficiary of his father's generosity; that's Frederick who, unlike all the generations of Umbertos since Oddo in the twelfth century, had failed to produce a son. This last Frederick had no firstborn son to be called Frederick in accordance to the promise made to Barbarossa's immediate successor in 1190. The last Frederick Umberto had died without any heirs – male or female – and so the line of legitimate Umbertos was ending with Niccolò. Of course, Niccolò's unknown bastards did not count, so though much was ending with him, the fact that Niccolò was the last legitimate Umberto standing was to him a source of great satisfaction.

Niccolò now lived in the Umberto's ancient keep in Piedmont, the very same crumbling heap from which he had been banished by his brother Frederick all those years ago. What sweet revenge it was to have lived long enough to have it all. In this, Niccolò was exaggerating, for the *all* he was having was not much, so he had in fact had all of almost nothing. Nothing save the crumbling keep of draughty rooms, some battered trunks with faulty locks, some faded Belgian tapestries and his memories. And like the keep, the trunks and the tapestries, his memories were disintegrating, faulty and faded. He had his imperfect memories. And whether those imperfect memories were concocted fragments didn't matter. What mattered to him was to live long enough to solve the puzzle that had been his life. In matters of reminiscences, there is not one true sequence of events. Umberto's memories were his, and his alone. To him it was his version of truth that counted.

Being old had no compensations. Umberto's days were running out in the same way as the wooden furniture that he burnt in the hall's giant fireplace; soon there would be neither days nor furniture left him. He found it disturbing that he had more yesterdays than tomorrows.

Being old brought Umberto more than the physical ailments that plague the elderly. Being old brought him a crisis of spirit and, try as he might to avoid it, he couldn't avoid an evaluation of his life.

What was Venice but three women and a merchant? What was Bologna and all those books and the old Jewish librarian? And there was something about Bologna and books. Many books and there was one book of special importance: *God's Agreement with Man*. Some things you never forget. *Yet another thing I'll never forget – I'll never forget Emel of Constantinople and her tricks. Emel whose name and body equalled desire. What I wouldn't do now for just one sniff of her crutch. But why settle for just one sniff? During the days you did for everyone and I didn't mind. But the nights – the nights you promised were for me alone. Come on, girlie, do for me as you once did, Emel. Give me more and more. Even an old man like me should be allowed such memories.*

Other journeys of my life? Today I don't remember. I'll think about it all tomorrow. Today I want to think about Emel and her magic cunt. But first I'll sleep and hope to dream of Emel and Constantinople.

⊷

Tomorrow came.

Why have the book God's Agreement with Man *and Emel remained with me when I can't remember other things? The three women of Venice. Can't remember their names; can't even remember their faces. Who was the Venetian merchant? What was the Jewish librarian in Bologna called? I've forgotten so much. Yet Emel and that book remain.*

Then the next tomorrow came and that was followed by yet another tomorrow. It worried Umberto that one day there'd be no tomorrow. Then all that would be left would be his yesterdays. But no matter how many tomorrows would be left, he had already outlived everybody of his past. Of them all, surely he alone had lived into the seventeenth century.

His father was dead. His brother was dead. The Venetian merchant must be dead. The Jewish librarian in Bologna was old even fifty years ago so without a doubt he must be dead. And the three women of Venice? He wasn't sure as he couldn't remember much about them other than they were the three women of Venice. He felt nothing about any of them. If they're dead then so be it. But how could it be that Emel be dead? Surely that would be an impossibility. She was born to be forever young and vital. Wouldn't God have decreed Emel was to be eternal? And if by Divine decree she was not eternal, then Umberto's mind could make her so.

A day came when he had a memory of a Greek called Spiro who had stolen from him while he slept in a room above a tavern in Constantinople, the room where Emel had done her Eastern magic. Spiro had stolen from him but then, wasn't it Spiro who had first brought him Emel and other sweet dreams? Emel who danced like the smoke that brought him sweet dreams. Rising with the smoke the sweet dreams wormed into his nostrils and ears all the way to penetrate his brain. Perhaps Spiro was not a thief but his true brother; they stood together on a hill to overlook the Horn when Constantinople was a sparkling diamond.

And for the first time ever, many years after the events of Constantinople, he figured Spiro's theft was not theft but fitting recompense for Emel and the sweet dreams.

～

Today a memory returned. It came in shards so sharp that cut deeply. It was of an island where he had stayed. There was an Ottoman garrison. How or why he should have been there eluded him. And it bothered Umberto that he did not know how he had come to be on that island. Had he been a prisoner of the Ottomans? Or perhaps he had been a slave? How could he, a Christian, been a slave to a heathen Turk? Prisoner or slave? Either explanation was possible but neither suited him. So he abandoned these explanations and settled that in all likelihood he had been a guest of a hospitable Turk. *Yes, I must have been his guest. And the Turk, what was his name? No doubt the Turk's name was something Turkish. But what?*

From his brain to the tip of his tongue he struggled for that name. Then after a while he gave up until without any further trying sometime later he mouthed the name Milyaz. Then as if to convince himself, he shouted Milyaz! Milyaz! Milyaz! The name Milyaz sounded right but was it that? Surely it had to be as to his ears it sounded Turkish?

Milyaz the Turk may have posed as his friendly host, but Umberto recalled that his host had been critical of him. Though the criticism was obviously unfounded, it had stung at the time. What had Milyaz said? Mulling on this Umberto, recalled it was not what Milyaz had said but what he had written – written in a notebook that Milyaz had left on his desk, a notebook that Umberto had found by accident; a notebook where the Turk had made a scientific study of Umberto's behaviour; a scientific study that found his guest lacking.

The Turk turned me into an insect in a jar; an insect to be examined, poked and prodded and then dissected. He examined and dissected me for no other reason than he had been bored by his posting to a godforsaken island of peasants. Fucking Turk!

By next morning, though he again suffered the hurt he'd felt when he had read the Turk's notebook, he once again forgot the Turk's name. What had come to him yesterday was again gone. Whatever the Turk's name had been, it would now not come to him. Throughout the day he struggled to retrieve the Turk's name and nothing came.

Then one evening some weeks later while slurping his gruel, the name Yilmaz emerged from the milky slops. The Turk had without a doubt had been called Yilmaz, not Milyaz. It had been Yilmaz the Turk. And the name provided him entrée to memories of his time on that island in the company of Yilmaz, his beautiful twin daughters and his two unpleasant looking attendants.

Apart from the hurt of Yilmaz's notebook, what were Umberto's memories of his time on that island? Umberto wondered why the island should seem so important to him now with the end not so far away. Were the events on the island really so important? Perhaps nothing notable had happened, or whatever had happened was not important, but they occurred at an important point in his life?

He remembered that he had left the island on his own accord. He had left with Yilmaz's copy of *God's Agreement with Man* and the Turk's instruction to return with the book to Bologna and place it in the old Jewish librarian's hands. If that was not an imposition enough, the Turk had implored him to go to Venice and make amends with a certain merchant and three women. *What an overstepping on the Turk's part!*

Umberto recalled the book was at that time considered to be of great value, or was it a book of considerable academic interest? Whatever was the case, why did he have to go all the way to Bologna, a town for which he had no liking, to give it to some Jew librarian? As he remembered it, Bologna was nothing but books and dust. And as for going to Venice, why did he need to make amends to some merchant there and three women whose faces and names he could no longer recall? He concluded that Yilmaz the Turk must have become unhinged by his posting to an insignificant island. Island madness must have been the price the Ottoman had to pay for his nation's occupation of stolen islands.

To hell with all Turks. Every one of them except for Emel! Oh Emel, even today the thought of you quickens my pulse. The thought of you leaves me short of breath. The thought of you robs me of my balance.

Strangely, Umberto failed to see that his quickened pulse, his shortness of breath and his faltering balance were also the natural dominion of old men. But then, what greater joy was it for him to ascribe it all to the carnal delights of a Constantinople strumpet rather than old age.

⌦

When working for the Umberto household, a servant received payment which outweighed the loyalty given by that servant. With the death of his older brother Frederick, despite dwindling money to keep servants, a servant's requirement to earn a livelihood remained. Niccolò Umberto's begging for servants to stay in his service was of no help, for whatever loyalty existed to the Umberto household when Frederick was alive, it did not extend to his brother Niccolò. And so servants left for employment elsewhere and over a short time, the pool of servants evaporated. All were gone save the gatekeeper and his wife, and between the two of them they ran the keep and attended to Niccolò Umberto's needs.

The offer of a gift in the hope of a reward or ongoing rewards knows neither era nor social standing. Many centuries earlier the Umberto progenitor, Oddo Umberto, had gifted the Holy Roman Emperor Barbarossa a signet ring sporting an oversized *U*, in the hope of rewards. Oddo Umberto had told Barbarossa the oversized *U* stood for *über*, the Germanic word for superior – an apt letter on the ring worn by someone of Barbarossa's superiority over all men. Of course, the ring's oversized *U* also stood for the first letter of Oddo Umberto's family name. In a similar act of ingratiation, Niccolò Umberto's gatekeeper had offered Niccolò his own wife. To his wife the gatekeeper had said first of all it was to keep their jobs and second it was to keep the old fellow warm at night. To which he added, after all, what harm could an old Umberto do? To keep their jobs and to please her husband, the gatekeeper's wife agreed, and so it came to pass that she became Niccolò Umberto's nightly bed warmer.

All those years ago, Spiro had brought me Emel; Emel performed so many wonderful tricks for me. The gatekeeper brings me his wife Leonora. At night I have her and a warm bed. There is something else. Something new for me. From the gatekeeper's wife I've learnt that some women are created to be appreciated with the eyes. But others are created to be appreciated with the hands, in bed and in the dark. Leonora is the latter type of woman. Once upon a time Emel thrilled the young me and now under my hands Leonora's curves and valleys and bulges thrill the timeworn me. The vastness of her dimpled thighs, the fullness of her pendulous breasts and the softness of her large rounded belly are explored under my ancient hands. Musky clefts, front and back, draw my fingers in and I am not only young again but lost again in woman. Oh, I swear to God though my eyes are cloudy and hands tremble, I will never tire of the female form. And if my eyes should fail and my hands lose their sense of touch then surely I am ready for death. And so we sleep, Leonora and me.

~◈~

A morning came when Niccolò Umberto asked himself why he had gone to Constantinople as a young man. Much of what he had of late been thinking concerned his stay in Constantinople: Emel, Spiro and hashish-borne dreams – all these were associated with Constantinople. His Constantinople experiences must have been important, but apart from his adoration of the shameless Emel and the smoky dreams of her city, there was no obvious reason he should have been there. After all, he was a native of the Italian peninsula so why had he found himself in Constantinople? No answer came to mind. Further, why had he been a guest of Yilmaz the Turk in an Ottoman garrison on some forgettable shithole of an island? Then there was the Jew librarian of Bologna; Bologna and its books. And there was something that happened in Venice. At least Bologna and Venice were closer to home, but Constantinople and an Ottoman-controlled island were not. What was the chronology of the events and places, and who were the people lost to him in time's fog?

I'm an old man so does any of this matter now? Why am I bothered by my thoughts? Thoughts, only thoughts. Nothing of the past can be changed. My knowing answers won't change anything. What happened, happened a long time ago. I don't need answers. All I need is my warm bed and the bountiful countryside of Leonora's body.

⇒

More than fifty years earlier a Turkish boat had visited an island to supply its Ottoman garrison with provisions. When the boat left the island, on board was a young Niccolò Umberto. The young man had left the island with Yilmaz's copy of *God's Agreement with Man*, a generous donation from the wise Turk. Though the boat was headed from the island back to its home port of Constantinople, the plan was for Umberto, once in Constantinople, to seek passage back to the Italian peninsula.

The self-centred Christian boy owed many people a lot. And yes, though Yilmaz had studied Niccolò Umberto, for Niccolò had presented an interesting example of self-absorption, he also felt that he could help the young man become a better man. An honourable man, whether a Jew, Christian or Moslem, would not have behaved as Umberto had in Bologna, Venice or Constantinople.

Then further north of Bologna there were the three women of Venice and a merchant. It was a night by the island's ruined temple high up on the windswept plateau that Yilmaz heard it all. Under the influence of mysterious vapours emanating from a fissure that ran deep to the earth's heart and the use of a Persian inhalation of truth, Yilmaz heard of Umberto's dalliance with these women. He learnt of Niccolò Umberto's two-fold cuckolding of the merchant Lorenzo Delmare – with Delmare's wife Rosetta and with Delmare's mistress the Duchessa di Palma. And there was also his betrayal of Delmare's daughter Cherubina. Bizarrely, though the sexual dalliances with each of the three women had been once, three pregnancies had resulted. In each case Umberto had left it to each woman to sort out the complications of their ensuing predicaments. And though the two mature women solved their problems using their wiles and connections, Cherubina, barely out of childhood herself, was not so lucky. Umberto had callously shrugged all of it off as none of it being his problem as that was the way of the world.

When Niccolò Umberto left the island on the Turkish supply boat, as far as Yilmaz knew, although the boat's first stop was Constantinople, Umberto would be subsequently bound for the Italian peninsula. And Yilmaz hoped that by his counselling the young man would make amends to those he had wronged – the librarian and the Jews of Bologna, the Venetian merchant and his wife, his daughter and his mistress. Yilmaz was wrong.

From the deck Niccolò Umberto saw, through the mist, the magic city slowly and shyly reveal itself – just as Emel had revealed her charms to him on the first night she had come to his room. And as the boat approached closer to the city – district by district, tower by tower and fragment of wall by fragment of wall – it became sharper. The features of Constantinople sharpened until he was finally caught in the city's seductive embrace and it whispered in his ears: *Welcome back traveller.*

⌘

> *'Bliss was it on that dawn to be alive,*
> *But to be young was very heaven!'*[*]

---

[*] From the poem 'The French Revolution as it Appeared to Enthusiasts at its Commencement' by William Wordsworth.

In any epoch, what joy it is to be young. But in any epoch, the greatest joy is to be young with sufficient financial resources and a lifetime of glorious possibilities ahead of you. Niccolò Umberto was such a person, for he was landing in Constantinople young, in possession of a valuable book and an infinity of glorious possibilities ahead.

On his first landing in Constantinople, Niccolò Umberto had arrived with money the Jews of Bologna had given him to buy *God's Agreement with Man*. He had wasted all that they had given him on his own wanton pleasures. This time he was arriving in Constantinople with Yilmaz's copy of *God's Agreement with Man* and he knew that the book was valuable – valuable enough to make his second time in Constantinople as equally pleasurable as his first visit.

Umberto knew well that the book was valuable and of academic interest so he would be able to sell it for quite a sum. And where in the entire world is there better to sell something than in Constantinople. You have to understand that Constantinople was a city not only of carnal delights but also commerce of all kinds. Umberto remembered how impressed he had been by the Grand Bazaar when Spiro had taken him there. He remembered the shops and the stalls, the noise and the smells. Big markets and little markets of Constantinople, he had seen them. And he remembered the other markets near the Grand Bazaar – the slave market, the strange Long Market that clung to the side of a hill, the covered markets and, of most relevance to him now, he remembered the old book market.

If it came to the number of books, then Constantinople's old book market's count would put Bologna's combined libraries' count to shame. Then there were other contrasts. Bologna's books were stored in the university's libraries and these were places of silence; these were places of solemnity and of dark corners. Books came to Bologna to stay put forever. Whereas in Constantinople, books came to be bought and sold; to move from owner to owner. Books in Constantinople acquired a life. In Constantinople's old book market, the laneways of books were abuzz with sound of many conversations.

People of all types browsed. There was colour everywhere and there were no dark corners. But as in Bologna, there was dust everywhere. To Umberto it was as it should be. He had once theorised the dust in Bologna's libraries was spawned by the wisdom held in the books, and there was no reason why it was not so with the books in Constantinople's old book market. So much for the arrogance of the West to think that it had the monopoly on books and what lay in them; after all, dust is dust in the East as it is in the West.

⥱

There came a night when old man Umberto dreamt of dust. It covered everything. In his dream it lay over Leonora as she slept alongside him, their bed floating on a sea of dust. The dust was heaped in the corners of the keep, and in the shafts of light the motes danced until they became little fairies, fit enough to inhabit the light shafts of an island's forest glades. And there was a book called *God's Agreement with Man* which, when it was opened, sprayed dust everywhere and made him sneeze. The sneeze woke him and he remembered the old book market in Constantinople.

Why haven't I thought about it before? The dust. I remember there was dust. The dust was so long ago. I was in Constantinople and young and longing for Emel and there was that book – God's Agreement with Man – *I'd gone to the market to sell Yilmaz's copy. You see, I needed money for Emel and hashish. But what happened next?*

Old men are permitted to have holes in their memories, but for Niccolò Umberto that hole was not just a hole but an abyss from which this early morning he could only salvage a tart named Emel, the name of a book and the smell of hashish-laden smoke. Oh and dust, lots of dust.

Journey to Find Out
What Happened

THE WAR ENDED AND the Americans marched through Paris in tight formations down the Champs Elysées just as the Germans had done four years earlier. To tell the truth, the Germans had marched in tighter formations; they were more serious about it than the Americans. Maybe that's the difference between invaders and liberators. All that aside, what's the difference? Germans or Americans? Each time for us it was foreigners marching down the Champs Elysées. Foreigners who wore different uniforms. Foreigners who spoke a different language. So, at least for me, apart from that there was no difference; they were both strangers.

I suppose I've always sat on the fence. Nothing wrong with that, is there? Sure, you get a sore arse but you also get a clearer view of what's on either side of the fence. One side thinks their side is a manicured park and the other's an unkempt weed-ridden abomination. Well, I can tell you for starters they're both wrong. Sit on my fence and you'll see a maze of messy hedges on both sides.

As I said, the Americans came to Paris and there were crowds dancing in the streets and all that *fin de la guerre* release of emotion. The invaders had been driven out but after the jubilation was over, which by the way I didn't experience, and after the last liberator had left France, I was still wading through treacle. All my life I had waded through treacle; you don't get anywhere fast and it saps your energy.

I was ready for my life to improve. That's not to say that I didn't do well enough during the war. There had been many ways to look after yourself and please your readers at the same time. They say war is hell and maybe it is, but war can be good for an enterprising writer; I found that it was so.

Look, I've forgotten to tell you my name. It's Martin Houx and if you haven't heard about me, then all I can say is you've been reading the wrong newspapers. In 1940 I was writing for *Paris Matin*. The Germans came in and my style of writing went out; I suppose the *Paris Matin* owners wanted to be careful of what appeared in their paper. Look, I don't blame them for that. A consequence of the coming of the Nazis was that I was ingloriously dumped by the paper. I took it on the chin, as the cliché goes. After that I had to live by my wits. I even stooped to writing advertisements. Well so what! I'll defend myself and say that someone has to write advertising junk – otherwise nobody would buy *Eau de Javel*, would they?

As for as my metier? Well, I did a bit of freelancing here and there for any rag that had the nerve to take me. Some might say I'd become a journalistic whore. Most of us do some whoring just to get by. Nevertheless, I defy anyone to say I was a hack. I managed to sell articles despite the Germans. And I'd say those articles were good, very good. It's strange but the occupation had improved my writing. I even started a novel but then don't we all. How many times have you heard someone say they're writing a novel? Too many times, no doubt. What's more, they'll keep saying it year after year after year and blah, blah, blah. I reckon it's the refuge of the would-be writer, because for as long as you keep saying you're writing a novel, no one can say you aren't a writer. Enough said about that. So where was I? Well I was with the Germans gone, the Americans gone, me wading through treacle and it was the summer of 1947.

That summer, July, after the fireworks at Versailles on the 14th, I first met Madame D'Eze on the train back to Paris. You know how it is – a festive evening, some wine, maybe a bit too much wine, and a plump, jolly woman on a rocking train. Of course you get to talking. And Madame D'Eze and I got to talking about this and that, so much so that by the time we got off the train at Saint-Lazare, she had invited me to visit her at her apartment in the 19th arrondissement the following day. Don't get me wrong. Nothing sexual here at the time. She was just a jolly, plump middle-aged woman I found amusing.

By the autumn, you could say Madame D'Eze and I were friends. That's not to say that even by autumn I knew much about her. I knew that she lived off the Rue Manin. Her apartment was small – just a kitchenette, a lounge room and a bedroom. And, as it was so unfortunately common in those years, a communal toilet and washroom off the landing. I suppose the apartment seemed smaller than it was owing to the furniture. The lounge room had a large, tall, canopied sideboard, a dining table with seating for eight, and wedged between the wall and dining table there was an enormous glass-fronted bookcase. I deduced that Madame D'Eze was no reader, as the bookcase was devoid of books and instead contained a jumble of hats, scarves and shoes. And framed photos. I mustn't forget her all-important framed photos. To further add to the crowding of the lounge room, there was an oversized comfortable sofa and two heavily padded armchairs. Her bedroom, well I wouldn't be a gentleman if I told you more than the fact that the bed, like the lounge room's sofa, was large and comfortable. All things considered, Madame D'Eze was like her sofa, armchairs and bed – amply padded and comfortable to sink into.

Did we eventually love each other? No, we didn't love each other. It was more that we enjoyed the occasions we spent together and at the time, I couldn't imagine I required anyone else's company other than hers. She was the armchair, sofa and bed I needed at the time. Plump, soft and pliant for a man wading in treacle. And for her, I suppose I was … well, I don't really know what I was to her, other than I made her laugh. I suppose if I made her laugh then I must have made her happy. And so tell me, does any woman need more?

Were we in lust? I don't think so. There was no wild madness in our physical passion; instead, it had all the mundaneness of an itch that needed scratching. It was necessary. It felt good and when it was done, an irritant had been satisfied. An itch satisfactorily put to bed, so to speak.

You might find this odd but throughout our time together, I only called her Madame D'Eze. Only Madame D'Eze, that's all. There was never any need to enquire what her first name was. I ask you, if I'd known would it have made any difference? Our relationship would have been just the same whatever her label, and Shakespeare had something to say about that many years ago. But if she was a Madame D'Eze, where was Monsieur D'Eze?

Despite there being a wedding ring on her ring finger, she never mentioned a husband and I didn't ask. Bizarrely, or perhaps out of some sense of decorum, a prelude to our lovemaking was for her to always remove that ring. For all I know, the absent Monsieur D'Eze may never have existed and the wedding ring was an affectation. It is possible the putative husband may have abandoned the marriage or he may have died in the war. You see, it was a time when many spouses left the marriage or had died in the war. There was, however, an adult son, the subject of all those framed photos. Her son – Patrick D'Eze – I was to meet later.

❖

Winter was upon us and I was still with Madame D'Eze. Most people hate winter but I don't. I don't mind the early darkness, the cold winds and damp air. I find it's a time of withdrawing into yourself. It's a time for savouring a modicum of luxury such as the warmth from the orange glow of a single-bar radiator. It's a time for planning but not acting.

Madame D'Eze had the same liking for those cold dark months as I did. We discovered that what we really liked about the season was that the universe had closed in around us. It was like the perfection that comes in lovemaking when the rest of the world could go to hell or vaporise. All that mattered was that moment and the two of us. We, Madame D'Eze and I, lived through that winter as if we were the only people in existence. Nothing else existed.

Her poorly heated apartment meant that the only warm place was under the feathered doona of her bed. Our winter passed mainly in that bed. Time passed in the paradise of the large comfortable bed. Time passed in the warmth of our embraces. Time passed punctuated by blanket-wrapped excruciatingly cold dashes to the landing's WC.

It was a time we made plans and promises to each other, promises we knew would never be consummated. But that didn't matter because it was the making of those plans and promises that helped keep us warm. In the end it was obvious, to me at least, that what was good about winter was the proofing yourself against winter.

She'd made a broth which we drank from bowls. Placing her bowl on the bedside table, she said, 'I made this for you because I like doing these sorts of motherly things. It has been said I'm a natural mother and who am I to disagree. Do you know I have a son?'

I didn't answer but I had already guessed as much because of the many framed photos in her bookcase. They represented the progression of the same individual from infancy to a young manhood.

'Patrick. His name is Patrick. My big baby boy-man now. To a mother, they never grow up. But he's a man now out in the world by himself and you have to let go. He's had his troubles but that was only because of the company he kept. Since the war, he's been getting his life in order. He's even got a job on a lawyer's farm near Fontainebleau. You must meet my boy one day.'

By the time she'd finished, her eyes had watered over and all I could say was, 'Yes I must meet him one day.' I know I should have said more but I'm not good at emotional support. Good at jokes, yes, but not emotional support. What's more, I wanted to think of her as *my* Madame D'Eze and not some man's mother. Not very gallant of me I know, but that's me.

With winter behind us, we were now into spring. In late March on the way to our bistro, with the footpaths still slippery, Madame D'Eze fell and broke a leg. In an instant I was transformed from amusing lover to reluctant carer. Look, I make it no excuse but up to that moment I'd only looked after my own interests and no one else's. Now it was different. Madame D'Eze's needs had become my responsibilities. Being the person I am, I found it hard to suppress my wants in the service of her daily needs. It just wasn't my way. So now the hours dragged, the days lasted forever; a monotonous succession of nights and days and all the while outside the apartment spring unfolded from its wintery cocoon.

It was spring in Paris but it was neither our spring nor our Paris. We might have as well been cave dwellers in the wilderness. And though by May she was able to walk again, no amount of coaxing could entice her to venture out of that cramped apartment. She'd lost interest in the things that used to delight her – window shopping, restaurants, clubs and me. For her it was still winter.

Is it any wonder that now even mundane activities, such as shopping for our provisions, was a welcome relief as it got me away; it was an opportunity to escape Madame D'Eze and her claustrophobic apartment with its oversized and overstuffed furniture. Don't get me wrong, I don't consider myself a selfish person but perhaps my self-centredness hastened the withering of our relationship just as a new Paris spring blossomed. And though I needed to get away, there was enough decency in me to see her through her crisis. Her crisis now not being physical but one of an extinguished spirit. I'm no expert in what ails people. I can say that caring for her physical needs was not easy but I managed; on the other hand, caring for her emotional needs was beyond me.

I didn't know how to handle her bouts of rage and melancholia, rage and melancholia that seemed to me to descend from nowhere. Surely melancholia was the domain of a belle epoch consumptive poet, and rage the domain of a gaunt revolutionary storming the barricades. Melancholia and rage did not sit well on a plump middle-aged woman who used to laugh at my jokes. Look, I'm a black and white type, so who knows, perhaps a stray word, a careless phrasing from me was the trigger to her moods. I longed for someone else to carry the burden of her moods. She'd often mentioned her son Patrick, so I suggested that she write to him. Finally on the last day of May she wrote a letter to him explaining her situation. She read the letter to me and I commented that although she had written positively about our relationship, she had not made any mention of her emotional state. To which she answered, 'News of the broken leg is enough. I don't need to worry the poor boy about anything else.'

I suggested that she should visit him but she felt she was not yet ready to leave her apartment. Instead she begged me to visit him.

Is it any wonder then, that when I knew she was capable of looking after herself, I made a journey to a farm near Fontainebleau? Yes, I knew I was running away but I justified myself with the knowledge that I was merely carrying out her heartfelt request.

❖

A leather-jacketed Patrick D'Eze was waiting for me on the tarmac outside the train station at Fontainebleau. He was astride what looked like a US Army-issue motorcycle. A stinking *Gitane*, gangster style, hung from the corner of his mouth. I suppose he was trying to either impress me or frighten me. His appearance did neither, but piqued my curiosity as to how he had come by the motorcycle. The motorcycle was some American job – probably a Harley Davidson. Its military khaki had been painted over in black. An amateurish attempt, I suppose, to give it a civilian air. But then, I really don't know much about motorcycles.

That night at the table in the farm, with a bottle of the roughest red I've ever had the misfortune to have forced on me, we talked. After I reported to him on his mother's health status, Patrick D'Eze opened up with what was really bugging him – not her health, but my relationship with his mother.

He started straight off with, 'Okay, she says you make her happy.'

I knew she'd written this, as in Paris she had read me her letter before it was sent. Still, now as then, I found this odd in view of the most miserable few months Madame D'Eze had experienced. He continued, 'I suppose that's as it should be. Making her happy, I suppose that's all that matters these days. She's not had it easy. Do you know you're one in a long line of lovers she's taken on board? A long line of hopeless cases. She attracts the hopeless.'

'Not speaking for the others but have you ever thought the contrary? Perhaps she's attracted to the hopeless.'

'Perhaps. But even if you're not a hopeless case, I'm surprised you're to her taste. What about you? Surely you'd be interested in

130

someone younger – surely. Someone closer in age to you. Stands to reason.'

Here he was, a twerp, quizzing me as if he was a father and I was dating his daughter. But I let him go on. 'If you're after her money, well she's got none. She's got nothing. As for this farm, it's not ours. It's not hers and it's not mine. I just look after it for a lawyer who's lying low at the moment. He's had problems with certain people. I get free accommodation here so long as I keep the place ticking over while he's out of sight. We, the D'Ezes, have nothing. My mother's got nothing apart from her apartment and I've got even less. So there's nothing to gain out of the D'Ezes, if that's what you're attempting. My advice is to just keep on making her happy.'

Well, I ask you, where do you go from there? Splutter and blather on about my intentions being noble? Talk about things that were none of his business? I wouldn't be me if I didn't go on the attack.

'I'll leave it to your mother to decide what she wants and not you. Just be happy that she's happy. I could say that it's really none of your concern. By your own admission and delightful turn of phrase, I'm not the first she's taken on board. She's a mature woman and I'm sure she knows how to protect her interests.'

I've learnt that a bit of flattery never goes astray so I added, 'Let me say this, she's a very lucky woman to have a son like you. These days such devotion to a mother is quite rare.'

Silence followed as if he was weighing what I had said, then he rose from the table and brought over another bottle of the disgusting red. He poured himself a glass and pushed the bottle in my direction. Out of politeness I poured myself another glass, and out of concern for my health I didn't drink it. The silence continued and I heard the grandfather clock chiming another hour.

To break the silence I asked, 'Your motorcycle? US Army issue, isn't it? How did you come by it?' Because it had been repainted, I suspected some illegality may have been involved so I added, 'I'll understand if you don't want to talk about it.'

Patrick D'Eze did not say anything other than, 'The lawyer,

Lucien Blondell, the guy who owns this farm, gave it to me for some things I did for him.'

I pressed him and in a garbled way he said he'd once introduced an American called Sam Rose to Blondell and that it turned out well for a business Blondell was in. And by the way, Sam Rose spoke good French for an American. But Rose was now dead. They found his burnt body in the Bois de Boulogne and that was that. Being curious I asked, what kind of business?

He looked at the bottle, poured himself yet another drink and after drinking it in one gulp said, 'It's time we called it a night.' I guessed he'd said too much.

❖

From time to time Nature has a way of vomiting up the foulest of individuals. Fortunately these people survive for a short time to be eventually destroyed by those they have wronged; think Caligula. Sometimes, however, these individuals are canny enough to live out a full life span; think Stalin. The lawyer Lucien Blondell was of the latter kind. You see, Nature is neither fair nor caring – it doesn't care whether you're a slimy bastard or not.

Lawyer Blondell was the lowest form of life who thrived during the pre-war years, then shrewdly flourished during the war and, except for a brief time in the mid-1940s, he continued to thrive in the post-war years.

Surely people are more complex than to allow for a grading as good, neutral or bad. There was certainly a lot of bad in Lucien Blondell. So was there any good in him? On that score one could only say he treated his dogs well for, like Hitler, Blondell was devoted to his dogs. So much so that when a current dog died he actually shed some tears. But after a few days of grieving, the dog was replaced by another of the same breed to which he always gave the same name as the deceased one. In that way Blondell felt he had cheated the canine Grim Reaper. As far as Blondell was concerned, life was all about power and access. Power over others and access to the means by which that power could be exerted. As for Blondell, if evil is forever then he probably would have chosen to go on forever. As much as he had worked at it, some things were even beyond his control.

Unfortunately for him, on New Year's Eve of 1963 he died. A fatal heart attack ended him while he was slurping bouillabaisse in the Negresco's dining room. His passing was received throughout France with a collective sigh of relief. But we get ahead of ourselves, as during the time most of this story takes place, Blondell was still well and truly alive and very evil. It should be said that even in death, it is not impossible to imagine Blondell suing the Devil, and winning. Suing the Devil for taking him before he thought he was ready to go. And it is not impossible, imagining the Devil settling a large compensation in Blondell's favour, for such was Blondell's ability to argue a case. You see, Blondell was that type of fighter who came out punching and hitting his opponent harder and for longer than he had himself been hit. In the parlance that was common on the battlefront, he didn't take any prisoners. If he had his way, then his prisoners would not have been lined against a wall and shot but completely obliterated by the largest cannon available.

Of course, lawyers play to win but Blondell played to win at all costs – even if that meant breaking the law or destroying the innocent. For him, life was all about winning and paradoxically, he played to win for himself even if it meant a client lost out in the process. In his mind defeat was never possible. He once confided to an associate that the way for advancement was to never admit defeat but instead announce loudly to all around that a victory had occurred and then to repeat this at every opportunity. You could say his motto was: *Truth never matters in the pursuit of success.*

Before the war Lucien Blondell had built up quite a reputation in the legal circles of Paris. Using the measure of his successes in the court room, one might have thought he was on the way to becoming a judge. Using the measure of morality, one might have thought he was on the way to a prison cell. He attracted a clientele from both sides of the Paris social register. Criminals were drawn to him as the lawyer who, with a nod and a wink, was a brother criminal. He knew their world and they saw him on the shady side of life often funding certain enterprises unbefitting a man of the courts. On the other hand, he also attracted clients from the wealthy families, in particular, families with old money. He was the darling of the industrialists and a useful man to have on your side drafting business deals where his skill at leveraging a good deal was valued. When the money was rolling in, little did it matter to his wealthy clients that his skills were based on blackmail, extortion and grainy photographs taken in hotel rooms. As he used to say: *Show me a man who says he has no weaknesses and I'll show you a man whose weakness is lying.* Blondell's successes lay in knowing everyone's weaknesses.

During the war he collaborated with the Nazis. Surprisingly, after the war he was able to make knowledge of the extent of his collaboration disappear – the usual blackmail, extortion and grainy photographs in hotel rooms. His collaboration with the Nazis had proved most profitable.

As a lawyer Blondell had had many wealthy and middle-class Jews as clients, and like a good lawyer, he had kept impeccable records. When making wills people make no secret of what they own. And why would they? Their wills list the assets they wish their beneficiaries to inherit – assets such as real estate, cash, jewellery and art works. The information stored in those wills was currency during the Nazi occupation, and Blondell made deals with the Nazis; one monster made deals with another monster.

Blondell set about exposing his wealthy Jewish clients to the Gestapo and in return the Nazis allowed him to acquire some of the property that was confiscated, property such as artworks, but most importantly titles to real estate. In this fashion, he acquired first dibs at artwork that was to be plundered in Herman Goering's name; he acquired some beautiful apartments in the 8th arrondissement and most importantly, he acquired access to strongboxes buried deep in Parisian bank vaults – strongboxes that held great amounts of Parisian Jewry's personal documents, cash and jewels. Bit by bit Blondell's team of informants obtained information about various high-ranking Nazi officers. The rent-boys of Paris, the drug dealers and black marketeers in Blondell's pay collected the sort of information those officers would not have liked circulated. As a consequence, a blind eye was turned to his own criminal activities. It was a demonstration of Blondell's wiliness that he survived the occupation and had not been shot by the Nazis or killed by anyone of the many others he had crossed.

One of Blondell's war time informants was Patrick D'Eze. In 1941, a young Patrick had run with a gang of toughs who, for want of something better to do, indulged in a bit of petty mugging. One night they attempted to mug the wrong man. The mugging led to an arrest which led to a court appearance.

Blondell, always on the lookout for potential gofers, often frequented the lobbies of the courts to scout for petty miscreants who shuffled through its doors. He had found that the hungrier and the more pathetic the accused, the more easily he could be perverted to whatever ends Blondell had in mind.

On the day of Patrick D'Eze's court appearance, Blondell was scouting. He had noted seated on a bench outside Court 5 a nervous, scrawny young man. Seated alongside this pitiable individual was his obviously distraught mother. For a while, the young man stared at the ceiling, perhaps wishing he was somewhere else. He then picked his nose, examined the resultant pickings which he then tried to flick away. When that didn't work he surreptitiously stuck it somewhere under the bench. When all other distractions paled, he started to jiggle his right leg as if there was an urgency to visit the toilet. Then he stopped and looked down to his shoes and on seeing a mud speck on the left, he spat on his thumb and attempted to rub away the speck only to leave a bigger and more noticeable smudge. Even the boy's attempt at adjusting his tie led to an ugly knot that was off-centre and centimetres away from where a tie's knot should have been. Mother and son – a doleful duo if ever there was one. A doleful duo for anyone who had a heart, yes, but for Blondell here was a young man ripe for the picking.

Blondell took the seat alongside Patrick and made his swoop. 'You're in court today?'

'Who wants to know?'

Good God. Plucky little bastard, Blondell thought. 'I do.'

'So what's it to you, old man?'

Good, good. Gutsy too. 'Who's defending you?'

'Why don't you fuck off before I job you one?'

The plump woman pleaded, 'Please, Patrick, stop it.'

Patrick D'Eze's request for Blondell to fuck off didn't bother Blondell; instead, he thought: *Perfect. I already like him.* 'I think I can help. I know my way around the system here. I'm a lawyer.'

Now the plump woman leaned across and spoke to Blondell, 'If you're a lawyer, then as much as my son ... Patrick, could do with a lawyer he ... we could never afford one.'

Capital. I've got him. In his smoothest voice Blondell said, 'Don't worry about the money, mother. I'll defend your son free of charge. And I'll get him off, that's a promise. Now quickly tell me the circumstances that led your poor boy, Patrick is it, to be here.'

When they entered the courtroom and the judge saw Blondell, he blanched. Blondell threw the judge a conspiratorial wink and mouthed a kiss. And Blondell was true to his word – the charges against Patrick D'Eze were dismissed. As for Blondell's services, no monetary remuneration was demanded. Instead he handed Patrick his card and said, 'Come and see me on Friday and I'll discuss some things you can do for me in return for today. Miss the appointment at your peril.'

❖

In September 1945, Patrick D'Eze hurried across the Rue de Rivoli to avoid the rain. He walked past Le Meurice, German headquarters right up to the liberation of Paris. The bullet hole next to the 'M' above the main door was still there. And why shouldn't it be? Paris was still full of bullet holes and ruin. *My whole life is full of bullet holes and ruin*, he thought. Like it was for many Parisians, the euphoria he had experienced in August 1944 had evaporated a long time ago.

During the war things had been clear, simple. For Patrick it was just like being back at school, but the masters were the Nazis. Learn to accept it as the status quo, for it's probably going to be the only life you'll know. Just like at school, he had figured out that all you had to do was not get noticed, not make a fuss and you'd be safe. If the Third Reich was to last a thousand years, then what other alternative was there? His mother had said that if the Third Reich was to last a thousand years then you could be sure there'd be more than a thousand tears. Mothers are like that – all emotion. It seemed to him that with liberation, he lived in a world of winners and losers and for the time being he was a loser.

Just like the Germans before them, the Americans had gotten all the pretty girls. The Americans had money. They had glamour and, strangely, they all had perfect teeth. He had none of these.

The Germans had said they were the master race. Obviously they weren't, as they'd lost the war. If anyone was the master race, the young man figured, that it had to be the Americans. Well, why wouldn't they be the master race? Americans were perfect-teethed individuals. Every American was a film star. Every American caroused around Paris dripping girls, money and charm. If only some of that master race magic could rub off on to him, then maybe he could be a winner also.

It was a time of music, American music. Music in clubs and bars. To the young man, every American, whether black or white, had music in his blood. Swing, boogie woogie and jazz as hot or cool as you liked flowed through them. Yes, the Americans had the music. For these Adonises from the New World the Almighty had made the rest of the world theirs and the young man craved some of it.

❖

Americans demi-gods? Surely not. American demi-gods, really? That's how a young Frenchman Patrick saw them, but that's not

137

to say they were as he saw them. The plough boys from Iowa were hardly demi-gods, neither were the former haberdashery assistants from Missouri nor the red necks from Kentucky. And the short Jew from New York definitely wasn't.

Sam Rose, Sammy to those who liked him and sometimes Rosie to those who liked him even more, was short, Jewish and from the Bronx. And before that? Before that in 1904 his Polish grandparents, Gustav and Brucha Rosenzweig, had found themselves shivering with anticipation and fear in a queue on Ellis Island; arriving with them was their only child, a-twelve-year-old son Moishe. Gustav and Brucha Rosenzweig remained Gustav and Brucha Rosenzweig all their lives. But by the time their American grandson Sam was born in 1920, their son Moishe Rosenzweig had become Moe Rose.

Sam was a studious boy with a gift for languages. Even as a teenager he had enrolled in extra language classes offered at his school. His hope was to eventually become a language teacher which, by the way, Moe Rose saw as a sure path to mediocrity and poverty. By the time he was drafted Sam spoke not only Hebrew, Yiddish, Polish and German but also, and most importantly, French. Wisely the army had not seen him as real soldier material. He just didn't show any aptitude for soldierly duties. To a large extent that was because he had intentionally failed at all aspects in the art of soldiering. Wondering what to do with him, some military genius checked Sam's academic records and noted Sam's superior ability with languages. To hell with Hebrew and Yiddish and perhaps to hell with Polish, but German and French could be useful. So armed with no weapon but with some documents and a pile of dictionaries in his kit bag, Sam Rose was sent off to do his bit for Uncle Sam.

Trailing the US forces from Normandy to Paris – always at a safe distance of many days behind the action – Sam was now comfortably entrenched behind a desk at US Military Headquarters Paris. If his days had been slow, then his nights certainly weren't. How wrong his father had been about his opposition to the language studies. With his command of French he had become the go-to man to have tag along for any night-time fun on offer. You see, in Iowa or Missouri or Kentucky or pretty much anywhere else stateside other than parts of Louisiana, there was no call for French. To quote one of his night-time companions, 'There ain't no need for that froggy jabber in the civilised world back home.' So Sam was the man. But to their credit, those boys tried to make sure the little Jew boy from the Bronx could one day truly say he'd had a wonderful war.

The army's need for Sam's language skills, if that need had ever existed, had faded by the time he got to Paris. His days involved moving paper from one filing cabinet to another and not much more. He begged his superior for something more stimulating. He argued that a trained illiterate could have done his work, only to be told, 'This is the US Army and if paper pushing is what the US Army says you do, then that's what you'll do. Now get me the report from Washington.' And barely audible, as the major had muttered it to himself, Sam heard him say, 'Pushy upstart little Hebe.'

You might wonder how a boy from the Bronx teamed up with a boy from Paris to scam the US Army. The answer is that it was all in the chemical reaction that occurs when you mix two special ingredients – an American in Paris whose talents weren't recognised with an insignificant Parisian itching to be more. Both of them had their motivations. As far as Sam Rose was concerned, he was out to make the army pay for overlooking him; all his studiousness had led to disappointment so any revenge would better than none. And making money out of it couldn't hurt. As far as Patrick D'Eze was concerned, he was out to live out any script that resembled a Hollywood movie; though the action of his movie wasn't set in America was a disappointment, he had to start somewhere.

Sam Rose had figured that a Goliath like the US Army must have had issues when it came to keeping track of supply requests, supply deliveries, supply storage and finally distribution of those supplies. Four vulnerable steps. Four vulnerable steps where a few strokes of a typewriter's keys could wipe out more equipment than an entire panzer division ever could – poof and anything from a can of beans to a Sherman could disappear. What's more, starting from the first of those four steps the amount ordered of any supply item could be increased or decreased. You see, documents requesting supplies and documents confirming delivery of supplies passed through Sam, and he was sure that he could falsify the numbers ordered and the numbers delivered. He had access to order forms and delivery forms. It looked so easy, he wondered why no one had ever done it before, so when the major had muttered, 'Pushy upstart little Hebe', he'd had enough and the army would pay.

I'm sure you're wondering how Sam Rose and Patrick D'Eze met. After all, though they lived in the same city, why would their paths have crossed at some point? The truth of the matter is there were many nights when their paths more than just crossed – for both of them, lengthy periods were spent where their paths coincided.

For Sam, tagging along with some of the good ole knuckleheads to the clubs had already palled. Montmartre strip joints had become boring. Jazz clubs were too smoky, too noisy and besides, he had no love of jazz hot or cool. And as for waiting in the cold outside Madame Zsou Zsou's establishment while his evening charges discharged their bodily fluids inside was undignified. Surely he hadn't crossed the ocean with the army to play good uncle to a bunch of rowdies. And he wondered how much he could put up with.

For Patrick, anywhere the Americans congregated was the place to be, and that meant hanging outside the strip clubs of Montmartre, the jazz clubs and places like Madame Zsou Zsou's. Here he could see his demi-gods in their clean uniforms, smoking their American cigarettes and walking their *I-own-the-world* swagger. For the moment this was the closest he could get to his fantasy of heaven.

One night outside Madame Zsou Zsou's, Patrick saw a small dark-haired man sitting on the hood of a jeep. The uniform was right but the man was wrong. He wasn't his idolised American. The man took out a packet of cigarettes. They were unmistakably American in their American-style soft pack. Army issue Chesterfields. The man then took out his lighter. A Zippo lighter. US Army issue again. Pewter black crackle, windproof with a flip lid, and though Patrick obviously couldn't see it, he knew the lighter had on its side the US five-star emblem and the letters spelling out *U.S. Army*. He knew it well. It was the same type as the one he had stolen from an unattended tabletop in Pigalle and was now in his pocket.

Sam tried flicking the grooved wheel of the flint once, twice, thrice and rather than try a fourth time he called to the youth loitering nearby. In perfect but faintly accented French he asked the young man for a light. Patrick handed his lighter to the small American who lit his cigarette and then without thinking, Sam put Patrick's lighter back into his own pocket; and that was the beginning of a strange friendship.

❖

Standing by the jeep, Patrick waited as the American quietly sucked on the cigarette. After all the months when he had looked on them from a distance, he had finally made contact with one of the demigods; granted, not a typical one but nevertheless one of them. That he had forsaken a stolen keepsake to that end was not a problem as he considered it a cheap entrance fee to the main event.

Sam glanced at his watch for the hundredth time and bristled that the others were keeping him waiting. *Why do they always do this to me?* He lit another cigarette, shook the Chesterfield pack at the young man and offered him one. Patrick took one and Sam lit it with Patrick's lighter which again he put in his own pocket. Then to explain why he was by the Jeep outside and not at Madame Zsou Zsou's, Sam said, 'I'm waiting for my friends. They're inside.'

Patrick was struck by the American's French – perfect except for a slight American accent. It struck him as odd because almost all Americans he'd overheard never spoke French even when speaking directly to anyone French. And the few who had spoken French had done so with such a heavy accent; even the Germans had spoken better French.

Time passed and still the rowdies hadn't come out. More time passed. More cigarettes were smoked. Having offered the young man a cigarette earlier, Sam now felt it was polite to offer the young man one each time he had one.

'Another?'

'Yes, thank you.'

And so it went, 'Another?'

'Yes, thank you.'

Until the packet was emptied.

'Can you recommend a cabaret I can take my friends to? Take them there if they ever re-emerge. You know, something traditionally French? French songs, folk songs, that sort of thing. It wouldn't harm them to get a dose of French culture. God knows at the moment they're probably getting a dose of something worse.'

Patrick knew of such a cabaret – Marcel's. He had been there a few times and if you wanted to hear that sort of music, it was the place to go. It was in the basement of a bistro in Rue Montorgueil, just a stone's throw from the Eglise Saint-Eustache side of Les Halles. It opened very late and stayed open until dawn. Generally it attracted would-be singers who sang traditional French songs. If that's what the American wants, then that's the place. But Patrick wondered why any American would want anything to do with French culture. Why would they? After all they had Judy Garland, the Hardy Boys and Laurel and Hardy. They had Hollywood. They had all those stars. It just didn't make sense.

Patrick explained to Sam how to get to Marcel's. There was much scope for Sam to get lost. It was getting late and the prospect of driving around Paris lost with his charges was not what he wanted to do.

'Hey, when they come out why don't you come with us? Show us the way and I'll stand you some drinks. Promise.'

The American extended his hand to Patrick. 'My name's Sam. Sam Rose. What's yours?'

❖

By early 1959 I was back writing for *Paris Matin*. All had been forgiven. I forgave them for dumping me way back in 1941 and they forgave me for being me. So it's amazing what a change of proprietor can do. They gave me a free hand to pick and choose what I wrote. They even gave me my own byline: *Le Monde de Martin Houx*. No restrictions, and the money was better than most people were getting then. All in all you could say it was working out well for me. In case you're wondering, I was still trying to write that novel but as I got older it no longer seemed important to me. Another thing about getting older is that you find yourself thinking about things that happened years back. You know, I used to find myself thinking about the short time I spent on that farm with Patrick D'Eze near Fontainebleau.

I have always been attuned to elements that could make a good yarn. Call it a newspaperman's nose. Patrick D'Eze's line about the lawyer Lucien Blondell rewarding him with a US motorcycle was such an element – a starting element. What was the connection between the boy Patrick D'Eze and Lucien Blondell? What had D'Eze done to be rewarded by Blondell?

Then there are the protagonists who make an interesting story. There's the evil combative pig, the lawyer Lucien Blondell who, and not before time, had finally been disbarred. Not that it harmed him – swanning it on the Riviera, rubbing shoulders with the rich and famous, and living the high life in his own suite at the Negresco in Nice. And they say nastiness doesn't pay. Then you've got the American Sam Rose. The mysterious and now dead Sam Rose. What business did he do with Blondell? Police records say the charred body found in the Bois de Boulogne was Sam Rose. Was it really? All they had to go on was essentially a hunk of barbequed meat, a dog tag and some burnt papers. That was all. Hardly a positive ID so there was enough room there for me to wonder whether the Bois de Boulogne body was indeed Sam Rose. With those ingredients, what story could ask for more?

As an aside, let me tell you that I've always wondered what

happened to the D'Ezes. Look, I feel bad about abandoning Madame D'Eze when and how I did. Sometimes I justify it to myself by saying that our relationship had run its course. But I must have caused her some pain when she was in need of affection. Yes, I'm a bastard when it comes to relationships. And Patrick D'Eze? What became of him? To me Patrick D'Eze was no more than a little boy trying to be a hard man. Maybe he changed for the better; maybe he even brought his mother some peace.

Well, where does this all bring me? It brings me to a pretty young thing, Marie Leblanc and her burst appendix. You see, Marie writes *Paris Matin*'s culture page for the Saturday edition and her burst appendix put her in hospital. So what's that got to do with anything? Well, coinciding with her hospital stay there was an international conference on linguistics at the Sorbonne. Marie was going to cover it to get material. She was hoping for an article on the linguistics conference for a future Saturday edition. Now I ask you, who reads stuff on linguistics? Linguistics, whatever that is.

Well, one thing led to another and the editor asked if I would go in Marie's place. Me? What do I know about linguistics or even care about it? Look, I'd never set foot in a university and now the editor had me going to a high brow academic conference. I suppose I could have gotten out of it but I felt sorry for poor little Marie with her burst appendix. So I went to the conference but not before telling the editor I was only doing it for Marie and her burst appendix and not the paper. I told him not expect too much from me.

Well, let me tell you what happened. As far as the stuff all those eggheads talked about, it was completely incomprehensible to me. Before going, I'd checked in the dictionary to see what linguistics meant and all I could glean was that it was the scientific study of language. Well, if that's so then I would have thought these guys could have used language in a way a novice like me could understand. The only technical word that I understood was the word *syntax*. No problems there, but they lost me when they started talking about *morphemes* and *clitics*. I ask you, what are *morphemes* and *clitics*?

Talk about the excitement those words generated in the question and answer time. I'd never seen grown men salivating over words. One even got so angry that he stormed out of the conference theatre, but not before calling the session's speaker a moron.

In the next talk some genius linguist from Montreal talked about *polysynthetic* languages. *Polysynthetic*? He might have well have been talking in Polynesian. By that time I was well and truly doodling, but most of all I was fantasising about Marie and her little appendix scar. I was still fantasising about Marie so much so that I had mentally disrobed her by the time the next speaker was introduced. I might have undressed her but there was no way I would have any material for her article.

The next speaker was a short man and introduced as an Israeli professor from the Hebrew University of Jerusalem. To hell with what he spoke about, I wasn't listening to the content, but what struck me was that he spoke in perfect French with a slight American accent. I recalled that all those years ago, Patrick D'Eze had told me that when he had first met Sam Rose he was impressed that Rose had spoken in perfect French albeit with a slight American accent. I hadn't caught the speaker's name as I had still been thinking about the now naked Marie and her cute scar. A wild thought was he could be the presumed dead Sam Rose, so I checked the program. No luck. The speaker was listed as Professor Shmuel Ver-Red. I spent the rest of the Professor Ver-Red's talk wondering why I would have ever thought he was Sam Rose. *Let it go. For Chrissake, Martin, just let it go!*

In the queue to collect our cups of coffee, I sidled up to Professor Ver-Red and lied, 'What a fascinating presentation, professor. I found it very thought-provoking. Oh by the way, my name is Martin Houx. I write for *Paris Matin*.'

The professor glared at me as if he had detected my deceit about his talk but answered, 'You think so?' and followed it with, 'Excuse me. I must go.'

'Before you go, are you by chance from America? From your accent.'

'I am an Israeli but yes, I am originally from the United States.'

'What place?'

And here it got interesting as he started to answer. He got as far as, 'New Yo ...' but quickly changed it to '... New Mexico.'

'Where in New Mexico?'

'Oh, you wouldn't know it.'

'Try me.'

Now he appeared nervous and blurted, 'Phoenix!' I'm no linguist and Professor Shmuel Ver-Red might be one, but I can tell you he was never from New Mexico. Even a dumb-arsed idiot like me knows that Phoenix is in Arizona. He turned his back to leave. With shaking hands he took a pack of Chesterfields from his pocket and placed a cigarette in his mouth. Then he lit the cigarette with a black US Army Zippo. That was the last I saw of him at the conference.

The upshot of my day at the linguistics conference was that I had nothing to write for Marie's column and I had met someone who might or might not have been the presumed dead Sam Rose.

Psychologists talk about Freudian slips of the tongue. Maybe there had been a slip of the tongue when the professor had hurriedly said he came from Phoenix. After all, hadn't the phoenix been a mythical bird that had risen from the ashes? So maybe Sam Rose had risen from those ashes in the Bois de Boulogne – risen as Shmuel Ver-Red. Then again, maybe not.

I felt I owed the professor an apology for my behaviour at the conference so I sent a letter to his address at his university. You know the sort: *Please forgive me for my somewhat rude interaction with you at the Paris linguistics conference ... etc. etc. ...* Well, that's what I wrote. As a creature of habit, I'd put my return address on the letter. I do that in case the letter had to be returned. I didn't expect a reply but a reply came.

The reply came in the form of a small parcel with a short letter. First, what was in the letter? He came straight out with it: *I do not speak to newspapers.* Then he wrote: *There is nothing I wish to say to you other than to be left alone. Of course, as it is no doubt for all of us who went through the war, there are matters about oneself that have long ago been left behind. These matters should be of no interest to you and, more importantly, these matters bear no relevance to me now.*

Then he wrote: I have enclosed this Zippo I borrowed from someone years ago and failed to return. If possible, please return it to a Patrick D'Eze. As a newspaper man I'm sure you'll track him down. He then signed off: Shmuel Ver-Red.

Not an admission but neither a full denial. So was Shmuel Ver-Red Sam Rose? If he wasn't, why did he risk all by linking himself and the Zippo to Patrick D'Eze? Let me tell you that in my business I've seen there is no accounting for the variations of human behaviour. I've reported on cases where serial killers purposely left clues to taunt the police. For the killer it was all a game of wits; call it an intellectual game if you wish. Also call it bizarre but it seems the higher the stakes, the more thrill a criminal experienced by always staying that one step away from apprehension. Then conversely, there have been cases where for the pettiest of crimes the perpetrators have gone to the most extraordinary and often convoluted lengths to avoid capture. People are strange. In the professor's case, it might have been that he had found it irresistible to throw the crumb of a clue into the wind and see what happened. That Zippo and its association with Patrick D'Eze was certainly a crumb of a clue.

I figured that for the time being, there was not much point finding Patrick D'Eze to give him the lighter and tell him how I came by it in the hope that he could tell me more than he had told me that evening long ago in Fontainebleau. As Patrick D'Eze had said that his association with Sam Rose had involved the lawyer Lucien Blondell, I decided to do what a good newspaper man should always do – I went to the top of the food chain, Lucien Blondell himself. If he would see me, then there would be a trip to Nice.

I knew Blondell had a suite in the Negresco so I a placed a call to him. I buttered him up, saying what a great asset he had been to all walks of French society and I was certain, despite his disbarment, that his *Légion d'honneur* must be just around the corner. I told him

I was a journalist who could help hasten up that *Légion d'honneur* by writing him up in the most positive way. He was flattered and agreed to meet me in Nice. It's amazing how vain the notables can be. Ah, the beautiful *Côte d'Azur* was calling and I was on my way south.

◈

I arrived in Nice the day before the arranged meeting with Blondell and checked into a pokey pensione overlooking a small park on Rue Josef Kosma. I hadn't been to Nice since before the war and its charm had not changed. I wandered the back streets of the Old Town, did some browsing in the market and took an aperitif in a small bistro by the harbour. I ask you, how can you be in Nice without having salade Niçoise? So I found a small café that catered to the tourist trade where I had the most disappointing signature dish of Nice. I should have known better than to eat at a tourist café. Then, though the evening was cool, I took a stroll by the shore along the Promenade des Anglais. My stroll took me past the distinctive domed Negresco where I was to meet Blondell the following day. I couldn't help but contrast my humble Parisian lodgings with where the scumbag Blondell lived in what certainly had to be a luxurious suite.

The next day I took the short walk from my pensione to the Negresco. On arrival I checked at reception, identified myself and asked for Lucien Blondell. I was told he was expecting me and he had asked that I be taken to his table in the Chantecler. A bellhop took me to Blondell's table in the restaurant. The Chantecler's tables were empty except for the one occupied by Blondell. What greeted me, however, was not what I had expected. Yes, I'd seen photographs of the man over the years. In fact, I'd be surprised if there was a person in France who hadn't. Of course I'd expected him to be much the same as in those photographs. What I saw was not. I had expected a slender man. But no, it was obvious he was enjoying the good life down south as he had put on weight. He had become a bloated toad. A napkin was tucked under his chin and an array of

Michelin star-class dishes covered the table. Apparently his avarice had now extended to high quality food, and by the size of him I'd say food of much quantity and any quality. Like those serving an Eastern potentate, standing each side of his chair were two heavies who looked like Turkish wrestlers – bodyguards, food tasters or both? His was the only chair at the table.

'You've arrived. Pleasant trip?'

I was still standing while with a serving ladle he scooped up some ratatouille from a tureen and tasted it. Addressing the tureen, he said, 'The kitchen here is superb. They know what they're doing.' Then as an afterthought he asked me, 'You eaten yet?'

Sensing a free lunch I replied, 'Not yet.'

Blondell gestured to the goliath on his left and commanded, 'Hop to it and get the man a chair!' When I was seated he commanded me with, 'Eat! Eat! Let's eat first and you can interview me afterwards in the bar over brandy and cigars.' The creep had certainly not fallen on hard times.

In the bar we sat in a cubicle while his henchmen guarded its opening. A friend had told me that brandy is the best leg opener in town. In Blondell's case I was hoping it would be an opener of another sort – a lubricant to answering my questions. It was my turn to start the conversation.

'Mr. Blondell you've had an illustrious career in so many fields. Law, business, a patron of the arts. And let's not forget your generosity to worthy causes. How would you describe yourself?'

I'm sure he'd already prepared his answer to this question before, because without hesitation he replied, 'I'm a renaissance man. Yes, without a doubt I'd call myself a renaissance man. You see, I'm a man of many abilities.'

The pompous prick, I thought, but I continued, 'Yes indeed. There have been so many facets to your life and they've all led to success.'

Here he interrupted me. 'Yes, I've been successful in any way one cares to measure success. Fame, money and influence. Do you know

I could have been a judge and sat in the Conseil d'État?'

I knew that to be a lie but I let him go on.

'As for money, well, I've got so much.' Then with an air of self-deprecation he added, 'It's only money. Now don't get me wrong, I appreciate it but I feel it's my duty spread it about. Charities, foundations, that sort of thing.'

Here he was telling the truth but his money was dirty money. As for charities? The money was only given away at the insistence of his accountants who'd convinced him of the taxation advantages of so doing. What's more, his donations were only given if it could be publicised that he had done so.

I wanted to steer the interview to the years that covered the time that Sam Rose was in Paris. I did so by saying, 'Paradoxically, though the war years were horrendous for many, the years after the war were also very difficult. For example, after the liberation and up to 1948. How did you find it?'

He hadn't expected this line of inquiry because it took him a long time to answer. So much so that it looked as if he wasn't going to answer. So I rephrased with, 'How did you manage after that heady August in 1944 and the start of Léon Blum's socialist government in December 1946? Not only till then but after that as well?' I thought that would cover the period in which I was interested.

Almost immediately I rued my mistake because I had inadvertently introduced a political issue by which he could divert the conversation. The canny bastard did just that.

'Don't get me started on Léon Blum and socialists. Bad for business, and when something is bad for business then it's bad for the creators like me.'

'But you still managed to thrive, didn't you?'

'I thrived only because of my drive, inventiveness and genius. But while we're on politics, did you know they wanted me to run?'

'They? Who do you mean by *they*?'

The clever scoundrel was now diverting me from where I had wanted the interview to go.

'Everyone. Right, left and centre.'

Of all the things that could have been said about Lucien Blondell, you might have to add delusional. He was a clever man but he was a dangerous man with shady connections. In those post war years when the memory of that other supreme villain, Adolf Hitler, was still fresh, Blondell wasn't the man any side of politics would have wanted. So I took his assertion to be a lie but answered, 'That's very interesting. I didn't know that.'

'Well, not many people do.'

I suppose he wanted me to take his reflection as an example of his modesty. I still had to guide him back to Sam Rose. I knew a way to guide him back on track and it was via Léon Blum.

'You didn't want me to engage you in discussion about Léon Blum.'

Here Blondell added, '… and the socialists.'

'Yes, yes, and the socialists, but what was it about Blum you didn't like?'

'Surely it's obvious. He was a Yid.'

I now had a way back to Rose. 'A Jew?'

'Yes, a Jew. A Jew who had too much clout.'

'Did that fact matter to you?'

'No, not if the Jew knows his place. But Blum didn't.'

Blondell was trying to draw the distinction between a particular Jew and Jewry as a whole. And now he made a classic error by saying, 'Some of my dearest friends are Jews.'

This raised my suspicion that it wasn't so. The claiming of having best friends in a group you despise is an old ploy aimed at throwing you off the scent. If that wasn't enough, he then said, 'You know, during the war I helped many Jews get out of France.'

At the time I couldn't fault him on that one. In a perverted way it was true. Only after Blondell's death did it become known the degree to which he had collaborated with the Nazis in the deportation of many Parisian Jews to the death camps. In that exercise he had profited immensely by the confiscation of their assets.

'So you helped many French Jews during the war.'

'Oh, yes. Many.'

'Well, that's something to be proud of. After the war, though, when the Americans were here, what then?'

'Then? With the Jews?'

'Yes, with the Jews. There were lots of Jews coming through France from the east. From places like Poland and Russia. Did you have anything to do with them?'

'They had their own organisations. Most didn't stay too long. In the main they were eager to get out of Europe. Anywhere but Europe. America, Canada even as far as Australia. Then of course there was the good old Promised Land. Palestine. They had their own teams running people out of France and getting them into Palestine right under the British noses.'

'What did you think of that?'

'Good riddance. The war gave us a chance to start with a fresh Jew-depleted France.'

The old anti-Semite was revealing himself. And here I set the bait.

'What about Jews with the American Army? There must have been some. Did you meet any?'

Here his eyes closed as he thought, and when they opened he looked around the bar. Clicked his fingers at his bodyguards and said, 'Leave us. Go sit on the stools at the counter but keep an eye on the door. No drinks!'

When his protectors were seated he turned to me. 'You're asking some very strange questions, Mr Houx. What's it with you and the Jews? You wouldn't be one? Houx is definitely not a Jewish name. Though those people have been known to change their names if it gives them an advantage.'

'No, I'm not Jewish. It's just that the time the Americans were in Paris was an interesting time, and as we were talking about Jews it led me to wonder about American Jews in Paris.'

'Okay, I'll tell you about one I met. If you mention it beyond here, forget seeing next year let alone tomorrow.'

Then as if to emphasise his threat, he waved to his heavies and yelled across the bar, 'Order yourselves some Evian.'

He then turned to me and said, 'Alright, I'll tell you something about what you've been fishing for in your inept schoolboy way. Once I've told you that will be it. This conversation never took place. You will never speak about it. You will never write about it. If you do, you will never do anything again. If you write about it, you will be destroyed first and then you will disappear. It will be as if Martin Houx never walked the earth. You understand?'

He then smiled and commenced his story.

'Way back in 1941 I used to amuse myself with court presentations in the lower courts. I was good at it and it was good for the ego. I defended the usual petty dregs who with regular monotony found themselves in and out of trouble. The little buggers were so grateful when you got them off the hook that they'd end up willing to run over hot coals for you. In one of those courts I defended a stupid kid, Patrick D'Eze. I got him off the charge. It was easy. I knew that the judge had a liking for little boys and he knew I knew. The charges were dismissed just like that! I recall the judge dreamed up that there was an irregularity in the charge sheet. The outcome was that this young Patrick came to do me favours, small things like keeping tabs on certain people, that sort of thing.

'The kid wasn't too bright. Sometimes I got the impression he was half a step up from an idiot. Anyway, he was a useful idiot throughout the war, doing this and that. Always trying to please. Then the war ended and we were in a whole new world. The Americans were here. They were everywhere like ants at a picnic. I suppose for many of them, Paris was a picnic.

'All of a sudden this thick punk Patrick is crazy about everything American. He goes hanging about wherever they go. Like a besotted puppy, he follows them all over Paris until in the end he befriends an American soldier. He comes back excited about his new American friend. Now, for the kid it's all Sam Rose said this and Sam Rose did that. All day long it's Sam Rose. In the end I'm intrigued so I said, why don't you bring your friend Sam Rose to see me. The day comes and I'm expecting some big strapping Yank soldier. I'm expecting a John Wayne or Clark Gable but in comes a small New York Jew. Patrick D'Eze had brought Edward G Robinson to see me.

'It turns out the stupid kid has blabbed to this Sam Rose about some of the lines of business I was running then. It was a time when a lot of odd merchandise was floating around and there was a demand for it. Stuff where you didn't ask the origin of but stuff with you could do well by on-selling. Really small stuff, stuff like socks, razors, even soap, but there was money in it because of the shortages.

'Now this American was not as straight as the army would have liked to believe. In fact, he was the one who put an interesting proposition to me. I know it's a cliché but those Jews really have a knack for business. Rose said he could get me various US Army supplies if I could sell them. If I could do that, then he'd be happy to enter into a fifty-fifty partnership with me. I didn't ask how he would get these things as I thought I didn't really need to know. It was safer for me not to know. The procurement of the goods was his problem and the sale of said goods was my problem.

'Patrick D'Eze might have been an idiot but this time he had done well. I rewarded him with a US Army motorcycle that had recently come into my possession. You don't need to ask me how it did, but I'll tell you the idiot was as happy as a kid at Christmas.

'But I digress. So more to the point, the American and I became partners. You'd say partners in crime but I'd say we were partners in a venture that was appropriate for the times. Do you think we were the only ones with our business model? No sir. There were worse scammers than us. There were others who were scamming the US Army of life and death items. They were stealing medicines. Things like penicillin, that sort of thing. That's not to say I wouldn't have done the same. But Rose couldn't get his hands on that sort of merchandise. No, we were stealing, I suppose you could use that word, but I'll rephrase it. We were redirecting mundane items – things like blankets, socks or canned food. Not as sexy as penicillin but perhaps in the long run more profitable. Just work it out for yourself. Suppose you make a hundred on an item and you can only get and sell that one item once a week then you'll make a hundred in a week. Now, suppose there is another item where you make ten per item and you can easily sell a hundred of them in the week, then you'll make a thousand in a week. Blankets, socks and canned food – everyone needs those often but not many people require penicillin often. And what's more, no sick and dying babies for lack of what we sold. Voila! Blankets and socks win over penicillin!'

Blondell broke into a broad smile, extremely pleased with himself. He continued, 'As I said, getting goods was Rose's job and on-selling was mine. Sounds straightforward, doesn't it, but there are two important in-between parts. How does he get the goods to me and where do I store them? We got around the first problem by Rose getting the army's delivery trucks to stop at a warehouse I had acquired from a Jew during the war.'

Lowering his voice and almost as an aside, Blondell said, 'I acquired quite a few things from the Jews during the war – apartments, shops, even the farm where you met Patrick D'Eze. Don't feign that surprised look. You see, I remember he told me you visited him at the farm. The fool couldn't keep his trap shut about anything. In the end that was his downfall.

'Now where was I? How did Rose get the supply trucks to go to the warehouse? Most Americans are a trusting lot. Naive and gullible, I'd say. They believe anything. So Rose had some fake US Army signs made up that looked exactly like the real thing. Whenever a delivery was due, my men would put those signs up all over the place. The gate, the walls and the warehouse's storage entry door. My men also put on US army outfits, which by the way Rose had got. My men would help with the unloading and they looked like the real thing. Well, as long as they didn't speak, they were the real thing. And as for the real US soldiers? The truck drivers. They were happy just sitting in the truck doing fuck-all or talking with Rose who was diverting their attention from what we were doing.

'You have to understand that when he was putting in orders for supplies, Rose would specify two drop-off locations, the first being our warehouse and the second being for the location where the supplies were intended to go. Now, suppose the actual delivery location had required a thousand of something, well, Rose would have ordered eleven hundred of that something. Of course, Rose had to be at our warehouse to sign off for those extra hundred items. The remaining thousand items went off to wherever they were intended where they were signed off by whoever had requested them. Uncle Sam was none the wiser; so, so simple and it worked … for a while.

'It was all going well until one day Rose came to see me. He'd lost his cockiness and was very shaky. He told me that questions were being asked. Apparently, some junior below him was doing an audit of the purchasing orders and noticed discrepancies. First he noticed that many goods ordered by Rose had two delivery drop-offs though the request for supplies had come from only one depot. He also discovered that the number of goods ordered by Rose was always greater than the number of goods delivered to the US supply depots. Because Rose had been the one filling out the orders, the junior thought it prudent to bypass him to go up the chain to an officer senior to Rose.

'Rose said that our business venture was dead as sooner rather than later the army would be coming after him. Then he asked me, if he deserted could I get him out of harm's way and better still, could I get him out of France. I had gotten many Jews out of France during the war. Sent them east.' Blondell looked at me directly as if I was a fellow war criminal, tapped a finger against the side of his nose and said, 'Of course, you know what I mean by that.' He said it as a statement and not a question. The man had no morals. He had sent people to their deaths with no more concern than he would have had taking out the garbage.

Blondell ordered another brandy for himself, giving me time to process what he had been telling me. The brandy arrived and we sat in silence while he savoured the drink. It was as if he was taking his time on purpose; he cupped the balloon, he sniffed the drink, he held it to the light and then he sipped it for a long time. Perhaps he was trying to impress me as a connoisseur of brandy, but all I could think of were the people he had sent east. He impressed me not as a connoisseur but as a dangerous poseur. Then he started again.

'I told Rose I could arrange something, but you have to understand what he was asking was not cheap. I said, surely you've done well out our little venture and no doubt you've done something with your cut of the money. Well then he asked how much did I want. Now he wanted to play that old game of haggling; goes back to Moses and I can tell you, the chosen ones are good at it.'

I felt uncomfortable by Blondell's anti-Semitic stereotyping. Surely the Nazis had taught the world where it ends. So I diplomatically said, 'Don't you think it's harsh to brand a group of people as all having the same characteristics? Are all Frenchman great lovers? I think not. We're as good and as bad as any other nation. And let me tell you, it's been my experience that very few Americans look like Clark Gable or John Wayne.'

But unfazed, Blondell continued, 'When a man like Rose has the dogs at his heels, he'll settle for any deal and I got a good deal from him. You see, the canny little Jew had used his cut of our venture to buy diamonds and sheets of gold leaf. Don't ask me how he had managed to convert his cut to such a treasure trove. As he put it, he had invested in something that was quite lightweight and therefore portable. Mr Houx, at a risk of upsetting your sensitivities, I say those people have a nose for business.'

He stopped at this point, called across the bar and asked his henchmen to order some more Evian for themselves.

I was eager to hear more so I prompted him with, 'So, you made a deal with Rose?'

'Yes, a very satisfactory deal. I wasn't upset at all by the exorbitant price I'd requested from him for his disappearance. In the long run, it wouldn't hurt him as his type always has the ability to bounce back and thrive no matter the circumstances.'

And now I added, 'Somewhat like you, Mr Blondell.' This didn't please him at all.

'Look, you've got to understand what Rose was asking was not cheap. There were a lot of people involved who would have had to be paid off. Not cheap whatsoever.'

He ordered another brandy and went through the same ridiculous process as with the one before. He showed no sign that the alcohol was having an effect on him, other than perhaps making him more talkative.

'Mind you, although what was going to happen would end our business venture, I relished the challenge posed by getting Rose out of France. To tell you the truth, I didn't have the vaguest idea how I would do it. But that didn't stop me promising him I would get him out. I've found that having confidence you can do something is more than half of what's required. For me, the rest always falls into place.

'Rose was insistent that he was going to have to go AWOL before the end of the week, otherwise it would be too late. I said, why wait? Go and collect your little hoard now. Bring it back to me here tonight and we'll do the transaction. That's all you have to do and the rest will be up to me. I then had a brainwave. I told him I'd need some of his personal papers, his uniform and his dog tag.

'I think it was clever of me to get those items from him. Remnants of these were found by the police with a burnt corpse in the Bois de Boulogne. It was the evidence used to assume the unrecognisable corpse had been Sam Rose. The Americans were on to what Rose had been up to, so by the time the body, or what was left of it, turned up, they were happy with the assumption that he had been killed by associates with whom he was dealing. The US Army's attitude must have been good riddance to their scammer. Believe me, I know bureaucracies, and the US Army or any army is just another bureaucracy. If something involves difficult or messy follow-up work, then bureaucracies look for the convenient way out. So for them, it was convenient to accept that the burnt remains were what was left of Sam Rose; convenient because it left no loose ends to follow up in their bailiwick.'

I had to ask the burning question, and there's no pun intended: whose burnt corpse was it in the Bois de Boulogne?

Blondell was taking his time with his answer, obviously he was weighing up how he would respond. Then he answered, 'Look, when you do business on the shady side, there are many who run afoul of their associates. Arguments happen. There are disagreements. Sometimes these disagreements escalate into violence and sometimes the violence escalates even further. You must remember that this was not long after the war had ended and there were lots of, dare I say it, shady ventures going on. It was a time when bodies turned up in the streets of Paris or floating in the Seine. In actual fact, there were bodies galore, ergo we had our pick of bogus Sam Roses.'

So there I had it – the corpse in the Bois de Boulogne was not Rose's. But that didn't mean that Rose was still alive or that he had even managed to get to somewhere that was safe for him. I was thinking about this when Blondell brought me back with, 'Enough said about all that! Now let me get back on track. Where was I? Oh yes. I told Rose about that farm of mine. The one outside Fontainebleau. I said I'd drive him down that night. He could hide out there until I arranged passage for him out of France.

'To justify the sizeable fortune I had extracted from him, I told him there would be very little of it for me. I told him most of it would be used to grease the many palms of those who would get him out to safety. It doesn't matter if I tell you it was a lie. The truth is that the so-called many palms I would have had to grease were in fact few. In the main, they were hands of people who owed me favours, so very little greasing was required. I did quite well out of Rose's disappearance. At the time our mutual little friend D'Eze was living at the farm, so Rose had company who idolised him.'

This brought me back to the time when at Madame D'Eze's

request I visited Patrick at the farm. Patrick had started as Blondell's runner in 1941. The Americans arrived in Paris in August 1944 and were gone by 1945. I met Madame D'Eze in the summer of 1947. So I figured that Rose had been at the farm sometime in 1945. I asked Blondell, 'So Rose was at the farm in 1945?'

'Work that out for yourself, great newspaper man. You don't need me to tell you. Go through your own newspaper's archives. I'm sure you'll find some mention of the burnt corpse. That'll give you the timing of Rose's disappearance.'

Although somewhat miffed by Blondell's telling me how to suck eggs, I pressed on. I asked him how Rose got out of France after he had hidden low at the farm.

'It took a while to arrange, but I've helped so many people, you'd call them shifty and I'd call them shrewd; as I said, most of them owed me favours one way or another. So I called in their debts as it were. There was a forger on the Left Bank who used to do beautiful work. He was a master of his art. You couldn't tell his forgeries from the real thing. I can tell you he'd forged many a document I needed. I defy anyone tell me they weren't the real thing. Magnificent work! Without a doubt I'd say artists like him only come around every hundred years. Unfortunately, in the end he was caught. Even I couldn't help him.

'But at the time I'm talking about he was still creating his masterpieces. I employed him to create some identity papers for Rose. Then at the stroke of a pen, as it were, Sam Rose, late of the US Army and the Bronx, became Marcel Lebeau, wine merchant from Bordeaux. I can tell you Rose was rather pleased with the forger's choice of *the handsome one* for the surname. So now Rose had a new identity and the former Sam Rose, as far as anyone knew, had ended as the charcoal grill in the Bois de Boulogne. The next job was to get Marcel Lebeau out of France.

'From '45 to early '47 I was running trucks from Paris down to the docks in Marseilles. My trucks would collect contraband from the docks and drive it back to Paris where my fences sold it. In those days things were very slack and easy – just a small bribe created many a blind eye. Oh, when I think of it, I miss those days. I had connections on the docks and on some of the boats coming in. So when the time was right we drove Rose – sorry, I should say Lebeau – from the farm down to the Marseilles docks. In Marseilles we were to put him on a boat headed for Rome. When he heard this Rose, sorry again, Lebeau, kicked up a hell of a fuss. Said it didn't suit him as his desired destination was Palestine. Ungrateful little bastard! Can you believe it? I'd fulfilled my part of the deal. I'd organised a means for safe passage out of France and now he's choosey about where he's going. So I left him at the docks and told him to sort it out himself. I'd done my part.

'As I never saw the boat's captain again I have no idea whether the ungrateful little bastard Rose sailed with that boat to Rome. We argued at the docks. I left in anger and that was the last time I saw him. Since then, I've never heard from Rose or Lebeau again and I don't care to.'

'What about Patrick D'Eze? I met him on the farm in '48, yes, it must have been '48. So what happened to him?'

Blondell quickly shot back, 'He's dead.'

This information came as a shock. I hadn't expected that. I'd been taken up by the mystery of Sam Rose and its resolution right up to the docks in Marseilles. As for Patrick D'Eze, well, when I had posed my question to Blondell I'd expected an answer along the lines of whether he was still on the farm or not. I'd completely taken it for granted that he was alive, if not on the farm then somewhere else. But dead? Never. Yes, I know a lot of things can happen in eleven years, but you don't expect an apparently healthy young man in peacetime to be dead. I wondered how Madame D'Eze had survived her Patrick's death.

I experienced white hot emotions, but coldly and perhaps with an undignified curiosity, I asked, 'How?'

'That kid was none too bright. Always thought he was cleverer than he was. Plus he was prone to blabbing untruths. That was his downfall. He started cutting himself in on deals behind my back. Said to others he had my support on some very unwise ventures. Though there's money in it, drugs were never my area. On the other hand, D'Eze thought he'd get involved. There was stuff coming in from North Africa through Marseilles. Lots of it. Funny, there's Marseilles again. Anyhow, D'Eze thought he would ship some of it from Marseilles to Paris using my trucks. Can you imagine? In my trucks. I'd trusted him and he's using my name to raise money to get his little business venture going. He talked to others in that trade, saying he had my backing. Utter bullshit! When I learnt of all this I took him aside and gave him a fatherly warning not to continue. I thought he'd taken my advice, then some months later I got a call from someone saying I owed them money for last month's shipment from Morocco. The kid had to go.'

'What happened?'

All Blondell said was, 'Motorcycles are dangerous machines.'

After saying this, Blondell claimed he had a pressing engagement elsewhere. He rose to leave but before he left, he said, 'Now remember to write something nice about me. Concentrate on my good deeds. Charities, widows and orphans. That and only that sort of thing. If you don't, who can say where you'll end up, if you get my meaning. So keep away from all those unproven stories you might have heard. And above all, no mention of Sam Rose and Patrick D'Eze. It's healthier for you if you want to be around to ring in another year. Take my warning when I tell you typewriters can also be dangerous machines.'

He then turned and, with one his heavies in front and one behind him, they left in single file. I was tempted to reply that an angel like him should have no need for bodyguards but my better judgement took over.

Well, what had I got from my meeting with him? I knew that the charred body in the Bois de Boulogne was not Sam Rose's and I knew that Patrick D'Eze was dead. Until my visit to Nice, I'd assumed it was possible that Sam Rose was dead and Patrick D'Eze was definitely alive. Now I knew it was otherwise. Anything else? Well, yes, another false assumption. I got a massive whack to my expense account. You see, I had assumed that the lunch in the Chantecler and drinks and cigars in the bar and even each henchman's Evian had gone to Blondell's tab at the Negresco. Not so. God knows, it would have been small change for him. I am usually unfazed but was stunned when I was presented with the bill for everything. Apparently on his way out, and unbeknown to me, Blondell had told the staff that he had been *my* guest and all expenses were on me.

Blondell had left me a lot to think about, but that's not all. As I was packing my case that night in preparation for my return to Paris next morning, there was a knock at my door in the pensione. Thinking it was the owner wanting payment now in case I should skip away without paying, I immediately opened the door. I recognised the man as one of Blondell's heavies from earlier at the Negresco.

He stood in the doorway and said, 'A message from Mr. Blondell.' And with that said, he delivered a swift and powerful kick to my testicles, and as I lay on the floor in agony there was another kick, this time to my stomach. He then said, 'Mr. Blondell wishes you to never mention anything about today's conversation to anyone. If you do, he said to tell you his boys in Paris aren't as gentle as me. The boss said to tell you he thanks you for the lunch. Oh, and by the way, from me and Ahmed thanks for the Evians.'

The door was still open, and though he had gone I continued to lie in pain on the floor where I had fallen. The pain was excruciating, but more than that, I was frightened by Blondell's threat. So that was how the bastard worked. He had climbed the ladder out of the shit where he belonged by lying, by inflicting pain, by threats and even by murder by proxy. He had, one way or another, done this to anyone who stood in his way – his rivals, the Parisian Jews and to the insignificant fools like Patrick D'Eze.

That stupid kid Patrick D'Eze wanted to be more but didn't know how. I had taken news of his death as just one of those things that happened when you play around with the hard men. But there must have been collateral damage – Madame D'Eze, Patrick's mother. That poor woman had loved her son, and perhaps even loved me; she must have suffered his loss alone. Both Patrick and I had failed her. The great journalist, Martin Houx, the great journalist with his own by-line in *Paris Matin*, was a coward and unable to love anyone. Then, feeling sorry for Madame D'Eze and her son and for myself, I started to sob.

In the morning I took that long train trip back to Paris; Nice to Paris with a change in Marseilles. I had half expected Blondell's goons would be at the station to give me a farewell beating or at least to see me off.

The trip was long enough for me to replay everything that had happened in Nice. The good and the bad of it. The good being the resolution of a mystery, namely that the remains in the Bois de Boulogne were not Sam Rose's. Sam Rose was in all likelihood alive somewhere. The bad? Well, there were a number of levels of bad. At the lower end of bad was that I had been bilked by Blondell into paying the restaurant and bar bills. But then again that was consistent with what I knew of Blondell as for him there would always be such a thing as a free lunch. The beating at my pensione was the next up in the ranking of bad things. In time I would of course recover from the beating but I was not so sure that I would recover from the threats to my life that came with it. These threats obviously lead to the next bad thing – I had a great story that if I valued my skin I could never write. Finally, at the upper level of badness was that Madame D'Eze's son Patrick was dead. I recalled her fragile state when I had left her. I doubt she would have recovered from the loss of her beloved boy. As for Patrick D'Eze? That was bad because he was only a silly boy and silly boys don't deserve to be murdered. Another thing he didn't deserve was his loving mother. Now, I'm not a person prone to the supernatural but the clickity-clacking of the train's wheels on the tracks were saying *Patrick D'Eze is dead, Patrick D'Eze is dead, Patrick D'Eze is dead* … Somewhere after Dijon I fell asleep and didn't wake until the train jolted to a halt at Paris's Gare de Lyon.

❖

I was back in Paris having spent more than a month's income in Nice. Even though I was *the* Martin Houx with his own by-line, there was no way *Paris Matin* would reimburse me. To top that, I was suffering an unrelenting ache in my testicles and I had no story to write unless I was willing to risk my life. At work, I was lost for words whenever anyone asked me about Nice. All I could bring myself to do was mumble that except for a lousy salad Niçoise, Nice was fine and left it at that. Even the pretty little Marie sensed I was not right. I told her that I thought I was coming down with a cold and I would stay home for a few days. I went home where I brooded about both D'Ezes.

Patrick D'Eze's death bothered me because the more I thought about him, the more I thought about Madame D'Eze. I don't know why I had taken Patrick D'Eze's death as I had, after all I had only briefly met him at the farm in Fontainebleau. I suppose I was disturbed because he was Madame D'Eze's much loved son. I knew how she cared for him and I knew of her fragility. I had treated her poorly and there was no way I could make up for that. Maybe it was that mother and son were linked that his death upset me. If it wasn't for my relationship with his mother, then to me he would have been just another insignificant punk who had run around with the wrong people. I had written about such cheap little shits many times. Let me tell you that without politicians, film stars, sportsmen, sex scandals and people like Patrick D'Eze, newspaper columns would be blank.

By my fourth day at home I had read every magazine I had lying around. Out of boredom I had smoked too many cigarettes and drunk too many coffees. I had acquainted myself with every ripple in the wallpaper, every crack in the ceiling's plaster and, for want of something else to do, I had sat on the toilet too often and for too long. I tried writing my never-ending novel. Writing it was something I'd often used to focus my mind. Call it a therapy if you wish. This time the therapy wouldn't work. Nothing would come. Finally out of anger with myself, I burnt every copy of it. In view of the crappiness of the real world, there had never been any point to that writing project. At best, it had only been a distraction. At worst, it had been a narcissistic undertaking. Oh, thank God I had saved myself from joining the ranks of the would-be writers.

Some men are made for relaxing at home; perhaps I wasn't one. But then there had been a winter, so long ago, I had spent with Madame D'Eze. We had spent it cooped in her crowded apartment without the need to venture out. Perhaps that was me of the past and Madame D'Eze of the past. What of Madame D'Eze of now? It was clear I had been a coward for too long and now I needed to see her again.

❖

I needed to see Madame D'Eze again. But how could I after all these years? I needed to see her, in part out of affection and in part out of curiosity. Affection because there was a time when we were inseparable. And though it was long ago, the cold winter we had spent in bed hunkered down against the cold had stayed with me as a pivotal time in my life. We had survived the war and then we were planning for a future. The possibility of better times with a new decade not far away. It doesn't matter that the better times never eventuated; what mattered was that we made plans for those better times. With the passing of time I reckon I've become more sentimental and it seems to me the bond we shared should never have been allowed to be ground away by intervening years.

Then there's curiosity, yes, curiosity. An old newspaperman like me is primed to follow the loose ends of lives to wherever they lead. Yes, curiosity. Curiosity because she was part of what brought me to Patrick and Blondell. Her beloved son was dead and surely I owed her some kindness. Even after all these years, I owed her something. But I ask you, how do you visit someone when you know their son was murdered, you know who ordered his murder and you know you can't divulge what you know? I wonder how much she knew of Blondell and her son's involvement with him. So I knew it wasn't going to be easy.

By now you've probably worked out that by nature I'm a coward. For a while I put off visiting her. *Coward!* I justified it by convincing myself that in all likelihood she no longer lived in her crowded apartment of overstuffed furniture, big bed and silver framed photos of Patrick's life. It took me weeks to steel myself to walk past her building in the 19th. And when I did, it was only a passing glance at the building before I quickened my pace to get away. *Coward! Coward!* When I was away from her building what I had planned to do seemed so simple. Away from the building, the nervous quiver was gone. The apprehension was gone and it was easy to think: *Martin, just walk up to the front door and if her name's on her buzzer, press it. Simple.*

Some weeks later I tried again, and this time I went to the buzzers at the entrance door. Her name was there. She still lived in that apartment. I also saw her given name for the first time; the label on the buzzer read Madame Jeanne D'Eze. So she was Jeanne. *Jeanne, Jeanne. Jeanne.* If I wanted, I could have pressed the buzzer. She may have let me in. And if she did, I could have walked past the concierge's station which had always smelled of celery soup. I could have climbed that old skewed staircase. I could have climbed the four squeaky flights to her door. But I didn't. *Coward! Coward! Coward!*

It was like that old hackneyed phrase where they say if you fall off a horse get up and try again. It took me many months to get back on that horse. This time, I was determined to ring her buzzer. I made it to her buzzer and was about to press it when I realised that if she answered, I would be visiting her empty-handed. After all these years, I needed to bring a gift, even if only as a diversion.

Paris in spring is a city of flowers and flower stalls, or it should be. Today this part of Paris was devoid of flowers. I wandered out of her district until I found a kerbside vendor and bought a bunch of creamy roses. I'm generally not a self-conscious person, but I felt ridiculous carrying a bunch of roses on the long walk back to her apartment. The irony of my self-consciousness was that it quelled all the qualms I'd had about ringing her buzzer. I pressed the buzzer of Madame Jeanne D'Eze and waited.

◈

After I had pressed the buzzer I waited but the street door had not opened. Reluctantly I pressed it again. This time the door opened without a voice at the other end of the intercom. The entrance foyer had not changed since I had first seen it that summer of 1947. The half-sized statue of the Venus de Milo still stood in the corner. On the other hand, the smell of celery soup no longer emanated from the concierge's station; instead, there was a pervading disinfectant smell similar to those yellow blocks at the base of the urinals at *Paris Matin*. At the foot of the stairs was the faux-antique Chinese urn with its unfortunate crack, the Chinese urn into which I used to drop my cigarette butts. I wondered if the butts were still lying in there.

I commenced the climb up the rickety stairs which still slanted toward the wall. The climb seemed longer and steeper than I had remembered. Had extra steps been added? No, I realised it was my age.

I arrived at her floor to see her apartment door open. In the doorway stood Madame D'Eze. But it was not as I had remembered. I had not expected this at all. I know everyone ages, but was that Madame D'Eze, Jeanne D'Eze? She had grown older than the intervening years should have allowed. In the doorway stood a woman who had only a slight resemblance to what I had remembered, but this Madame D'Eze had shrunken in size. Her plumpness which I had found comforting had gone and she had become a thinner woman. Too thin. From where I stood I saw that her hair was unkempt; it had become white, its quality had become wiry and in parts her scalp was visible. Madame D'Eze had aged.

I arrived at her doorway and we looked at each other for a while.

Her eyes narrowed and she was squinting. She was trying to work out who was this man with the flowers. And when she was certain she knew, she smile and said, 'I know you. You're an old friend of Patrick's. You're Pierre.'

I corrected her. 'No, I'm Martin, Martin Houx.' She didn't answer. Her mind was already elsewhere as she had noticed the flowers. 'What a lovely bunch. Patrick will love these.' Before I could say anything, she took my hand and said, 'Come, let's visit him. It's not far.'

Still holding my hand, she shuffled through the streets taking me to the Rue d'Hautpoul entrance of Cemetery de la Villette. 'Patrick will be pleased to see you.' She knew exactly where to find the grave. And why shouldn't she, as it was a journey she made regularly.

The grave and its monument were more elaborate than I thought she could have afforded. And Cemetery de la Villette? Yes, it was close to where she lived but after all, it was a small cemetery where the rarely available grave sites came at a premium.

She looked at the grave with its weeping angel monument, then she looked back at me and said, 'Pierre, don't you think it's beautiful? A beautiful spot for my beautiful boy.' She then took the flowers from me and placed them on the grave. I was touched. I felt deep into my pocket for the lighter the Israeli professor had asked me to give to Patrick D'Eze. When I found it I dropped to one knee and placed the Zippo on the grave. From my kneeling position I looked up at her and said, 'This was Patrick's.'

I rose, dusted the knee of my trousers and, motioning to the angel monument, said, 'That's quite a thing.'

'Yes, the gravesite, the monument and everything was paid for by a wonderful man. The lawyer Lucien Blondell organised it all. You know he treated Patrick like a son. Just like a son from the first day they met.'

'Lucien Blondell?'

'Yes, the lawyer Lucien Blondell. You've heard of him?'

'Our paths have crossed.'

I did not have it in me to tell her about Blondell's role in getting Patrick D'Eze to where we now stood. It would have been heartless and serve no purpose other than to destroy Madame D'Eze even more.

She told me that she wanted to stay with Patrick alone. Just a little longer. She suggested I wait for her at the cemetery's gates. While I waited for her I reflected on the complexity of human behaviour and the paradox that was Lucien Blondell. Maybe that stuff about Blondell and charities, widows and orphans was in part true and extended to grieving mothers of sons he'd had had murdered.

On the way back we passed the bistro that all those years back we had referred to as *our* bistro. It hadn't changed and I suggested we go in, if only for a coffee. She agreed and when we were seated she said to me, 'I used to come here with a friend a long time ago.' Then pointing across the bistro she said, 'Used to sit at that table over there – near the counter.' True. It had been *our* table in *our* bistro.

It was getting dark as she shuffled back to her building, all the time holding my hand. Outside her building, she let go of my hand and before I could say look after yourself, she said, 'It's nice to see a friend of Patrick's.' And then she was gone.

Though I had been moved by the day's events, I was still a selfish enough man to know I would never seek her out again.

❖

I know, I know I'm a stupid old fool but when a pretty woman comes along I'm a goner. I've been saying this a lot. Well, this old fool, Martin Houx, has got himself shacked up with little Marie. You know the one. The pretty thing who does the culture section for the Saturday edition. You remember? The appendix and all that? By the way, I've seen the scar and a lot more. Well, it's that Marie. We're getting on like a house on fire, as they say. Mind you it's hard to keep up with her demands but I'm trying. I mean, who am I to disappoint her? It'll probably kill me in the end but hey, it'll be a great way to go, don't you think? I'm doing a few things behind her back just to keep up appearances. It's a secret but I get my hair dyed every so often. Do you know I've grown a goatee? I get that dyed at the same time I get my hair done.

I try to keep fit. Well, we do that together. Weights, pulleys and lots of walking. Her favourite walk is in the Bois de Boulogne. It's not the location I would choose. But you don't disappoint a lady, if you get my message. She's even got me attending yoga classes with her. Yoga and Martin Houx, can you believe it? But once again you don't disappoint a lady, do you. The pay-off, on the other hand, apart from the sex of course, is seeing guys my age gape with envy when they see the two of us arm-in-arm.

By the way, another thing she's into is self-improvement. The apartment we share is full of those books, you know the sort. Crap like *Improve your memory using Zen* or *Learn to meditate your way to self-fulfilment*. Coming from someone who does the Saturday culture feature, it's a crazy paradox. Definitely not my kind of literature. I'm not going to raise that with her. Got to keep little Marie happy and that's what I do now.

And another thing about the way things are now. That 'what happened to Sam Rose' thing. Look I don't care whether it was Sam Rose who burnt in the Bois de Boulogne or if he left from Marseille to become an Israeli professor of linguistics. It's not important to me anymore. I really don't care one way or another. Anyway, it's all ancient history.

I'm thinking this when before I know it, Marie's on top of me, begging me to take her into the bedroom. And you don't disappoint a lady, do you? Now I tell you *that's* what's important.

My Journey with the Nixons and Others

Prologue

Last night I dreamed about Cliffy Nixon. Sometimes I dream about all the Nixons and my times with them. I dream about Cliffy's parents, Mr and Mrs Nixon, that's Clarrie and Joyce. I dream about his sister Noelene whom everyone called Gypsy, though she had pale Nordic features and not a drop of Romany in her. I dream about Melvin Marx who was with us just a brief time. And about Paddy O'Sullivan whose short time with the Nixons was far too long for Mr Nixon. I even dream about Asparagus. For years after Cliffy Nixon and I drifted apart, there were occasional thoughts like: *Why did Cliffy go? Where did he go?* Other than that, I've just lived my life.

Mr and Mrs Nixon

LIKE EVERY PREVIOUS OBSESSION Mr Nixon had embraced, he failed at singing. He took singing lessons from a Signor Garibaldi. Mr Nixon referred to his singing teacher as *The Eyetalian*. While Cliffy, that's the Nixon's son, and I knew that *signor* was Italian for mister, we thought the teacher's name was Gary Baldy.

Well, getting back to Mr Nixon and singing. The plain fact of the matter was that he didn't have a singing voice. If he attempted a deep baritone, he got chest pains and a sore throat. If he attempted falsetto, he went red in the face and felt that he would faint. Anything in between led to symptoms that were various combinations and to various degrees of the symptoms I've just mentioned. Let's face it, Mr Nixon just couldn't sing. He practised his *do-re-mi*-ing often, and when anyone heard him it was difficult to keep a straight face.

In the end the lessons and singing stopped. Mr Nixon told us he had had to fire Signor Garibaldi … *Utterly useless! The bloody Eyetalian didn't have a clue.* Cliffy suspected Signor Garibaldi did have a clue and he had fired Mr Nixon, rather than it being the other way around. No, singing was not Mr Nixon's strong suit, but it segued nicely to his next obsession – his magnificent new musical obsession. The harpsichord! And with the harpsichord came Miss Wanda, the very buxom harpsichord player.

Look, I suppose the bottom line was that Mr Nixon had wanted to find his inner musical soul. Liberate the artiste that might have dwelt deep inside a man who was more than good at any task so long as it involved his hands. Well, maybe Miss Wanda helped him there, though perhaps that's not all Miss Wanda liberated in him.

It had often been said of Mr Nixon something like: *That Clarrie, jeez he's fantastic with his hands. Give him anything of a practical nature and he'll master it. Ever seen him work on a car, make a trailer or just mend a toaster? He can do it. He can do it all. The man's a master with his hands.* So is it any wonder he wanted to succeed at something that was different – like something in the arts?

After his failure at his singing obsession, he decided to build a harpsichord. When you look at it, the way Mr Nixon must have, it wasn't such a stupid idea. It was a perfect choice for him because it involved something that he was good at using, namely, his hands. There would be two elements at work here, something practical that would lead to something of artistic use. You see, his failure at singing had not extinguished his need for self-expression in the arts. In fact the failure had enflamed it. His plan was to build his own harpsichord (that's something practical) and then he would learn to play it (that's something practical and artistic). To cap it off, once he had mastered the instrument, he supposed, naturally, he would go on to compose music for the harpsichord, and that's something very artistic.

After he had parted ways with the singing Italian Signor Garibaldi, somehow and somewhere he got blueprints for making a harpsichord. In no time the blueprints were laid out on the workshop floor and he was ready to start. Mr Nixon worked long into the night on his harpsichord goal. He even took his meals out in the workshop, and throughout most of the night Mrs Nixon kept him supplied with endless cups of tea and Salada crackers with cheese, tomato and salt and pepper: *Lots of salt but just a sprinkle of pepper, Joycie.* On weekends he worked at it all day.

Being a genius with his hands and given the time he put into it, it's no wonder Mr Nixon actually ended up making a fully working harpsichord. The drawback, however, was that he couldn't play the harpsichord even if his life or the fate of the universe depended on it. Well, it's one thing to make a musical instrument and quite another thing to play one, but he was on his way to harpsichord paradise. Enter Miss Wanda – the angel of harpsichord paradise!

Well, Miss Wanda was a hefty lady who had answered Mr Nixon's ad in the local paper for a harpsichord teacher. One wouldn't say she was beautiful but she was prettyish in a flat-faced, high-cheek-boned Magyar way. She was blonde, though it was suspected that came from a bottle, but what was significant to Cliffy was that she had substantial breasts … huge, in fact.

On the one hand, Mr Nixon couldn't play the harpsichord, and on the other hand, Miss Wanda played a mean harpsichord. You think harpsichord and you automatically think Bach and all that classical stuff. Sure, Miss Wanda played classical but she also played jazz on Mr Nixon's harpsichord. Jazz on a harpsichord! According to Cliffy's suspicions: *She probably could play a mean organ – namely the upright organ.*

Cliffy suspected his father was tickling more than the ivories. If all roads led to Rome, then for Mr Nixon this was a time when all roads, streets and laneways led to Miss Wanda. When talking about her to others, Mr Nixon would start with: *Miss Wanda, that fine cut of a woman …* then … *blah, blah, blah …* on and on about her. It pissed Cliffy off so much so that whenever she came up in our conversation, to mimic his father he would start with: *Miss Wanda, that not so fine cunt of a woman.* Look, to be honest, Cliffy did not have any evidence that something other than a mutual interest in the harpsichord was cooking on the stove between Miss Wanda and his father.

To cut a long story short, things came to a dramatic end in the following way. First Mrs Nixon was pissed off after Mr Nixon hired a signwriter to paint the name *Miss Wanda* in copperplate on the lid of the harpsichord. It was done in gold paint and very arty. There was even a scroll-like flourish under her name, sort of like the one you see under the word Coca on Coca-Cola signs. Next, probably after encouragement from Miss Wanda, Mr Nixon joined the Bayside Harpsichord Society where she was an office bearer.

This meant he was out with her every Tuesday night at the Society's weekly meetings. And if that wasn't bad enough, he was away all one entire weekend, presumably with her, at the Bayside Harpsichord Society's Annual Weekend Live-in Intensive. Now who's to say what happened at the Intensive? But it's certain that subsequent to that weekend, intense things happened.

Mr Nixon could not conceal the fact that he had been drummed out of the Bayside Harpsichord Society. Cliffy suspected his father had been fiddling when he should have been harpsichording. Mrs Nixon was devastated, but she was not devastated because Mr Nixon had been kicked out of the Society – oh no, her devastation came from thinking what might have lead up to Mr Nixon's expulsion. The closest Cliffy got to it all was overhearing Mrs Nixon accusing Mr Nixon of hanky-panky with that harpsichord slut. Maybe out of guilt or to appease Mrs Nixon, he burnt his harpsichord in a backyard bonfire. And Cliffy had the final word at the bonfire, saying, 'Well, there goes the hot harpy's *pissy* accord' – only to receive a withering look from his mother and a clip over the ear from his father.

Did Mr Nixon fail or succeed at the harpsichord? One can't say, but I can say as far as Cliffy could tell his parents became frostier with each other thereafter. So long harpsichord and so long Miss Wanda.

Gypsy's wedding bash

NOT LONG AFTER MISS Wanda left the scene, a certain Patrick O'Sullivan, usually just known as Paddy, entered the Nixons' world.

I can't exactly pinpoint when Paddy O'Sullivan came into the lives of the Nixons, and more to the point, into Gypsy Nixon's life. I can say that it happened after Mr Nixon's harpsichord obsession but before 1969. Why 1969? Well, that was the year that the Palais de Danse in St Kilda burnt down. What's the Palais de Danse got to do with it? That's where Gypsy met Paddy O'Sullivan at an urban version of a Bachelors and Spinsters Ball. As Cliffy used to say, 'She met him at a BS and it's fitting because he's full of BS.' You see, Cliffy didn't like Paddy much.

It was a while before Gypsy's phantom lover eventually materialised in the flesh at the Nixons. Of this phantom, Cliffy said, 'The bastard's probably a space alien visible only to Gypsy and, to tell you the truth, although she's my sister, I haven't worked out what planet she comes from.'

As the time being written about here predates social media and all that other stuff, the only evidence for Paddy's existence were the perfumed letters Gypsy posted addressed to Mr Patrick O'Sullivan, C/- Arnold & Sons Trucking Company, 224 Chapel St, Prahran. Cliffy knew this because there were times Gypsy gave him letters to post at the corner letterbox. That's not to say Cliffy actually posted every letter she gave him, as some found their way to the rubbish bins of the flats between the Nixons and the letterbox.

Paddy O'Sullivan was no phantom or alien from outer space

and so a human Paddy eventually was invited to the Nixons for a Sunday lunch roast. Though first impressions should be important when meeting your girl's family, they must not have been important to Paddy. He didn't bring any gift for the Nixons. So no flowers or box of chocolates for Mrs Nixon; no bottle of wine or bottles of beer for Mr Nixon. Nothing. When Mr Nixon offered him the choice of sweet or dry sherry as a pre-lunch glass, he unashamedly requested, 'You wouldn't have something better, would you? Perhaps a single malt whisky or if you don't have that, I suppose I'll have to settle for a blended variety.'

When the food was being dished out, he held his plate under Mrs Nixon's serving spoon and asked for more than had been given to him. Not wishing to seem mean, Mrs Nixon complied with the request at the cost of giving everyone else a half portion. This Paddy accepted without giving a word of thanks.

When he wasn't filling his face, Paddy held the floor, in this case the table, with his opinions on everything from world politics to football teams; from the Archbishop of Canterbury to the Pope; from science to art. Cliffy just switched off: *the prick's a bore.* Mrs Nixon was puzzled by the subjects and his appetite. Mr Nixon, on the other hand, was still bristling at the rapid depletion of his birthday present whisky; whisky he had enjoyed only on special occasions and even then allowing himself no more than a thimble at a time.

All through Paddy's monologues, Gypsy held onto every word he uttered, and though like her mother she didn't understand a word of it, later that night she said to her parents with pride, 'Isn't Paddy just so knowledgeable and clever? He's a genius. He's divine and the one and only for me.'

At the end of the main course, after having eaten everything he had been given at the expense of everyone else's servings, he said to Mrs Nixon, 'Meat was a tad too salty and rather tough, and I prefer my vegetables less mushy. What's for dessert?' To Mr Nixon he said, 'By the way, a nice red wouldn't have gone astray with the lamb.'

After that Sunday, Paddy became a regular feature at the Nixons for Sunday lunch. Even though he continued to receive larger portions than everyone else, and even though he had drained Mr Nixon's precious whisky empty, he never brought a gift with him. While we're on the issue of Paddy's consumption of Mr Nixon's prized spirits, it should be commented that the Sunday after the whisky had gone, Paddy asked for Mr Nixon's brandy. 'On the one hand, I'll have none of that foul medicinal hospital brandy I see you have in the drinks cabinet, Clarrie. On the other hand, I note that you have some Napoleon way at the back of the cabinet. I'll have some of that. I take it you've got the good sense to serve it in a proper brandy balloon.'

The more Cliffy despised Paddy, the more Mrs Nixon was puzzled by him, the more Mr Nixon fretted about his declining collection of spirits, and the more Gypsy was enchanted by Paddy. These states of increasing 'more-ness' continued until one day Gypsy announced, 'Paddy and I are getting married and he wants the wedding to be held here. What's more, we can have Reverend Mount officiating, he doesn't cost much.'

Who can tell whether Gypsy harboured disappointment at having her wedding festivities in the house where she had lived all her life – perhaps her agreeing to do so was a testament to the degree to which she thought she was in love with Paddy. How else could you explain her giving up her girlhood dream of a big wedding as the bride-queen in some fancy reception palace? To tell the truth, it must be said that Clarrie was not pleased with Gypsy's choice of future husband.

'He's rude. He's a bloody know-it-all and full of hot air.'

'Not at all, Dad. In fact, he's very well bred. He's told me that his people have much land in the Western District. They're graziers. Wealthy ones, he's told me. I'll have you know Paddy went to Xavier in Kew.'

'I don't like him.'

'Well I do and you won't be marrying him.'

'He's an O'Sullivan, right. He's been educated at Xavier, right.

That school's run by bloody Jesuits, right. For Christ's sake, can't you work it out, girlie? He's a bloody Catholic! What's more, he's a flaming Irish one. Catholics are bad enough but Irish ones are the worst sort; he's a dyed in the wool, flaming Mick. You'll have the Pope in your bedroom before you know it. And what about his people – his highfalutin people? If his people have all that money he claims, then why haven't I seen him spreading any of it within cooee of me?'

'Dad, I love him and we want to get married and that's that.'

'Then why don't the two of you get engaged first? Take it slowly. See how things develop.'

'Gee, Dad, don't be so old-fashioned.'

'Well, I'm not happy. How do you know there isn't something nasty lurking in his background? For all we know, he could be a kiddie fiddler or something like that.'

'Oh, Dad, now you're just being silly.'

'Alright, just tell me where are the two of you going to live? Tell me that. Out in the Western District on a bloody sheep station with his people?'

Mrs Nixon now spoke up to give her twopence worth, which today, as far as Gypsy was concerned, turned out to be worth much more than two pennies. 'Clarrie, of course they won't live on a farm or anywhere else other than here with us. I don't think we should have it any other way. We'll fit them in somewhere here until they put away enough money to find a place of their own.'

Gypsy beamed. 'Oh. Mum, you're a gem.'

As far as Mr Nixon was concerned, the marriage to Paddy was wrong on many levels. The only positive for him was that Gypsy had requested the wedding be held at home and as such, he would be relieved of footing the bill for a big wedding in some fancy reception place.

Maybe all weddings have problems when it comes to deciding who should be on the invitation list. In the case of Gypsy's invitation list, it consisted of her family's side only.

Mr Nixon pointedly asked, 'Why aren't any of his wealthy Western District family invited?'

To which Gypsy said, 'Paddy says they're in the middle of something to do with sheep crutching and all his other family members have gone to England for the Test Series.'

'Likely story, I'd say. Well, what about his friends? He must have some.'

'Yes, he's invited an old friend, Bruce who used to be a monk.'

'A monk. A bloody monk! Please tell me you're joking.'

'Dad, he *used* to be a monk but he left his order.'

'If he's a friend of Paddy's then his order most likely kicked him out.'

To tell you the truth, Mr Nixon was pleased with Paddy having only one guest and no family members on the guest list; it would keep the catering costs down. Not that catering costs would be high because Mrs Nixon and her sister Lizzie would be doing all the food preparation. Of course, Gypsy promised to help but that turned out to be help only by way of her instructing her mother and aunt what should be on the menu. Unfortunately some of Mr Nixon's costs crept up. You see, he had counted on Paddy chipping in for the drinks. Unhappily for Mr Nixon, Paddy countered by arguing that since the only person attending from his side was a teetotalling former Cistercian monk, it would be unfair for him to contribute to the drinks bill.

Gypsy's big day arrived; a brief ceremony at Saint Joan's officiated by Reverend Mount, and a few hours later guests arrived at intervals at the Nixons for the evening's festivities. The guests brought carefully wrapped gifts which Gypsy, now Mrs Patrick O' Sullivan, stacked neatly on the hall table. Gypsy received the gifts, displaying more interest in the gifts than their bearers. Last to arrive was Paddy's friend Bruce, a non-gift bearing ex-Cistercian monk.

Nature has ordained that whether one was an ex-monk or

practising monk there should only be two types – short, round, fat and jolly like friar Tuck or tall, thin, emaciated and mean-looking like Savonarola; Bruce the ex-Cistercian monk was of the latter variety. To be honest, there should be no issue with the fact he was extremely thin and lanky; so many people were in those days. One could say he looked sort of like Fra Bartolomeo's portrait of Savonarola; mainly it was the nose and lips. What was very odd, though, was his outfit.

Mr Nixon puzzled why anyone would turn up at a wedding wearing a long yellow cape and a red beret, a long yellow cape and red beret he wore all night. This ex-monk confirmed Mr Nixon's discomfort about his newly minted son-in-law. What sort of person is Paddy if an obvious nutcase like Bruce is his best friend? Mr Nixon considered himself a free thinker. He'd say he was a live-and-let-live type of person but in the case of Bruce the former Cistercian, he felt compelled to circulate among the guests and whisper in their ears, 'Whatever you do, don't mention the cape or the poncy beret. Just don't mention the cape and beret.' Then, making a circular motion at his temple with his pointing finger said, 'He's a nutcase, you know.'

As far as weddings at home go, this one was going well until Reverend Mount took it upon himself to be the master of ceremonies. He started with, 'Ladies and gentlemen, charge your glasses, be upstanding and let us toast her majesty the queen.'

There followed a general hubbub as glasses were filled or refilled and as those who had been seated stood up. After silence was established and before the good reverend could say another word, the ex-monk shouted, 'Fuck the queen!'

In these circumstances, people respond in different ways. You'd think that the monk, I mean ex-monk, would have been told to be quiet, be respectful or something like that. At rowdier weddings he may have been taken outside and roughed up by some of her majesty's more loyal or more inebriated subjects. At Gypsy's wedding, the surprise value of his outburst was such that everyone fell into an embarrassed silence. The responses ranged from looking at the floor to looking at the glass in hand, to just skolling the glass's contents and then looking at either the floor or ceiling. The best that the queen's more loyal subjects present could muster were hateful stares at Bruce the former monk.

Having recovered from the shock of the outburst, Reverend Mount continued, 'To the queen!' at a volume equal to that of the ex-monk's disloyal outburst. He then gave a rambling speech about Christian values and the benefit of Christian marriage. That last bit enabled him to go on to his current hobby-horse, namely the evils of unsanctioned cohabitation which he felt would eventually bring down civilisation. The ex-monk was not to be silenced by stares and murmurs of disapproval, and at random times he interjected with choice phrases that espoused views always opposite to those held by the reverend.

The worst part of the reverend's speech, as far as Cliffy was concerned, was the comparisons made between him and Gypsy.

'... and Mr and Mrs Nixon's daughter Gypsy – what a credit it is to them for having raised such a delightful and dare I say beautiful girl, I mean, beautiful young woman. She's a fine person indeed. I only hope that Mr and Mrs Nixon's son Clifford can learn from his sister's shining examples of duty to one's parents and see the rewards that come from selflessness ...'

The worst part for Mr Nixon was all the talk about Christian values. He would have preferred it if the speech had not dwelt on religion. He was concerned that though Paddy was a Christian of sorts, it might draw attention to the fact Paddy wasn't of the reverend's sort.

The worst part for Mrs Nixon was that Reverend Mount had filled his face with the food she and her sister had spent days preparing yet he hadn't uttered a word of thanks.

For Paddy there was no worst part as he had left the room to go to the toilet before the proposal of the loyal toast and returned after the reverend had finished his speech.

Meanwhile Reverend Mount, believing he was a bit of a psychologist and a skilled counsellor, and most of all certain in his

Christianity, turned his very Christian other cheek and said to Bruce the ex-monk in the gentlest but insincere voice, 'My son, I see you're greatly troubled, but tell me why do you hate yourself?'

To which the ex-monk replied, 'Not your son, don't hate myself and so go fuck yourself.'

After that and the debacle of the loyal toast, Reverend Mount sought solace in the free grog. The drunker he became, the more annoyed, vocal and louder he became. As far as his shouting, well, to some extent you couldn't blame him, because by this time the room had become very noisy and you had to shout to be heard. Despite the noise, not many would have missed him saying, 'What a travesty. What a travesty indeed!' and 'This is the worst wedding I've ever had the misfortune to attend, let alone officiate,' and 'Mind you, I would never have let a daughter of mine marry out,' and 'Who invited that rabid foul-mouthed disloyal Rome-loving monk?' and 'You'd think he was from the IRA judging from his behaviour during the loyal toast.'

Just in case one corner of the room had missed what the reverend had said, he said almost exactly the same in the other three corners of the room. After this he went to the ladies in the kitchen who were making tea and coffee with his message.

Although now well and truly peeved off, it didn't stop the good reverend from handing Paddy the bill for his services. 'Make sure you don't dilly-dally paying.' With that done, Reverend Mount put another party pie into his mouth, stuffed a handful of them into his pocket for later and left. Not content leaving the bill, he also left a knocked down a gatepost. You see, on the way out of the driveway and somewhat worse for drink, he had backed his car into the gatepost and sent it flying into Mr Nixon's prized rose bush.

Paddy was undeterred by what was an obvious overcharging for the reverend's services; undeterred because he wouldn't have to pay. He handed the folded over bill to Mr Nixon, saying with a wink, 'Here, Clarrie, I think you can deal with this.' Sure, the bill annoyed

Mr Nixon but what annoyed him even more was that Paddy had winked at him.

With the gatepost down on the ground and Reverend Mount on his way home, the time had now come for Mr Nixon, as father of the bride, to give his speech. This was the moment he had fretted over in the week leading up to the wedding. He had fretted so much so that he knew he could never give the speech without crib notes – just to make it look off the cuff. As a consequence he hadn't bothered to memorise the speech because he would have those notes.

He had prepared a speech complete with dot points and committed it to paper. Safely tucked away in his back pocket, he'd placed the neatly folded sheet of foolscap before any guests had arrived. He now reached into the back pocket where his notes should have been. Empty. Nothing there. He must have put it in one of the other pockets. He tried another pocket but it only contained a used and very grubby handkerchief. Another pocket yielded the reverend's exorbitant bill. Rummaging through all his other pockets, he found a folded sheet of paper deep in the last pocket he checked. He could see the dots of the dot points through the paper. Saved! Saved be buggered, as it was the *To Do* list of things he had never gotten around to doing and what's more, it had been written around the time he last wore the trousers – at least a year ago. So he would have to ad lib.

The best he could manage was, 'Bride looks lovely … yes, the bride looks lovely … Uhhmmm the bride looks lovely …'

Before he could say the next of his foggily remembered dot points, the former Cistercian interjected, 'Certainly didn't get her looks from you. Let's hope she didn't get her brains from you either.'

Though his brow now had beads of sweat, he remembered one of his missing dot points: 'I'm not losing a daughter, I'm gaining a son.'

The ex-Cistercian came back with, 'Cliché! Cliché! Cliché! We've all heard that one before.' With his armpits now damp Mr Nixon continued, 'Yes, Paddy has been like a son to me.' No interjection from the former Cistercian this time. On the other hand, Cliffy was livid; *If a shit like Paddy can be considered like a son then what does that say about me his real son?*

On a roll now, Mr Nixon continued: '... and the food. Ah yes, the food. Mustn't forget the food. Wasn't it all just so fantastic? Thanks for the delicious food. Credit and thanks must go to my lovely wife Joyce and her beautiful sister, my sister-in-law, Lizzie. Thanks for that. Take a bow, girls.'

Now the former Cistercian came out with, 'Food? What food? I didn't see much of it. Bring out the cake for Christ's sake before we all starve to death!'

Mr Nixon couldn't remember any more of what else he had written that he was supposed to say so he finished with, 'I'm sure my new son Paddy would like to say a few words.'

Paddy stood up and made a deep theatrical bow to those standing around. He started with, 'Thank you, Clarrie, I mean Dad. Dad? Come to think of it, I am gaining a father.'

At this the ex-monk yelled out, 'Hey, Paddy, you might as well call him your dad because no one else has so far owned up to being your father.'

Paddy laughed and continued, 'I've been asked by Clarrie my new da to say a few words. Well, here are a few words – thanks everyone for coming.' Then in a lewd way he added, 'By the way, if you want me to tell you what married life is like then ask me tomorrow morning.' Having said those few words, Paddy sat down.

Not to be silenced, the Cistercian retorted, 'Bloody hell! I hope you put in a longer performance in bed with Gypsy after we're all gone home. Otherwise you can send her my way.'

Mr Nixon couldn't stand it any longer and demanded the ex-monk to shut up once and for all. For the first time in the night, Paddy lost it and, jumping up from where he had just sat down, said, 'Shame on you, Clarrie. Bloody shame. Brucie's an old mate of mine. We've known each other since Christ played fullback for Jerusalem. Come to think of it, earlier than that. He's our guest. He's *my* guest.

Don't you realise the poor sod's dying? He's got a terminal illness. No one knows how long he's got. He's been a Cistercian monk. Don't you know anything about them? Because if you don't, let me tell you. They're sworn to silence! Before tonight he hadn't spoken a single word for a long time. Only God knows for how many years. It must be at least ten. Got it, Daddy?' Then in a faux pidgin English Paddy said, 'Brucie he no talkie talkies for big longum time gone. After all those years he's just venting now. For goodness sake, show him some Christian charity, just cut him some slack would you? Just cut him some slack, Daddyoh!'

As the party was thinning out, somebody asked where the bride and groom were going to for their honeymoon. At this point, Paddy clinked on a glass with a teaspoon to get everyone's attention. 'Ladies and gents, girls and boys. And all other creatures.'

The mention of all other creatures brought a quiet chuckle from the remaining guests and from the dying ex-Cistercian monk. 'All other creatures?' Then glaring at Mr Nixon he added, 'You wouldn't be wrong there, Paddy!'

Paddy continued: 'I've just been asked where my lovely bride and I will be going for our honeymoon. Well, I've got a small confession to make. Just a teensy weensy one.' To emphasise this point he made a gesture of a small gap by placing his thumb and pointer finger close together. 'We're not going anywhere.'

From Gypsy, 'What! But you promised me we'd be going for a week to Mt Buffalo. To the Chalet. I've told everyone.'

'No, my dearest cupcake. The love of my life. My sweet darling. No Mt Buffalo. No Chalet.'

'Not Mt Buffalo and the Chalet? Then it's a surprise. A surprise destination, isn't it? A surprise for me. Where are we really going? Please tell me.'

'We're not going anywhere.'

'Why?'

'Lots of reasons.'

At this point the newlyweds, as newlyweds do, had become

oblivious to the fact that there were other people in the room.

Gypsy demanded, 'Reasons? Like what?'

'For starters, it's winter and the place is full of honeymooners and piles of snow. Just honeymooners and snowy ski runs and that's it. You'd hate it up there, my little beach-loving baby. Besides, if one can't ski, which neither of us can, then what's the point? We'd end up spending time in our room together.'

'So what's wrong with that? It's meant to be a honeymoon. Our honeymoon. My honeymoon. So where are we going? Up North? You're just teasing me, aren't you?'

'No, not teasing. Just no honeymoon. In my opinion it's an unnecessary expense. In my opinion it's a waste of time. In my opinion it's a very outdated tradition.'

'I don't give a rat's arse about your opinions!'

Having screamed that last bit out, Gypsy grabbed the nearest plate, which happened to be someone's half-eaten serve of pavlova, and threw it at Paddy. It missed him and hit Mr Nixon in the chest.

Gypsy wailed at Paddy, 'You're a cunt!'

From the laughing monk came the shout, 'Hey, Paddy, you're well and truly getting fucked over now. Probably the only bit of hot action you'll be getting tonight.'

Slamming the door, Gypsy rushed to her bedroom where, locked in, she spent her wedding night fuming and planning her revenge. Finally Paddy was no longer knowledgeable, clever, a genius, the one and only for her. He'd become just another disappointment.

Paddy's' confession, Gypsy's outburst and a laughing, not long for this world, former Cistercian heralded the end of the wedding festivities. Guests politely left, but not before Cliffy overheard a guest say to another, 'Bloody best wedding ever but I'm sure they won't last – you can't mix Proddie and Mick.' To which the other replied, 'Yeah, I know. It's like oil and water.'

Cliffy had had enough of Gypsy's wedding and all that had happened. Luckily for him, on the sideboard he found an unopened bottle of sweet sherry and an almost full packet of Marlboros complete with matches. It was time to leave the shambles for the peace of the backyard. Armed with the pilfered bottle and cigarettes, and despite it being winter, Cliffy made himself comfortable on the patch of grass near the lemon tree. After his first swig from the bottle, he shouted to his friend the lemon tree and to any space aliens who might have been around, 'Bloody stupid arseholes! Arseholes the lot of them, Paddy O'Sullivan, and Gypsy, and Reverend Mount and Dad and that shit-streak monk and everyone else! Paddy O'Sullivan mainly but maybe not Mum, definitely not Mum.'

With more swigs and puffs came a bonding with the lemon tree and further cursing. So, emboldened by the alcohol and cigarettes, Cliffy got himself well and truly drunk under the stars and the lemon tree.

He had finished about two thirds of the bottle and was on to his eleventh consecutive cigarette when he became aware that the stolen sickly sweet sherry and Marlboros had worked their magic to give him a magnificent erection: a whopper. Unfortunately for him, before he could act on it he had his first vomit of the night.

Later as he lay on the grass to collect his thoughts, the flat world tilted until it was at an unpleasantly steep angle. The rest of the night, or what he can remember of it, he spent clinging to the long blades of grass in an effort to stop himself sliding off the surface of the tilted flat plate earth. To do otherwise he would surely slide into the open mouth of a giant space alien holding the tilted saucer-like earth to its foul-breathed mouth.

The chirping of dawn birds brought him back to the vomited remnants of party pies, saveloys, Pavlova and the mystery of the dried-out crusty blood caking his mouth and nostrils. Try as he might, he couldn't figure out the origin of the dried blood. He stopped worrying about it when he started vomiting again. This time it was dry retching as he had already eliminated all the festive food from his stomach. It has to be said that most disturbing to him was the discovery that his marvellous erection of the night had gone. Vanished just like that, not to return for another four days, and when it did it was just a poor imitation of what he remembered.

Later that morning, Cliffy snuck back into the house to head to the bathroom only to find, amid the devastation of the lounge room, Paddy snoring on the couch and the dying ex-Cistercian on the floor twitching in his sleep.

At this point it should be mentioned that twenty years after Gypsy's first wedding, Bruce, the supposedly terminally ill ex-Cistercian, was still around, however by then he was married, had numerous children and hosted a talk-back program on community radio.

A story told to Paddy by Bruce the ex-Cistercian monk after Paddy was refused entry to the matrimonial bed on his wedding night

AFTER THE LAST OF the wedding guests had left and Paddy was locked out of Gypsy's room, and consequently denied access to what would have been the matrimonial bed, he was relegated to the couch in the devastated lounge room. Paddy figured that if he couldn't spend his wedding night with his bride, then it was fitting that he should spend it with his old mate Bruce. In the spirit of mateship, he had insisted Brucie stay over. That's the Australian way with mates, isn't it? But because he was the groom, it was right that he should have the more comfortable of the sleeping arrangements, so Paddy got the couch and Bruce got the floor.

'The floor? That's okay with me. I'm used to it. In fact, it's probably more comfortable than what I had at the monastery. You've got enough to contend with, Paddy. But I'd have to say it was a bad move on your part about the honeymoon. Though to be sure, Gypsy flew off the handle a bit. For your sake, I hope it's not a promise of things to come. But then, I've always found the female of our species hard to fathom. Anyway, don't feel bad about it. It'll work out okay. By tomorrow evening, if not before, you'll be in bed with Gypsy. You're much better off than a headmaster I once knew. I'll tell you about it and you can consider it a bedtime story if you will.

'In an earlier life I taught for a while at a high school in Buckland.

Country town. Bloody small place really – the sort of place where everybody knew each other's business. Awkward. Well, the school had a headmaster. Joey Crandon was his name. Before he rose to the lofty position of headmaster, he had been a teacher of Geography and English. Can't tell you whether he was a good teacher or not because by the time I arrived at the school, he was already the school's headmaster. Believe it or not, the school ran well but not because of timid Joey Crandon but because it had a competent deputy headmaster.

'You see, Joey had a problem – he was an overly timid individual. He wouldn't … no, he couldn't look you straight in the eye. Shit no. When he addressed the school at assembly, it was with a quaking, nervous voice. When he held notes to deliver a speech, the paper would quiver in his shaking hands. The poor bastard just couldn't pull off sounding headmasterly. I suppose not everyone has to be an impressive public speaker. By the way, your father-in-law's speech was pure crap. But back to Joey Crandon. Let's just say public speaking was just not in his nature.

'I felt sorry for him so one Friday after school I decided to take him to Turners Commercial for a few drinks. I thought it would be a pleasant man-to-man thing. After I'd got a few beers into him, he opened up and do you know what he told me? As he put it: *I've never had relations with a woman.* Could you bloody well believe it? He'd never been with a woman. At that time he was well into his fifties, whereas I was in my twenties. To be honest with you, I found it somewhat flattering that this mature man was talking to me about such personal stuff. But being in my twenties and speaking to my boss, I was ill-prepared with what to say next. The best I could manage was something useless like: *Strewth, that's hard to believe. Have another beer.* He must have been embarrassed by his confession and declined another drink, got up and left, saying he had something important to finish off for school.

'The next term a new teacher came to the school and into his world, Miss Lynne Driscoll and she taught Australian History. As far as I was concerned, she was the plainest looking individual I'd ever seen. To be honest, I've never been attracted to women with prominent foreheads – as far as I'm concerned the forehead on a woman is where plainness has the chance to meet up with ugliness. In her case it did, and let me tell you it was unappealing. Little squinty eyes and no eyebrows. Wispy non-descript-coloured hair. She was not attractive at all. Not like your Gypsy. But irrespective of her lack of beauty, Joey Crandon fell for her in a big way.

'He was like a besotted teenager around her. He was like a bounding Labrador pup. It got to being uncomfortable to see him hovering about her in the staff room at morning tea. I'll tell you that while everyone got their own drinks and biscuits, he'd get hers. Can you believe it – here was the headmaster of the school being a servant to the most junior of the teaching staff. Bloody incredible! Talk about being smitten, he was smitten alright. He'd hang onto every word she said like they were pearls from the Almighty: *Oh, how marvellous, Miss Driscoll. How clever of you, Miss Driscoll. I wish I'd thought of that, Miss Driscoll.* Things like that. It was so embarrassing. His lack of dignity made us all feel uncomfortable. There was no task that he didn't offer to help her out on – lesson preparation, doing her stints of after-school detentions and even taking over her turns at yard duty. If a headmaster doing yard duty for you, collecting the filthy crap kids had dropped isn't a sign of love, then what is? There wasn't anything he wouldn't do for her. And that's only what we saw at school.

'Apparently outside school he did his share of wooing. He tried all the conventional, old-fashioned things. You know, things like the pictures on Saturday nights in Wangaratta, flowers and chocolates. Someone said he'd written letters and poems declaring his love for her.

'I suppose I shouldn't mention the Mt Buffalo Chalet in view of your non-realised honeymoon plans, but he took her away to the

Chalet for a long weekend. Mind you, not a dirty weekend. No, it was all above board. Separate rooms – after all he was very proper and decent.

'Can you imagine the courage it must have taken a timid man like him to do all this? In the end he must have drummed up enough courage to propose marriage because they married at the end of third term. All the school – staff and pupils – turned up to the ceremony in Wangaratta. Then they had a function at a vineyard in Milawa. Sorry to add insult to injury, mate, and mention the word honeymoon, but they managed to have a honeymoon; they spent a week in Melbourne.

'You'd think after they married he would have had a normal sex life, but no. Their marriage was never consummated. He told me that although he tried, she just wouldn't have a bar of it. Look, he must have trusted me because he told me all this. You see, after he opened up to me that first time in Turners I must have been the only person he felt comfortable telling about such a personal thing. Mind you, once again, this happened after a few beers; well, actually after more than a few beers.

'Now here comes the oddest part of it all. Once she'd married him she was on, sexually speaking, with almost every man in town other than Joey Crandon. It was as if getting married had given her the licence to be promiscuous. It was claimed she was having it off with the cricket team, the football team – though to be fair, there must have been some overlap as some men were in both the football team and cricket team. They also said she was giving it up to the entire drinking school at Turners and even did the publican with the gammy leg. Well, I lie, I'm not sure about the publican. Maybe she even had it with men who passed through the town. Who knows, she might have been a virgin up to the time she married but after she married, she'd more than reversed that status.

'It was said her needs were insatiable, but the truth of the matter was that for some weird reason her needs didn't include her husband. Apparently she didn't include him no matter how nice or kind or understanding he was. He was invisible as far as being one of the many sexual bodies that orbited around her, trapped by her sexual gravitational pull. It's weird because I don't know what the attraction was. It beats me because as I said, she wasn't much to look at.'

'So what eventually happened?' Paddy asked.

'In the end it was said she'd left him for an entire basketball team from Melbourne that was visiting to play a team at the prison in Buckland. Well, that's what everyone thought. Now here's the strange part to the story. Years later, long after I'd left the school, I read Joey Crandon had been arrested for her murder. Apparently he had not been too timid to kill her. You see, during one of the dry spells they get up that way, it was so dry that the water levels in the farm dams dropped a lot. It was then that her body, or what was left of it, was found in a dam on a farm near Milawa. Strange, because Milawa is where they'd had their wedding reception.

'She'd been weighed down with gym equipment from the school. At about the time she supposedly had run away with the basketball team, gym equipment had gone missing from the school. Suspicion for the disappearance of the gym equipment fell on the school's caretaker who, despite pleading his innocence, was fired over allegations he had stolen the equipment.

'As for her running away with the basketball team? Well, that had been accepted as a fact by everyone until her body turned up. And why shouldn't it have been? We all knew she had form. When we thought she had run away, everyone felt sorry for the headmaster. As I recall, he had some sort of breakdown and went on a substantial amount of sick leave followed by long-service leave. In the time he was on leave he travelled overseas a lot, mainly to America. You know the deal – Disneyland, the Grand Canyon and New Orleans.

'When he returned to the school, we all said he seemed a changed man. He could look you in the eye, his voice had become stronger and he started to do things like having parties at his place. He seemed happier, sort of lighter. Then the sly bugger started keeping the company of a very pretty widow in town with whom he spent frequent weekends in Melbourne. Once after one of his weekends away with the widow he said to me, proudly and with a conspiratorial wink: *No separate rooms now, Brucie my boy*. I'd have to admit that by the time I left the school, his timidity had completely disappeared.

'After discovery of the late Mrs Crandon's body, police were able to locate every member of the basketball team that had visited Buckland to play the prisoners. Follow-up interviews with players of the basketball team, and I may add its support staff as well, established that though they had, to a man, enjoyed her charms, she had definitely not left with them. And of course how could she, as her body had lain at the bottom of a dam on a Milawa farm.

'Eventually, of course, after I'd parted company with the school, suspicion fell on the headmaster. When confronted with the facts, things like motive and means, he confessed to murdering his wife. Buckland is not a big place so it must have been quite a day in town when the police came up from Melbourne to take him.

'So don't worry, Paddy, you'll be better off in your marriage than Joey Crandon was in his. You'll be right with Gypsy. By tomorrow night if not before, you'll find that the two of you are in bed going hammer and tongs. I guarantee it.

'By the way – bloody nice wedding you threw tonight, mate. Must have cost you a packet. Oh, and another thing. Thank you for getting that stupid get-up for me to wear tonight. I reckon it caused quite a buzz. That was a good idea of yours. It certainly pissed that prick father-in-law of yours. And that bit about me having a terminal disease – that was pure Paddy O'Sullivan genius. So truly thanks for inviting me. I enjoyed myself but I can't say I liked your in-laws. Creepy lot, especially that Clarrie. Now, no more rabbiting on from me I've got to get my beauty rest.'

When Elvis was king

LIFE WAS NOT ALL about Mr and Mrs Nixon, Gypsy or even Paddy O'Sullivan, but also for a short but impressionable time for Cliffy and me there was Melvin Marx. Melvin Marx came into our lives around the time Cliffy's dad gave up bonsais for photography and Cliffy and I were fourteen. Maybe it was a question of geography and Melvin had always lived nearby, just another neighbourhood kid who for no obvious reason we'd never met before. He wasn't at Cliffy's school and he wasn't at mine. At seventeen he didn't have to be at any school. Maybe the rumour about him was true. It was said he had been expelled from a number of schools, with the reason leading to his last expulsion from school being the most dramatic. Rumour had it he had tied a kitten to a tree and used it as target practice with an air rifle. If that wasn't bad enough, he had finished off the poor animal by pouring kerosene on it and setting it on fire. But like I said, it was only a rumour.

Perhaps at the time it was an advantage to look like Elvis and if so, then Melvin Marx had that advantage. Melvin Marx was the Elvis Presley clone of our neighbourhood. He was our Elvis. Some unknown quirk of genetics and the gods had enabled him to channel Elvis to a tee. Melvin had mastered the skill of curling one side of his top lip in an easy smile which could also pass as a sneer. Nature had given him the blackest hair which he wore Presley-style – slicked until it shone, brushed back at the sides and finished with a quiff like a veranda above his forehead. He wore tight stove-pipe black denims when, at the time, all of us wore standard loose indigo Levis.

His tight jeans gave him a bulge in the pubic zone; apparently he thought it was a much desired bulge. He wore fluorescent-coloured socks while most of the time we wore boring grey school socks. Then there was his three-quarter-length black coat, a dapper coat he always wore with its collar turned up. Yes, he was our Elvis.

He was our Elvis with perhaps one physical flaw. Somehow he had lost his two top front teeth and wore two false replacement teeth on a plate. How he had lost those teeth added a touch of mystery about him. We were told various stories – his father had knocked them out in a fight; he had fallen off a motorcycle he had stolen; he had tripped in the gutter while drunk. So take your pick – victim of family violence or motorcycle thief or drunkard – by any account, a colourful Elvis. You'd think two front teeth on a plate would be a disadvantage. Not for Melvin Marx. Melvin turned those false teeth into an entertainment device. He had perfected the technique of loosening the plate and somehow rattling it in his mouth against his natural teeth until it sounded just like ice cubes clinking in a glass. Then with the clinking, he could rattle out a good rendition of 'You ain't nothing but a hound dog' and 'Jailhouse Rock'. His rendition of 'Love me Tender', on the other hand was barely passable. Like I said, he was Elvis and if not a musical genius then something of a musical oddity.

Then there were his other skills, not the least of which was spitting. No one could spit like Melvin. No one could produce such volume or the consistency. No one could match him for distance or accuracy. Like a true artist or athlete, he needed special preparation to generate his masterpieces. Apparently, so he claimed, for the best results he had to drink at least half a pint of milk; the more milk he drank, the better the result would be, however this required the delicate estimation of his bladder's capacity. Suitably tanked up on milk, he would wander down the shopping strip where, after some snorting from the back reaches of his nasal cavities, he spat globs on shop windows. Gelatinous heavy blobs that would eventually slide down the window leaving milky bird-shit-like streaks. I couldn't spit to save my life. If I could, I wouldn't have dreamed of spitting on shop windows, and if I had then I would have been caught doing it and without a doubt I would have been dragged off to be punished. Melvin could spit beauties; Melvin spat on shop windows and without exception, Melvin got away with it. He was after all Elvis – the king.

Then there was Melvin's scientific side. To be more accurate, I should say there was his proof of something by way of a demonstration. If he stated something we didn't believe then there would follow a demonstration. He would say something like, 'With the following demonstration I will demonstrate my proof of concept.'

Cats always land feet first.

Apparatus – a stray cat, a convenient roof.

Method – (1) hold stray cat away from body so as to not get scratched and (2) throw said cat onto a convenient roof.

Conclusion – cats (well at least that cat did) land feet first.

The 'cats landing on their feet demonstration' proof of concept is one I still feel ashamed to have witnessed. I now know, however, that only given certain conditions will cats land feet first.

There were other proofs of concept such as:

- With a suitable (shop-stolen of course) firecracker it is possible to blow up a domestic letterbox. Observe as proof the box at 17 Carlingford Street, the box at 212 Glenhuntly Road and the box at the corner of Shoobra Road and Rowan Street. The same is not true of public mailboxes – the most that can possibly happen in that situation is some smouldering of the letters within.

- On a sunny day using only a magnifying glass you can torment and eventually ignite a spider.

- You can render someone unconscious by judicious pressing of the thumbs on that someone's temples.

For demonstration of proof of concept of that last one, I was the someone on whom it was demonstrated, and though it was painful, I can tell you Melvin's proof of concept was faulty because in the interest of curtailing my pain, degradation and above all to please

Melvin, I slumped to the ground and feigned unconsciousness.

When it came to phrases, Melvin had a way of delightfully twisting them. Melvin could turn a phrase on its head so that it turned your head. He had phrases like: *Let sleeping dogs lie – all other dogs must tell the truth* and *That prick is such a cunt* and *It gives me the shits so much so that it pisses me off.* Talking of piss, Melvin used say a good piss was the equal of half a fuck. In our virginal days and in respect to our virginal curiosity, that was a cool thing to know. What struck me about it was if it was true, then a fuck must be equal to double a good piss. If that was so, then, though we might have been busting for one, a fuck wasn't much to look forward to.

On the other hand, there was a mysterious but sexual thing he referred to as tunalingus. I now know what he meant but at the time all he would say was it was the measure of a true man as it would drive the girls wild. Melvin knew those sort of things as he was our expert in such matters.

Melvin Marx was also the ultimate swearmeister. Cliffy and I sometimes talked dirty, but only to each other and then only with sniggered whispers. Melvin, however, bellowed sex talk all the time. Not only sex talk but also swearing. Cliffy's dad, Mr Nixon, occasionally swore in semi-polite English: *Bloody hell* and *Oh es-aitch-eye-tee.* More often he blasphemed in Standard English: *Jesus wept* and *For Christ's sake.* Melvin, on the other hand, swore real swearing: *Fucken cunt!* and *Fucken cunt face!* and *Go fuck yourself you fucken cunt faced arsehole!* Because of Melvin, it wasn't until adulthood that I learnt the word was *fucking* and not *fucken.*

Not only could he swear in English; he claimed he could swear in Dutch and Chinese. How exotic was our multilingual Elvis. There was: *Poot ein orz preeck in yew rasre!!!* delivered in a heavy faux-eastern European accent. He gave rise to outbursts, according to him to be Dutch: *Mah seepa arhl!* and *Donah radah mooscow!!* and *Sidaway a potzah nookah!!!* – or supposedly Chinese: *Chow chow chipaye!!!!* Melvin did a lot of bellowing and so these phrases were delivered at full volume. Whatever they meant, if they ever meant anything, according to him they dealt with fucking and being fucked by someone or something with some body part or device in some orifice or other.

To date I have not been able to find any remote connection between these phrases and Dutch or Chinese. More to the point regarding fucking, Melvin Marx was the sex machine. At the time he was the only one of us who had had sexual contact with another living thing other than oneself. Melvin fucked and he let everyone know about it. Melvin was *the* SEX MACHINE and as such, for the time he was around us, he was the alpha male. Being the alpha male allowed him many privileges.

Those privileges included having Cliffy and me putting up with his bad behaviour anywhere and anytime. If you believe the rumour about his last expulsion from school, then you can take it from me that not everything about him was nice, not very nice at all. Sitting alongside him in the movies, which at the time we called the flicks, could be an ordeal. His thing was audience participation. A romantic scene which, by the way, Cliffy and I usually found boring, would often result in Melville yelling out at the female character: *Watch out, girlie. We know what the dirty bugger's after!* For quiet suspenseful scenes he could muster up massive burps or farts and loudly declare to the entire theatre: *Pardonez moi! I shouldn't have had those baked beans.*

Once with a current girlfriend on his left and me on his right, it was in the movies I learnt the meaning of humiliation. I suppose Melvin must have thought fingering his girlfriend at the movies was cool. Definitely not cool was him then running his wet finger under my nose and yelling with increasing volume *Stink finger! Stink finger! Mah seepa arhl!!!* Ours was a nasty Elvis who meted out humiliation all round – to his girlfriends and to us, his disciples.

Despite Melvin's burping, farting and bad behaviour, apparently few females could resist his other charms. Maybe the girls were attracted to the wild bad boy and if not to that, then perhaps it was his Elvis-like good looks. Our faux Elvis seemed to have the same pulling power as the real Elvis when it came to girls, and Cliffy's cousin Meg was no exception. She fell for his questionable charms. She succumbed and for a while she was Melvin's girlfriend. One day in the middle of school holidays, Melvin, Meg and I were sitting at Cliffy's in the TV room watching afternoon TV. Without warning Melvin lifted Meg off the couch and placed her on the floor between me and the TV. The best way to describe what happened next is to say that he started to dry hump her in front of me. I'm not sure who he was trying to embarrass, me or Meg. Whatever. But as I've already said, ours was a nasty Elvis.

So as to not embarrass Meg further, I got up and went to join Cliffy who was sawing wood in Mr Nixon's workshop. Sometime later, an exuberant Melvin, adjusting his crotch, probably to impress us, and a sheepish Meg joined us in the workshop. From Melvin: *Shit, that was good. Fucken good. Donah Radah Mooscow fucken good. Sidaway a potzah nookah!!!*

While Meg was Melvin's girlfriend, Cliffy grew closer to Melvin and I was slowly edged out of the way. Cliffy and Melvin shared jokes at my expense and started to exclude me from their activities. Secret activities. The message that I was the third wheel on a two-wheel bike was made clear when I was walking behind the two, perhaps tagging along when not wanted, when Melvin picked up a loose gutter stone and hurled it at me. *Piss off you little fat kike!* True, at the time I was a touch podgy but a kike? I didn't know what a kike was so maybe I was or maybe I wasn't. The hardest part of it was Cliffy thinking this was hilarious. I got the message.

Their secret activities? I'm glad they excluded me from their secret activities because the upshot of the secret activities was that Cliffy and Melvin each scored a Children's Court-ordered good behaviour bond. For a time after his court appearance, Cliffy was forbidden to hang out with Melvin which was good for me. For the time being, Cliffy had satiated his need to live on the wild side. At the time no one told me what they had done and though we were close, unless Cliffy told me I wasn't going to ask. It was only sometime later Cliffy told me about it – for over a month he and Melvin would sneak out of their houses in the early morning and armed with Melvin's air rifle, they roamed the neighbourhood blasting out car windshields.

Sometime between sixteen and seventeen, around the time Cliffy's dad gave up raising canaries and took to painting insipid water colour scenes, we outgrew Melvin Marx. Melvin was still the same Melvin but we had changed. He no longer impressed us with his burping, farting, spitting and talk of chow chow chipaying this girl and tunalingus with that girl. We were over it. We had discovered girls and were into some chow chow chipaying of our own – well, at least Cliffy was. The days of Elvis being the king were over and our days pretending to like the real Elvis's music had passed, and what's more, the Beatles were coming with a whole different look and sound.

Gypsy's apparently immaculate conception

SCENE 1: STAGE STETTING has the bare minimum. At centre stage there are two women, one in her forties and the other in her twenties. The older woman is Mrs Nixon. She is seated at her sewing machine unpicking a hem. While she works at the unpicking, a conversation is taking place between her and the younger woman, her daughter Gypsy.

At stage left and unbeknown to Mrs Nixon and Gypsy, Cliffy (Mrs Nixon's son and Gypsy's brother) is eavesdropping behind a door that has been left ajar.

The time is a Saturday afternoon about four months after Gypsy married Paddy O'Sullivan.

Gypsy: Mum, I'm pregnant.

Mrs Nixon: Are you sure?

Gypsy: Of course I am.

Mrs Nixon (looking over the top of her glasses): But you're taking precautions, aren't you?

Gypsy (shouting): Yes, of course, but nevertheless I'm pregnant!

Mrs Nixon (takes off her glasses and puts down her unpicking): The pill? You're on the pill, aren't you?

Gypsy: No, I'm allergic to something in it so I couldn't take it.

Mrs Nixon: Then are you taking other precautions?

Gypsy: Of course! Mum, it's not as if we didn't take any precautions. Paddy uses frangers.

Mrs Nixon: You mean condoms.

Gypsy (angrily): Condoms! Frangers! Dingers! Frenchies! Johnnies! It's all the same, Mum. Whatever you want to call them, I'm pregnant!

Mrs Nixon: All right, all right, don't bite my head off.

Gypsy: Anyhow, Paddy is a bit iffy about them. He says that the Pope wouldn't approve. I don't care about the Pope. Sometimes I even make Paddy put two on, just in case. He doesn't like that. Says they take the edge off it all. But we always use them and Paddy is always careful.

Mrs Nixon: Well, what can I say other than maybe he should have put on three. I can't explain it.

Gypsy: Well neither can I.

Mrs Nixon: How far are you gone?

Gypsy: About two months.

Mrs Nixon: Have you told Paddy about it?

Gypsy: Not yet. It's still early days.

Mrs Nixon (thinking out loud): Maybe it's a sort of Immaculate Conception. Do you think Paddy would like that idea?

Gypsy: Oh, Mum, get real!

(Cliffy sneaks away from behind the door unnoticed by the women.)

Cliffy was great at overhearing things. He'd hide behind doors listening or put a glass to a wall to hear through it. When he was older and we went to cafes, he could listen to conversations going on at three or more tables simultaneously and later tell me about it.

He was good at things like that; he'd have made a great spy. Anyhow, more to the point, he had overheard that conversation.

The next conversation was between Cliffy and me.

Scene 2: Later that day Cliffy, after overhearing the conversation between his mother and sister, talks to his friend, the Narrator. The conversation takes place in Mr Nixon's workshop where Cliffy is aimlessly sanding a piece of wood.

Cliffy: You know that Gypsy's up the duff?

Narrator: You're joking.

Cliffy (sands more vigorously and then holds the piece of wood to the light and feels for bumps): No, I'm not. I heard Mum and Gypsy talking about it. What's more, it was me who did it.

Narrator: What! With your sister?

Cliffy (he stops sanding): No, not in the way you're thinking, but it's still me who did it. I'll tell you about it if you want to know.

To put you in the picture, I should tell you that until Gypsy married Paddy O'Sullivan, Cliffy lived in the large detached asbestos bungalow the Nixons had at the back of the yard. Everyone called it the sleep-out. It was fully equipped with a shower stall and toilet. It also had a kitchenette that Cliffy understandably never used. Today you'd call it a granny flat. Cliffy called it his sanctuary. Well, when Gypsy married Paddy, Cliffy was evicted from his sanctuary. He was back inside the house and if that wasn't bad enough, he was given Gypsy's old bedroom with its wallpaper of little red hearts and cutesy winged pink cupids with bows and arrows. Mr Nixon made a half-hearted attempt at consoling Cliffy: 'Yeah, son, I know it's not that good but I'll strip the paper and repaint the room. I reckon a nice manly blue will do the trick.' Mr Nixon never got around to doing that, and right up to the time Paddy O'Sullivan disappeared

(I'll tell you more about that later), Cliffy slept in a room with girly wallpaper.

I'd better get back to Cliffy's eviction from the bungalow after Gypsy married. To say that Cliffy was unhappy at having to give up his sanctuary for his sister and her husband would be an understatement. Every night, the hearts and cupids reminded him of what he had lost. Every time the newly wedded O'Sullivans said goodnight and retired to the bungalow to enjoy their privacy or whatever else newlyweds enjoyed, he bristled with anger. As the weeks went by, the grudge he held against Paddy O'Sullivan increased. He considered Paddy the reason for his eviction: *If Paddy wasn't so mean you'd think he would have moved with Gypsy to a place of their own by now.*

The anger at his eviction grew in proportion to the time he spent thinking about it; and he thought about it a lot: *what right have they got to the bungalow? It's been mine for yonks and then that shit Paddy comes on the scene and I'm chucked out.*

Cliffy just had to get his own back against the injustice that had been dealt him. His focus became exacting retribution.

Scene 2 (Continued):

> *Cliffy*: D'you know how we used to go to the Lucky Dragon
> for dinner each Friday night? We went as a family. That's
> the four of us: Mum, Dad, Gypsy and me. We did that
> for years and years. It was a family tradition. Then that
> shithead Paddy O'Sullivan comes on the scene. It's still a
> table for four, but now not the same four. It's them and
> Paddy O'Sullivan but not me. Not me! Dad reckons it's
> because there's limited car space to take an extra passenger.
> I reckon that's bullshit as it's a big car. I reckon it's because
> Dad's a tight-arse. He's budgeted for four and that doesn't
> include me. Mind you, if Gypsy sat on Paddy's knees there'd
> be plenty of room for me. And if Paddy at least paid for

himself, Dad's budget would be okay. Come to think of it, if Paddy paid for Gypsy as well, she's his wife after all, then Dad's budget would be looking even better than it used to.

Every single Friday night I'm left at home to fend for myself. I'm lucky if they bring me back some leftovers. I tell you, I'm treated like a dog. It's just not fair the way it's gone since that bastard hitched up with Gypsy.

Well, about three months ago when they went out to the Lucky Dragon, I snuck into the bungalow – let's face it, *my* bungalow. Snuck in just to have a quick squiz.

They'd changed things around. There's a double bed in there now and a dressing table in the corner where I had my HMV and weights. As no one was around I thought I'd have a look in the drawers of the bedside tables; you know, just to amuse myself. They've got one on each side of the bed. A sort of his'n' hers setup. One side is his and the other hers. The first one I checked out must have been Gypsy's as it had feminine stuff – stockings, make-up – that sort of stuff. The other side was obviously Paddy's. Do you know what I found? I'll tell you. Packs and packs of dingers! No kidding, there were enough to issue to an entire sex-starved army battalion and still have plenty left over. They must have cost him a fortune. Goes to show the bastard is willing to spend money to satisfy his horny self.

Well, I got my own back on the bastard. I got a pin from the dressing table and put small pricks through random packets. I must have hit the sweet spot on some of them and hey presto, as they say, the rest is history. I suppose I didn't really think it through. I wasn't thinking of the consequences. I suppose I didn't think it would get Gypsy pregnant. I was just very angry when I did it. On the other hand, you know, I'm sort of looking forward to being an uncle, so long as the kid is nothing like Paddy.

Mr Nixon's business ventures

IN ADDITION TO MR NIXON'S never-ending progression of obsessions, I can tell you that Mr Nixon was always on the lookout for a business opportunity. Unfortunately for him, he always found himself on the wrong side of the opportunity. Take the time Gypsy's then husband, Mr Nixon's then son-in-law, Paddy O'Sullivan, talked him into going 25/75 in a mushroom farm venture. That's Paddy putting twenty-five percent into the venture and Clarrie putting in seventy-five percent.

According to Paddy, 'Clarrie, you put in seventy-five percent of the set-up money and you take seventy-five percent of the profit. Think of it, Clarrie. That's three-quarters of the profit! Not bad for you, don't you think? Mind you, I would have gone in fifty-fifty with you but you know, with Gypsy expecting, I have to be careful with money. You know what I mean.'

They set up the mushroom farm in a shed on one of Paddy O'Sullivan's brother-in-law's farm which was located where the suburban outskirts met the countryside. By the way, Paddy's brother-in-law and sister were still smarting because they hadn't been invited to Paddy and Gypsy's wedding. Paddy placated them with, 'So sorry about that, but Clarrie's such a miserly old bastard. He's the worst sort. Can you believe to keep costs down he wouldn't allow me to invite my side?'

Because he was good with his hands, it was Mr Nixon alone who built the shed in which to grow the mushrooms; he also built the racks and the trays for the developing mushrooms to grow on. The entire fit-out was a hundred percent his effort. Then because Paddy had said, 'Clarrie, you're going to have to pay for this. What with Gypsy expecting, I have to watch my cash flow now. You know what I mean?'

And so Mr Nixon paid for the air conditioner, thermostat, insulation batts and such things. He also paid for starter spores and whatever else was needed. Another hundred percent effort. Look, to be fair, I think Paddy arranged for all the horse shit that was delivered to be used as fertiliser, though I'm not sure whether he paid for it.

That's well and good, but when it came to physical effort Mr Nixon had to put in a hundred percent of the effort. 'You know, Clarrie, what with Gypsy expecting she needs me around so I can't help you out for a while. You know what I mean?'

Still, there was the prospect of seventy-five percent of the profits. Well, I don't know anything about growing commercial quantities of mushrooms, and more to the point, I suspect that the *Nixon and O'Sullivan Mushroom Company Pty Ltd* didn't know much either. They were plagued with problems, and for every problem Paddy would say, 'Teething problems, Clarrie. Only teething problems. Nothing more than that.'

Despite all the teething problems and despite Paddy's much less than twenty-five percent input in matters financial and labour, the mushroom spores took on and grew. Finally, when it looked as if there would be a harvest or whatever they call it for mushrooms, Paddy not only forgot to make sure the temperature gauge on the thermostat was set accurately, he also forgot to close the door of the shed after one of his rare visits. The entire mushroom crop was ruined. Every tray on every rack housed miserable shrivelled knobs that once had been marketable mushrooms.

'Sorry about that, Clarrie. My mind must have been on Gypsy – what with her expecting.'

To which Mr Nixon responded with, 'Yeah, I know exactly what you mean.'

Everything was lost and as for Mr Nixon making money, well,

seventy-five percent of zero is still zero. If there was any money made out of the mushroom farm, it was done in an oblique way and made neither by Mr Nixon nor Paddy O'Sullivan. A fortune was made not long after the failed mushroom venture and it was made by Paddy O'Sullivan's brother-in-law. For a phenomenally high price, the brother-in-law sold his land to a property developer. For your information, the land where the mushroom shed once stood is now part of Melbourne's urban sprawl.

Look, maybe Mr Nixon was just plain unlucky in money matters. Take for example the silver cutlery episode. When his mother died, he cleaned out her house and in the process he found a tarnished silver cutlery set. Like the very elderly are prone to do, his mother had stuffed the complete cutlery set into an old bag and hidden it in a wardrobe. The cutlery, though tarnished, nevertheless was silver and what's more, it was hallmarked silver.

After a trip to the library, this being the time before the internet, and a hunt through the relevant books, Mr Nixon found out that the hallmark indicated the silver was German. The hallmark had the number *800* and that meant the silver was eighty percent pure. How his mother had come by the cutlery was a mystery to him, but surely there was money to be made by selling the cutlery set.

Mrs Nixon was put on silver polishing duty, and after one rainy afternoon of vigorous rubbing the cutlery set was transformed. Her hard rubbing had paid off and that cutlery set had come up nice and shiny. So much so that when Mr Nixon checked out his reflection in a large serving spoon, he was moved to say, 'You've done a sterling job there, love.'

Mr Nixon's next step was to visit the antique shops along the street where those shops cluster. You know the sort of shops – places where you pay an arm and a leg for crummy sticks of furniture you chucked out last year because they had belonged to Aunt Fanny and, like her, they were ancient and rickety. Eventually Mr Nixon settled on the shop that gave him the highest price. Though he got less than he thought he would, he was happy enough with the deal. He even threw in the old bag as he didn't need it anymore, and besides, it was too sissy to be seen walking around with it.

Good business? Well, not really, you see with the silver price being what it was, he would have done better selling the set for its silver content to a bullion company. To make matters worse, he would have made by far more than the silver's value by selling the bag at auction, which was what the antique dealer did. You see, the bag was not just any old bag. It was a seventeenth century beaded bag made in England in 1630 with an embroidered inscription: *If money go before, all ways do lie open.* I can tell you that today the bag is on permanent display at the *Museum of Bags and Purses* in Amsterdam, but don't worry, the Nixons never found out about that.

I suppose I could go on with his many other business ventures but I'll tell you just one more. Around 1974, Australia changed distance and weight measurements from British Imperial to metric, and it was with this change that Mr Nixon saw another business opportunity. Unless a car was new, it had its speedometer in miles per hour rather than kilometres per hour. He figured that pretty soon, people driving old model cars would need to know their speed in kilometres per hour: *No one's going to change their perfectly good car just so they've got a metric speedo but I reckon they'd be happy to change that car's perfectly good but old-time measurement speedo for a metric one.*

He figured that changing the speedo from British Imperial to metric would be easy and his plan was as follows. Get transparent plastic sheets made up so that they were blank replicas of the original speedometers. Calibrate them and then they could be stuck over the original speedometer dial. He knew what to do as he had already looked up the formula for converting miles to kilometres: *Easy peasy! Where the original speedo had the number 25 I'll paint the number 40 on the transparent cut-out, where it says 50 on the original I'll paint 80 on the transparency and so on and on. As I said, easy peasy.*

The ever handy Mr Nixon got hold of the appropriate transparent plastic sheeting and, based on his extensive knowledge of makes and models of cars, he made up blank replicas of a variety of speedo dials. As I might or might not have said before Clarrie was very talented with his hands. In his workshop he set up wooden fruit crates labelled Ford, Holden, Austin, Hillman, Vauxhall and the names of other popular car makes of the time. Each car make had its own crate. Within the crates he placed cardboard shoe boxes and within each shoe box he placed the freshly cut-out plastic and appropriately calibrated speedos of various models within makes.

You might find this unbelievable, but he actually sold all of the speedometers in his first shot at trading from a stall at the Sunday market. *Joyce I'm on a bloody winner here. Mark my words, we'll be rich in no time. Pack the suitcases – I reckon the holiday to Port Fairy is happening this year.*

I suppose this business venture might have worked but unfortunately he had failed to check the accuracy of his calibrations. You see, when it comes to speedometers, the saying close enough is good enough does not apply. On the next Sunday he went to set up again at the market, only to find a group of last week's very excited customers already waiting for him. *You beauty,* he thought, *repeat customers.* On the contrary. These were angry customers and they were demanding their money back. Not only demanding their money back, but also demanding that he pay their speeding fines.

Mrs Nixon develops a lean to the left

LET'S NOT FORGET THAT Mrs Nixon had a life and it wasn't just as Mr Nixon's little woman at home. In 1970 during the Vietnam War (or as it is known in some places, the American War), well before Mrs Nixon displayed any signs of a sinister affliction, she got all political. To be more precise, she discovered politics just before Friday, 8 May 1970 – the day of the big Moratorium Marches across the country. I suppose she went all political for lots of reasons. You see, though Cliffy and I had not been balloted in for National Service, it troubled her that Asparagus, her sister's son, had not been so lucky. So that might have been one reason. Look, we thanked our lucky stars that our marbles had not been drawn, and though it was a deadly serious business, we thought it hilarious that Asparagus had been selected to protect the national interest – here and abroad – and by abroad, at that time it meant Vietnam. As for that name Asparagus, everyone called him Asparagus despite his real name being Alan. He was called Asparagus because he was born thin and long with a pointed head like an asparagus tip. At the time of his conscription, he was no longer like an asparagus. He was more like a turnip but he was stuck with Asparagus. Then again, who'd want to be called Turnip? The other thing about Asparagus was that he wasn't too bright. You see, Cliffy and I had come across a book where you could test your own IQ. You did these tests that were in the book and at the back of the book there were graphs where you could read off your IQ based on how you did on the tests. Cliffy did okay and I won't brag but I did quite a bit better. When it came to Asparagus, his results were never high. In fact they were low.

So the prospect of her dull nephew being sent to a war must have been one of the reasons why Mrs Nixon had found politics. Another reason was Dr Jim Cairns; the politician Dr Jim Cairns; the Labor Party's Dr Jim Cairns; the very left-leaning Jim Cairns; the charismatic Jimmy Cairns; and, according to Mrs Nixon, the genius James Ford Cairns. Look, Jim Cairns was such a genius that if he had done the IQ tests from that book just mentioned, his results would have been off the scale – off the scale beyond the high IQs.

Mrs Nixon always referred to Dr Jim as the good and handsome Doctor Jim Cairns. Maybe she did this to pay back Mr Nixon for the Miss Wanda episode. Perhaps she had done so one time too many when Mr Nixon came back with, 'He's not a real doctor. Couldn't fix you up if you're sick, let alone do your fillings or cure a dog. He's just a lefty, intellectual – just a useless intellectual pinko, you stupid woman!'

To which Mrs Nixon replied, 'Well, I think he's not only clever but also handsome. In fact, very clever and very handsome. He can park his slippers under my bed anytime.' Up to then it was probably the only time she had ever spoken back to Mr Nixon. You see, Women's Lib and all that bra-burning stuff was yet to arrive in the Nixon household.

Anyhow, let's get back to the Moratorium March organised by Dr Jim Cairns – the Moratorium, which by the way, Mrs Nixon pronounced as the Mordychorium. All around, the talk of the day was the upcoming big rally and march through the city. As for Mrs Nixon, in the days leading up to the big march all she talked about was: *Mordychorium this … Mordychorium that … Good Doctor Jim this … Good Doctor Jim that … and bring our boys home …* She also started spouting the slogan *Make love not war*. Mrs Nixon and *Make love*? For Cliffy and me, the thought of Mrs Nixon and *Make love* was a thought too hard to imagine. According to Cliffy, the thought was stomach churning. 'Easier to imagine Mum making war and not love. Who knows, maybe she doesn't think it means having sex. Maybe she thinks it's like in the Bible, like love thy neighbour.'

In the days leading up to the march, Mrs Nixon made a roll-up banner on which she stencilled the slogan *Bring Our Sons & Nephews Back Home … by the AAW*. If you're wondering what *AAW* stood for, you're not Robinson Crusoe there. We had to ask her, as we didn't know. Apparently it stood for 'Aunts Against War'. On the day of the big march, Mrs Nixon, the sole representative of the AAW, and her banner headed off to the rallying point in the Treasury Gardens. Well, there you go Asparagus – Auntie Joyce cares about you.

Look, I don't know much about the march other than what I saw on the TV and read in the newspapers. I can tell you it was a big success for Dr Jim, and the march had an effect on the government's understanding of the degree to which the public disapproved of the war in Vietnam and conscription. I can also tell you it had a great effect on Mrs Nixon. A cynic might say that if she couldn't have Doctor Jim, then she could have his baby – the left-wing of the Australian Labor Party, the ALP left. So how did that come about?

Well, first, not only did she come back from the big march glowing with political motivation; she also came back with a Madge, Madge Niven. You see, Mrs Nixon had marched alongside a woman who seemed to know everything about politics and the personalities in the ALP. Not only was this woman a member of the ALP but she had once met the good doctor. Madge helped with the AAW banner by holding one side while Mrs Nixon held the other. By the time their contingent turned from Bourke Street into Swanston Street, Madge Niven had been told all she needed to know about Joyce Nixon and suggested that Mrs Nixon join the local branch of the ALP. 'Join up. You won't regret it. You'll meet some nice folk and you can do the world some good at the same time.'

At home after the march, Mrs Nixon brewed up a cup of tea for Madge and herself. When Mr Nixon came into the kitchen, he saw the table set with two cups and assumed one must have been for him. As he reached for what he thought should have been his cup, Mrs Nixon said, 'No! That one's for me and the other is for Madge. Oh by the way, Clarrie, this is Madge, Madge Niven. We met at the march. I'm afraid you'll have to get your own cuppa.'

Such a small thing like missing out on his cup of tea sparked an instant dislike of the usurper. From that point on, it was a downward path for his feelings for this lefty man-destroyer Madge Niven; bloody fat Madge Nixon with downy cheeks and a hint of a moustache.

To tell the truth, you'd have to say Mr Nixon was a Liberal man through and through. Not that he had much interest in political things, but if pushed he would have, using a sporting analogy, said he barracked for the Liberals. As far as he was concerned, politics was like football. You followed one team and that was your team for life. Over the years the players might change but the constants were the team's history and its name. In his case, the team was the Liberal Party. For Mr Nixon, they were the best team and what's more, over the years they had had more than their share of good captains – the great man Menzies, the playboy Holt and mercurial Gorton – though he wasn't so sure about Gorton. He thought the team might have made a mistake in choosing Gorton as its captain. Come to think of it, he wasn't that sure of Gorton's successor McMahon either: *There's been some poor selections for captain since Holt drowned but by and large it's the team that matters and the team's still solid.*

A week after the march, Mrs Nixon announced she was going out with Madge to the ALP's local branch for their meeting. 'And what's more, I'm signing up as a member.' Obviously the Moratorium March, which by the way she now pronounced correctly, had given her backbone to stand up to Mr Nixon. She thought if she could thumb her nose at the government, then thumbing her nose at Clarrie was no big deal. So Mr Nixon's, 'You stupid old cow, don't you realise that's bloody treachery? Mark my words, woman, one way or another, all this will end in tears,' had no effect on her.

Mrs Nixon had now found politics and not more than a month later, she told him to keep out of sight on Thursday evening as she was going to host a Women for Labor night at their home.

'Have you lost your bloody mind, woman? Those Laborites, they're all traitors. Communists one and all. Most of them are spies for the Eastern Bloc. It's wrong! Bloody wrong!' and he finished with what was now becoming his stock phrase when berating her regarding her new-found political zeal, 'Mark my words, woman, one way or another, all this will end in tears.' Look, I suppose like many husbands, Mr Nixon finally took the course of least resistance, and in his case the course of least resistance on that night was to disappear into his workshop.

God now takes over the pages to speak to the Reader –

HEY YOU! YES YOU READING THIS! GOD SPEAKING HERE! SORRY, I KNOW THAT I'M SPEAKING IN BOLD CAPITALS BUT THAT'S TO DESIGNATE A BOOMING VOICE BECAUSE THAT'S THE WAY I SPEAK. SORRY? HANG ON, I'M GOD AND BEING GOD MEANS I DON'T EVER HAVE TO SAY SORRY TO ANYONE. SO SORRY ABOUT THAT. I'LL TAKE BACK ANY SORRY I'VE BOOMED. AND ANOTHER THING ABOUT BEING GOD IS THAT I CAN SEE AND HEAR EVERYTHING THAT'S GOING ON EVERYWHERE IN THE MULTIVERSE AT ANYTIME AND ALL AT THE SAME TIME. SO I'LL GET THE AUTHOR TO TELL YOU BELOW WHAT WAS SAID AND DONE WITH THE NIXONS.

I, GOD, SAW AND HEARD EVERYTHING. TO PUT IT IN A WAY THAT SOUNDS BIBLICAL: AS IT IS WRITTEN BELOW THEN SO IT WAS SAID AND DONE. YOU HAD BETTER BELIEVE IT OR ELSE YOU'LL BE THE ONE WHO'S GOING TO BE SORRY!

To tell you that Mrs Nixon understood much about the ins and outs of the political scene after the election of the Labor government on 2 December 1972 would be an overstatement. What did she know? Well, she knew that Asparagus was not going off to Puckapunyal or Holsworthy or wherever they sent those poor boys and he certainly wasn't going to Vietnam. Apart from that, politics for her was about fundraising events and not much else. The turmoil that led to the 1974 double dissolution went above her head. And though she thought that it was called a double disillusionment to match her growing disillusionment with politics, she knew that there was to be a bigger than usual federal election coming up in May of that year. More relevant than the forthcoming election for her was receiving an invitation to attend an evening pre-election party in Eltham. As far as Mrs Nixon was concerned, such an invitation meant she was on her way up in the world of politics.

Rumour had it that Dr Jim Cairns or perhaps Don Dunstan would be there. In fact, as it turned out neither attended. By the way, that's the artsy-fartsy Don Dunstan, premier of South Australia I'm talking about. More relevant than Dunstan's arts-driven policies, and to the point as far as Mrs Nixon was concerned, was Dunstan's sartorial elegance. In particular his safari suits. So elegant, so, so left of centre and so, so, so modern were Dunstan's safari suits. If Dunstan could wear safari suits then why couldn't Clarrie? Somehow and don't ask how it followed that not only did she talk Clarrie into attending the function – *Look Joyce, understand this – I'm only going out of sufferance and to perv on those damn lefties. I'll show them how a true Liberal and loyal subject of her Majesty behaves* – but she also talked him into buying and wearing a safari suit to the party in Eltham.

'Why do I need that crappy-looking sack outfit? You wouldn't have ever seen Menzies wearing one. Double-breasted, well-cut pinstriped suits were Menzies's style. Safari suits are only for wankers!'

'Don Dunstan wears them all the time.'

'There you go. That's what I mean, woman.'

Well, he did go with Joyce to Myers in the city to buy a safari suit and he wore it to the function. In the process of purchasing the suit, he had refused a beige safari suit, refused the baby blue one, refused the lime green one and refused the orange one. He should have gone for a khaki one – 'At least that would make me look like a big game hunter.' In the interest of compromise, he settled on a pure arctic white safari suit – 'I suppose this will have to do. At least it makes me look like a polar bear hunter.'

On the night of the function he wanted to wear his old belt with the safari suit's trousers but he was talked out of doing that by Joyce. 'Clarrie, the trousers don't need a belt. First of all, the jacket already has a belt and so another belt for the trousers would spoil the line of the outfit. Second, the fit around your waist looks fine to me without a belt. No, you don't need your old belt; that sturdy button above the fly will do the job of holding the trousers up. Finally, why wear that worn-out old belt of yours with that beautiful new suit? And please, please, Clarrie, promise me you'll behave yourself.'

'Yes, I promise, but I can't promise I won't speak my mind if the need arises.'

'Please. Just be nice for once.'

'Don't worry, I know how a true Liberal man behaves. I'll behave with class.'

On the way out to Eltham, Mr Nixon remained silent while Mrs Nixon babbled trivia in her excitement at the prospect of rubbing shoulders with Labor luminaries. As they entered the suburb of Eltham, Mr Nixon finally spoke and said, 'You know, Joyce love, only flipping lefties and hippies live out here.' And if Eltham being the home of left-wing hippies wasn't enough aggravation to him, he got lost on the unmade roads of Eltham trying to find the party's venue. 'For Christ's sake, Joyce, this bloody place is so bloody far away you need a passport or at the very least a visa just to be here.'

On pulling up in a bit of bushland near the house, the Nixons completed the journey to the house on foot.

'Jesus Christ, Joyce, look at the house. Why can't your Labor friend live in an ordinary house? This isn't a house. It's just a series of giant boxes staggered at odd angles. Giant boxes with glass walls and with flat metal roofs.'

'Don't be so critical. It's very modern. Apparently some famous Danish architect designed it. Do you know it's been in *Home Beautiful*?'

'As I said before, your mob's just a team of wankers if you ask me.'

'Well, no one asked you.'

Inside, the house was ultra-modern and fashionable: huge glass floor-to-ceiling picture windows, vaulted cathedral ceilings, raw brick feature walls and big squares of black slate floor tiles throughout. Persian rugs and shaggy rugs were on the floors and medieval style tapestries with unicorns hung from the brick walls. There was even a sunken circular area someone called the conversation pit. In the middle of the conversation pit there was a wood heater that vented into the high ceiling via a long beaten-copper exhaust flue. Then there were the art works. Art works which appealed to neither Nixon.

'Look at those, Joyce. Bloody pretentious modern abstract art. Wanker art, I'd call it. Come to think of it, that one there looks just like the fence where I clean out my paint brushes.'

On the walls, in addition to the tapestries, there were macramé wall hangings and strange rusted metal objects somebody said were called mandalas. Neither the macramé nor the mandalas appealed to Clarrie. 'You know, Joyce, those mandala things might just as well be car parts. In fact, I think that one could be a hubcap off a '49 single spinner Ford.'

What appealed to Mr Nixon, however, was a triple life-size paint-brush-line stylised picture of a big-breasted nude female form done in an oriental style, on stark white paper and with thick black-painted fluid lines. Mr Nixon kept his thoughts on that one to himself. And though it was stylised, it was sufficiently realistic for him to think: *Jeez, cop an eyeful of those. Bloody enormous!*

Now that's what the interior of the house looked like. Outside was an extensive Australian native garden of the Ellis Stone variety. Therefore there were large rocks strategically placed among stands of native grasses, there were grevilleas, melaleucas, stands of lemon-scented gums and it all sloped gently down to a softly flowing creek at the bottom of the property. The pathways were edged by man-height bamboo poles with flaming torches at the top. The outdoor paths were covered in crushed Lilydale toppings that crunched pleasantly when walked on. Powerful outdoor lighting illuminated the tree tops and fairy lights were strung along the balustrade of the jarrah decking. Finally there was an enormous blazing brazier where people stood around chewing political fat and outrage over the Liberals' tactic of blocking supply.

Mrs Nixon gasped when she saw the outside. 'Oh look, Clarrie. This is so beautiful … and romantic.'

Mr Nixon, still thinking of that Amazonian huge-breasted nude indoors, could only manage, 'They're bloody lucky it's not total fire ban time.'

'Look, Clarrie, other men are wearing safari suits. I'm glad you're wearing one. You'll fit right in.'

'Fit right in be buggered. It's a wanker's outfit. I'll be buggered if one of those safari suits over there makes a pass at me. And I really mean bloody well buggered!'

'Please, Clarrie, don't be so crude. These people are intellectuals.'

Despite Clarrie's objections, Mrs Nixon was pleased that she had convinced him to wear the safari suit but thought another colour might have been better as in this lighting, the arctic white appeared definitely luminous.

To complete the picture outdoors there were three graceful salukis that nosed around the garden, quietly sniffing crutches here and there. 'Look Clarrie. Look at those beautiful dogs. They're so elegant.'

'Bloody fancy foreign fleabags, if you ask me. Not real dogs. Give me a kelpie or heeler. Even a bloody mini foxie has got more going for it than those three abominations. This Eltham is just strange houses, strange dogs and very strange people. Your lefty friends are supposed to be supporters of the working class so you'd have thought they'd live in a working-class house with understandable art on the walls. Why don't they have working-class dogs and not these flouncy walking sheepskin rugs? And where are the working people here? I haven't seen anyone here who looks as if they get their hands dirty, just your bloody intellectuals, and what would they know about anything real.'

'Well I think everything here is just right.'

'Well I don't.'

By the time food was available the party crowd had built up. Animated groups were dotted indoors and outdoors, clutching their glasses of cask red and talking loudly. The air was thick with cigarette smoke, Neil Diamond's 'Hot August Night' and politics. Mrs Nixon went off to help pass the food around on large trays. 'While I'm gone, why don't you mingle with the others and please, please, please behave yourself.'

When the food came around it was somewhat of a disappointment to Mr Nixon: *Christ, where are the saveloys and party pies?* As far as he was concerned, a party like this should have had, at the very least, saveloys and party pies. Instead, trays passed by him with things they called canapes and spicy meat on skewers that you dipped into some sort of peanut butter sauce. He was offered a kind of meat bun; he thought he heard someone say they were called pork bowels. Then there were things he recognised as dim sims. These were not the fried variety, which he would have preferred, but steamed. Even what he called dim sims were being referred here as dum sums: *Pretentious bastards!* But he was hungry and so he ate whatever was offered; in fact, he ate too much of everything.

Now the truth is that Mr Nixon was not a smoker, but sometime between his fifth pork bao and seventh chicken satay stick, a pretty young thing with flaming red hair and perfect teeth offered him one of those funny cigarettes that he had heard about. He knew it wasn't a standard cigarette as it was wide in the middle and tapered at the ends.

'Here, mister in that cool suit, have this fatty.' Was she saying, 'Here, mister in that cool suit, have this fatty' or was she saying, 'Here, mister in that cool suit have this, fatty?' With all he was eating, he was feeling fat in the middle and tapered at the ends but then he'd heard that these sort of cigarettes had weird names. Maybe fatty was one of them. Ultimately he reckoned whether he was looking fat or not, who was he to refuse this flaming red-headed beauty. Why should he refuse this braless Venus in a see-through cheesecloth blouse, this wonder woman who might or might not have been a famous actress? Mr Nixon wondered: *Maybe I've seen her in a film, or was it a TV variety show.*

With Joyce flitting around somewhere, balancing trays of food and him looking debonair, but perhaps a trifle bloated in his electric arctic white safari suit, he was flattered to have this offering. In his eagerness to accept this unusual cigarette, he bumped into a goateed left-wing intellectual who was holding a glass of red wine. The outcome of this clash of political ideologies was a large red artistic abstraction in the style of a Rorschach blot all over the front of Mr Nixon's white safari suit jacket. Instead of getting angry, he remembered Joyce's request to behave so he cracked what he thought would be a joke: 'Hang on, mate! Are you trying to turn me into a red?'

The goateed intellectual turned around, peered through jam-jar lenses at Mr Nixon's red blobbed jacket, didn't get the joke and said dismissively, 'Sorry, comrade.'

Goatee then turned to get his glass refilled with the corrosive red and continued with his opinion on whether the Senate was the states' house or a house of review. This was getting complicated and, as far as politics went, Mr Nixon believed it shouldn't be complicated and he would let goggle-eyes know.

'You know,' Mr Nixon said, 'If a party can't explain its economic platform in one sentence, not too long a sentence mind you, then it's not worth a nob of goat's shit.' The intellectual stared at him and then turned his back on Mr Nixon and walked away.

At this point, after thinking: *Bloody arsehole*, Mr Nixon noticed that the pretty young thing had disappeared after having lit his toke. Now with more than just a few hefty inhalations of the funny cigarette, his head was light and a bit dizzy. On the other hand, he was finding that the party was becoming more agreeable: *It's not too bad after all. None too shabby.*

So long as he didn't move his head around much and he didn't focus on all the political mumbo jumbo talk around him, all was fine. On the negative side, his stomach felt bloated and gurgled. *Cripes, these bloody trousers are too tight. Must have had too much of that wogish food.* He decided that the solution to his discomfort would be to seek a quiet spot outside, relieve himself of the rumbling air that was percolating in his guts and replace it with some clear, clean, cool, but unfortunately left-wing, Eltham air into his lungs.

Mr Nixon found a large flat rock out in a dark corner of the garden, but as he was lowering himself to sit down the button holding his trousers up exploded outwards. *Jesus! I have eaten too much for sure!* He then thought: *No problems*, and assumed he could use the safari suit's jacket belt to hold up his trousers. Unfortunately the belt wouldn't budge as it had been sewn into place by the designer; it served no other function than to be decorative: *Bugger, I should have worn my old belt. Bloody hell!*

He stood up to see if the trousers would stay up. They didn't. The only way to keep his trousers up was for him to hang onto the waist band. He had no other alternative but to sit down again and try work out how he could get out of his dilemma. If only this was his only dilemma. But no. He smelled shit. *Oh Christ, what's going on? Those cigarettes are meant to loosen your inhibitions. Loosen you up and all that, but they don't loosen your sphincter as well, do they? Jesus.* Well, Mr Nixon knew that it couldn't be his sphincter malfunctioning as he suffered chronic constipation. Any shitting on his part was an event not to happen by accident; in fact, it was impossible to happen without extreme effort on his part.

He had accidently sat in the dog shit that had been laid on the flat ornamental rock. Judging by the amount on his trousers' legs and seat, it was three salukis' worth of dog shit: *And those radicals want to clean up the country when they can't even clear their garden of dog shit! This would never have happened at a Menzies function. Never! Jeez, I knew it. I knew it. I should have bought the khaki suit!*

Dilemma now – trousers that need to be held up by clutching the waistband with the right hand and shit all over the electric arctic white trousers. He tried to flick the shit off and only succeeded in creating lines that looked as if they had been the work of the artist who had created the huge nude female form indoors. Could it get worse? Well, yes, because as he stood up to plan an exit, the red-headed lovely from maybe a film or TV variety show was approaching him with a toothy smile and cheerfully said, 'Hey, listen! You in the white suit. Yes you. I see you hiding in the shadows. They're starting up the music again. It's Daddy Cool! You know, 'Eagle Rock'. The actual band Daddy Cool is inside. Daddy Cool! They're tuning up their equipment. So you, cool daddy, come inside and let's dance.'

She grabbed his arm to lead him inside. It was the arm with which he was holding up his trousers. Three things happened. First she saw his artistically shit-stained trousers; second (and it was only a fraction of a second later) his trousers slid to his ankles; and third, the shit smell rose to greet her. Then the ravishing red-headed actress from maybe a film or TV variety show let go his arm, turned her back to him and headed indoors, but not before grimacing and giving out a very loud, 'Oh, yuck!'

It wasn't long before Mr Nixon saw the redhead through the wall of picture windows. There she was, gyrating to the thumping beats of Daddy Cool with the goateed goggle-eyed intellectual. She whispered something in goatee's ear and then she pointed in Mr Nixon's direction. Goatee followed to where her outstretched arm was pointing and they both laughed. Mr Nixon thought: *Bloody ginger-nutted bitch and bloody lefty four-eyes!*

Mr Nixon saw two laughing mouths looking his way, a set of perfect teeth in a sweet laughing mouth and the other a jumble of red wine and tobacco-stained teeth in a donkey's braying gob. *Talking about me, aren't you. Big bloody joke no doubt. I'm sure it's a leftist setup to humiliate a loyal Liberal.* For the one and only time in his adult life. He wished his mother was there and he was five years old. He wished Mum could clean him up, rub Vicks VapoRub on his chest and tuck him into his bed with fluffy Lambie, his woolly toy lamb. *Goodnight darling. Sleep tight.*

For the rest of the evening, Mr Nixon lurked in the darkest corners of the Ellis Stone-designed garden, hanging onto his trousers. Late into the evening Mrs Nixon found him shivering; it was May, and when all was said and done, not really safari suit weather. Stinking and slinking back to the car, he drove home furious.

'Well, I hope you had a good time with *your* bloody pinko degenerates, because I didn't!'

God now says goodbye –

NOW READER, BE GOOD AND GOD-FEARING. GOD SIGNING OFF HERE.

Look, I don't know how long Mrs Nixon's fascination with all matters Labor lasted, but I know it was definitely spent by the time the Whitlam government was kicked out of office in November 1975. The expulsion from power of the Labor government, well, I can tell you it was an event a gloating Mr Nixon relished. 'You see, you stupid cow. Just as I told you. All this bolshie stuff, one way or another, all this malarkey ends in tears.'

When it came to being bitten by a cause, Mr Nixon was not immune, and sometime after Mrs Nixon's flirtation with all things Labor had run its course, he found religion. Well, to say he found religion might be a bit of an exaggeration. He found religion on Channel 2 – only for a short time after watching a Billy Graham rally on TV. For a time there, Cliffy thought his father had gone nuts. Fortunately, like most things his father embraced with a passion, it didn't last too long.

In a matter of weeks God, Jesus and in fact all manifestations of the Lord were out the door and Mr Nixon was back in his workshop as his old self, blaspheming his way all the way to hell.

Mr Nixon opens up to Paddy O'Sullivan with his take on hate, love and sex … but mainly on hate

JUST A HEADS UP here to forewarn you that not long before Gypsy had her baby, Paddy O'Sullivan went AWOL never to come back. For now I'll let you know about when Mr Nixon gave Paddy O'Sullivan his take on love and hate. Well, actually about Mr Nixon's preference for hate over love.

Look, I wasn't present on the love-hate conversation Mr Nixon had with Paddy O'Sullivan that hot summer night. I got the gist of it from Cliffy and technically speaking he wasn't present either. As I said, it was a hot summer night and Mr Nixon and Paddy were sitting on the front porch bench knocking back some beers. Before I get any further I should let you know that Mr Nixon was not a beer drinker, but it being a hot night he must have thought it was right to have a cold one and right that he should share it with his son-in-law Paddy.

The lounge room window facing the porch was open and Cliffy was in the dark lounge room lying on the floor just under the window. He overheard the two men talking and his search for ceiling aliens was abandoned.

To tell the truth, I heard what was said on the porch from Cliffy who heard it through the open window and so as I wasn't there I have to make up the conversation from what Cliffy told me. I'm pretty sure that I haven't messed it up.

'You know, Paddy, I find it easier to hate than to love. Hate is such an easy thing for me. Hate's something I feel in my guts. Love? Well, I don't know. I find there are lots of people and things I hate and nothing I can say I truly love.'

Cliffy heard one of the men opening the Esky and the fizzy sound of another bottle being opened. 'You know, Paddy, I can hate for years. In fact, I enjoy hating.' Mr Nixon let out a loud beer-burp.

'Pardon me. Strange as it might seem to you, I love to hate. I can carry hate in me for years. I'll harbour a grudge for as long as it gives me pleasure; and I must say it always gives me great pleasure. It gives me something to focus on. It's great saying *I hate this* and *I hate that*. Love it. And I can tell you I will totally hate whatever or whomever *this* or *that* might be.'

'Like what?'

'Well, I still hate my father. I suppose Gypsy's told you why. And though he's dead I still hate the bastard. I hate most Continentals, especially those with money. I hate your brother-in-law Frankie.'

'Frankie? Why him?'

'I don't like his smugness but most of all I hate him for making us pay him, I mean, making me pay. For Christ's sake, we're family, aren't we? Well, maybe not family but certainly kinsfolk. It's not as if the shit spot where we built, I mean where *I* built, the mushroom shed was land he was using. That burns me up real bad and I'll hang on to it for as long as I enjoy the hating. Bloody mean act on his part I'd say.'

'Come on Clarrie, that makes you sound like a tough old bastard. What about love? You don't love anyone? I find that hard to believe.'

'I really mean it. Hate comes so easily for me. As for love? I s'pose I don't know what they mean by love. I don't think there's anything I can say I love.'

'But you love your family. Wife and kids?'

'The best I can say is that I tolerate them.'

'Really? You must have loved Joyce when you married, at least in the early days.'

'No, not really. I loved the sex that led up to me getting me marrying her. And it wasn't the actual sex as such.'

'If it's not too personal, what was it about sex that you liked then and not now?'

'It was the feeling of power.'

'That's it? Just power? Okay, that's with Joyce but what about other women?'

According to Cliffy his father didn't say anything for a while; he must have been thinking about it. Actually he hoped that they had stopped going on with that conversation. No such luck because his dad started up again.

'First of all, steady on. You're going to go on about that harpsichord woman, Miss Wanda, aren't you? Shit, I shouldn't have told you about her. So steady on.'

'Well, okay, I'm sorry, Clarrie, to have brought it up. I won't mention that again. Ever. Promise.'

'Good. Make sure you don't. So apart from that momentary, and I mean really momentary, spasm and spurt, it was that sex made me feel in control of the bloody universe. Sort of like a god. But now? The old mutton gun is firmly in the holster, probably never to be drawn again.'

By this stage, Cliffy said he wished he wasn't there to hear all this sex talk stuff: *Dad and his old mutton gun and its momentary spasm and spurt. I didn't need to hear that!* – but there was no way he could get out of the room without them knowing he was there. On top of that, there would be no way he would ever get his father's spasm and spurt out of his mind.

To leave the room, Cliffy would have had to go out via the lounge room door and because the hall light was on, it would have thrown light onto the porch as soon as the door was opened. So he was stuck there. Cliffy said he knew that his father was getting drunk because otherwise he never would have said a word like 'shit', let alone talk about sex. Mr Nixon talking about sex and love? Well, to quote Cliffy: 'It made me want to puke. As for not loving but only tolerating us, I don't care if he tolerates me or not. Most of the time I can't even tolerate him.'

Mr Nixon went on: 'Jeez, Paddy, this conversation is getting too personal. I don't go around asking you about you and Gypsy and that sort of thing.'

'Sorry, just curious.'

'Well, you know what they say about curiosity and the cat so watch it.'

'What about if someone said they loved you?'

'To tell you the truth, I wouldn't like that.'

'Why?'

'Well, first of all I wouldn't believe it. And second, if it was true there'd be the let down when they didn't love me anymore. Which would be sure to happen.'

'Jeez, Clarrie' you're a hard man.'

'You know' I like it when people say that of me. Now be a sport and get us another out of the Esky.'

Well, that's my recreated take on Cliffy's take on Mr Nixon's take on love and hate.

Madge makes a move on Joyce and eventually moves on

OKAY, SO YOU'VE JUST heard Mr Nixon on love and hate, so what about Mrs Nixon's take on all of this stuff? Well, I don't know.

HANG ON. JUST HANG ON A MOMENT. GOD HERE AGAIN. IT LOOKS AS IF SOME GODLY HELP IS NEEDED TO TELL YOU ABOUT MADGE NIVEN AND JOYCE NIXON. IT'S THE SAME DEAL AS BEFORE – THE AUTHOR WILL TELL YOU WHAT I'VE JUST PUT INTO HIS MIND. NOW LISTEN! SORRY TO HAVE TAKEN OVER AGAIN. NO, I'M NOT SORRY. OH GOD, I'VE GOT TO STOP APOLOGISING – I'M GOD, AFTER ALL! NOW I COMMAND YOU TO READ ON!

Did you know that Madge Niven took a shine to Joyce Nixon? Well, if we're talking shine it would be more accurate to say she was more interested in the act of polishing rather than the resultant shine, if you get my drift. From their first meeting at the Moratorium March to all those party meetings, Madge had, dare I say it, the hots for Joyce. Let me say upfront it was not reciprocated. But why would mousey Joyce inspire such passion in Madge?

When it came to matters sexual, you couldn't say Madge was univalent or even ambivalent – she was multivalent. As far as sex and she were concerned, it was about her and not about any partner of whatever gender. This was girl to girl territory and as far as Joyce was concerned such attitudes and happenings happened only with and only god knows (**YES, I KNOW TOO WELL**) where – maybe with adventurous women novelists, certain types of actresses and athletic netball players, but definitely not with a woman of Joyce's type.

234

Let me tell you a little more about Madge. First things first and that first thing, to put it in the kindest way, would be to say she was stocky or big-boned. An unkind description would be to say she was as wide as she was high; well, she was almost as wide as she was high. Her ex-husband described her as beach-ball-shaped but then, according to Madge, he was an unkind brute. One couldn't deny that she was bright. She called herself an intellectual and she had the degrees to prove it – *Madge Niven BA, BSc (Hons)*. She worked at the real university, the University of Melbourne and not the Farm out at Clayton. At the university she had her own little office, well, actually it was a windowless former storeroom in the Chemistry Department from which she occasionally ventured to work as a research assistant to the department's Reader.

In those days, smoking was the thing and while most smoked cigarettes and university types sucked on pipes, Madge went a step further and smoked cigars of the most pungent stench. Oh, and yet another thing, in the Chemistry Department the wearing of a lab coat was a matter of being practical. Oddly, Madge wore one although her work involved no exposure to chemicals or the laboratory. She wore it all the time – in her office, in the tea room, even at the Baillieu. The lab coat and the little name tag on it marked her as university staff. In other words, she thought, she could be identified as a member of a club of the intellectually substantial members of society.

If one would have found Madge's office a shambles then be prepared, be very prepared for her flat. The flat was the entire front room of the upper floor of a charming double-storey terraced house in Elgin Street. You'd call her flat a largish bedsit. She had chosen the flat not for its charm but because it was a damn easy walk to the university. Her flat stank of stale cigar smoke, explainable by the cigar butts in many overflowing and rarely emptied ashtrays. Much smoking had yellowed the frayed Terylene curtains. As she was always happy to eat but never happy to clean dishes, almost every horizontal surface of the covered-in veranda that served as her kitchen was covered with dirty crockery – dirty crockery that couldn't be put into the sink because the sink was never empty of dishes from earlier meals which were also waiting to be washed. In fact, she called the dirty dishes her memories of delicious dinners past.

Madge was no fashion plate and what clothes that she owned hung on hangers from the back of her entrance door or were piled on any piece of furniture that could be sat on. Some would say Madge was a grub. Madge would say that such an assessment of her was very bourgeois.

Then there were the wooden fruit boxes packed with unread paperbacks bought at church fairs or at the university bookshop sales. These boxes were located in random places around her room in such a way that one had to navigate an obstacle course to get anywhere. When it came to books, Madge was no different from everyone else who bought books. She bought them at a rate faster than they could be read. In fact, beyond reading a book's title, few books were ever read by her. It was sufficient for her to tell others she possessed them: *Oh yes, I've got Moravia's* Woman of Rome *and Sartre's* Being and Nothingness. Notice she never said that she had read them, but to give the impression she had she would say things like: *Make sure you get first editions and unless they're in the original language you miss a lot. Modern translators just aren't up to the task – they miss all the subtle nuances and argot.* As for Proust, though she hadn't read any of his books either, she felt it gave her an air of literary knowledge to say: *Mind you, talk about* In Search of Lost Time*! No need to search for that because take my word, reading Proust in any language is a complete waste of time.*

She'd heard of a recently published book called *Books Do Furnish a Room*, and though she couldn't remember who wrote it she was taken by its title. The idea that books could offer more than just the reading experience appealed to her so much that she had promised herself that the fruit boxes would have to go and her books placed on shelves so as to furnish her room.

Madge's feelings for Joyce dated back to the day of the Moratorium

March. On that day back at the Nixons, she loved the way Joyce's nostrils had flared when Clarrie went to take the tea that had not been made for him. What strength that showed. So sexy, especially when Joyce's cheeks flushed a beautiful pink. That particular moment was a moment that brought on a reciprocal flush of sorts in Madge. Showing a brute like Clarrie his place, well, that was ever so sexy.

As she got to know Joyce better, Madge was finding Joyce progressively more interesting. But why? Joyce had little education, no career and certainly no political nous. Joyce was a member of the proletariat class who didn't know what that meant. Here was Joyce who kept a tidy house, who had two useless offspring, an even more useless son-in-law and a prick of a very piggish husband. And here by contrast was Madge, who by her own reckoning was a substantial intellectual, unencumbered by bourgeois mores.

Madge and Joyce. North and South. Joyce and Madge. East and West. Surely they were exact opposites of each other and don't opposites attract? And so it came to pass that Madge invited Joyce to meet her after work at the tram stop at a Swanston Street entrance to the university. The plan was to go out to dinner in Lygon Street. Joyce had cleared it with Clarrie by saying that although it wasn't the usual Labor evening, there was an extraordinary and special meeting requiring her attendance in Carlton.

To make an impression that she was truly a gifted intellectual, Madge waited for Joyce at the tram stop smoking a cigar, wearing her lab coat and around her neck she had a stethoscope she'd borrowed from a third-year med. student. At her feet and firmly clamped between her ankles she had good old Mr Gladstone well and truly trapped, Mr Gladstone being her battered Gladstone bag. And with all that, she made quite an impression on Joyce as she hopped off the Number 62. Not the impression Madge had hoped as Joyce wondered why Madge was wearing a cleaner's dust jacket, had a piece of doctor's equipment while struggling to keep her balance astride an old bag. Rather than an intellectual Madge, Joyce saw an eccentric Madge – eccentric but nice.

Old Mr Gladstone could be used to further impress Joyce. Pointing to the bag between her ankles Madge said, 'Got to drop this off at the flat. I've got some very, very important scientific work in there and I'd hate for it to get into the wrong hands.' In actual fact, the Gladstone bag contained nothing of any scientific interest to anyone – other than leave rosters for the Chemistry Department over the coming term break.

At the flat Joyce made her next move. 'How about we have a wee drinkie or two before we go out to dinner? What's your poison? Red? White? Something stronger?'

Well, it would be wrong to say Joyce was a complete teetotaller. She enjoyed an occasional shandy in summer but wines of any colour were not for her. As for spirits, as far as she was concerned, Clarrie might on special occasions drink spirits but women did not drink such alcohol. Not wishing to be a killjoy, she pointed to a bottle of Stone's Green Ginger Wine that was only partially hidden behind a packet of cornflakes and a dried-out loaf of bread. She'd heard Gypsy mention that drink once and she figured it should be okay for her.

'Just a small one of the ginger wine, thanks Madge.'

Madge poured Joyce more than just a small one into a chipped glass.

'You sure? Well I'm going to have a stiff whisky.' Then adding with a wink, 'It's the only stiff thing nowadays I'll allow in my mouth.'

Joyce stifled a gasp with a hearty gulp of her drink and Madge made a mental note not to be so blatantly crude. But she couldn't help saying, 'Talking of things in the mouth, how about dinner? I've reserved a table for us at the Università Café in Lygon Street. They do fabulous pasta.'

At the restaurant, what an eye-opener for Joyce when she perused the menu. Up to then spaghetti for her was something that came in a can and best served on toast. Her naiveté regarding all the different forms of pasta was a godsend to Madge as it gave her an excuse to move her chair closer to Joyce. She put her arm over Joyce's shoulder and from that position, she went through the menu. She explained the differences between ravioli, cannelloni, lasagne and all the other pasta types found in Italian cuisine. Every so often her eyes glanced from the menu to various parts of Joyce's anatomy. She was even emboldened to brush a stray hair that had fallen across Joyce's forehead: *Mustn't be too brazen*, she thought. Joyce, on the other hand, found this level of intimacy with another woman most uncomfortable and was relieved when a waiter finally brought their pasta.

The pasta was followed by a garlicy rocket salad which in turn was followed by gelato and espresso coffee. All this food was new to Joyce, though she could have given the coffee a miss. But what was also new to her was Madge's attentiveness.

Finally, lighting up one of her foul cigars Madge said, 'I suppose Clarrie doesn't pay you much attention. I get the impression you're more than somewhat neglected. Men are like that, especially husbands. You know, I was married once and it was so very disappointing. That was long ago and best forgotten. It was a lapse of judgement on my part. I thought men, marriage and all that was something that was expected of a woman. I was denying my true self just to conform. I'd accepted all that bullshit they feed you when you're growing up. Let me tell you, as far as I'm concerned, marriage and men are not worth the effort. Men and marriage? Both overrated. And as for heterosexual sex, well that's a very sticky and messy business. Very sticky. Very messy. The bottom line is that even if they're given to the end of time, men will never understand a woman's need like other women do.'

Reaching out, Madge put her hand on Joyce's. She was so close that despite the garlicky meal and the cigar, Joyce could smell her whisky breath. 'Listen to me. Joyce, I think I understand your longings, your needs. Believe me. I do.'

Poor Joyce. This situation was so unfamiliar, just like the dinner, but unlike the dinner this situation was not pleasant. She withdrew her hand from beneath Madge's and said, 'No Madge, I like you but I'm not like you. Thank you for the dinner but I think I'd better go home now.' With that she left the table, left the restaurant and caught the Number 62 on Swanston Street back home.

A stunned and perplexed Joyce rode the tram, replaying the evening's events all the way down St Kilda Road. She certainly wouldn't be telling Clarrie about it lest he might think her as strange or, even worse, the instigator of what had happened. She could already hear him: *Strewth! I always thought that Madge was odd. Come on, come clean with it, Joyce. You must have led her on.* But then she thought: *It would be nice if only just in a while Clarrie felt the way about me that Madge did.*

Still sitting in the café, Madge was disappointed but resigned that she might have miscalculated: *Pity. Bloody pity.* But not too disappointed to order another *dolce*: *Cannoli for two and another coffee per favore.* She then went back to her flat and finished off what was left in the bottle of whisky. By two o'clock, she had pleasured herself aided by erotic fantasies about the reception girl in the Physics Department and by two fifteen she was flaked out on her couch, grateful that it was now Saturday.

Now here was the bind for Joyce – she liked Madge and she also liked the local ALP branch meetings, but after that strange Friday night in Carlton, how could she continue with both? The solution came about in the following way.

For the next two months, Joyce attended the branch meetings each time they were held; on the other hand, Madge didn't. Then Madge came to a meeting and throughout they avoided eye contact. It was up to one of them to break the ice. As they were filing out of the meeting, and with her heart thumping madly, it was Joyce with a jaunty, 'Hi, Madge, long time no see.'

'I know, I know. Haven't been feeling the best.'

'Sorry to hear that.'

In her mind Joyce was repeating: *Don't mention last time. Don't mention last time. Don't mention last time* – and Madge mentioned last time.

'About last time, I hope I didn't frighten you too much. Really I do. I know that sometimes I go over the top. All heart and no mind. Listen, why don't you consider this – as a Christmas present to you and to let me make it up to you. So … please be my guest at this fabulous little bistro in the city. I just love the place and I think you will too.'

Joyce really didn't think it out and accepted on the spot. Sure, Christmas was coming up so why not accept the offer. Perhaps? Maybe she felt sorry for Madge, maybe she wanted to be thought of as sophisticated and above a trifling thing like the event of last time. More likely it was the excitement of a trip out of the suburbs and into the city – in to the city and a meal at this fabulous little bistro.

This time the ruse to placate Clarrie was, 'I'm going to a special Christmas function for all the committees. It's at Trades Hall.'

Joyce took the 62 tram up Swanston Street just as she had when she visited Madge at the university gates. But then that was in the past and all that. Though come to think of it, it was nice to be thought of as desirable and that Italian restaurant had been a delicious eye-opener. This time Joyce got off near Little Bourke Street and of course in the city it was beginning to feel a lot like Christmas – the street decorations, tinsel, cardboard Santas and shop windows with Christmas displays. She walked up the hill past the Chinese cafes in Chinatown; even they had gotten into the spirit of the season. They seemed more exotic to her than the Nixon's usual Chinese cafe, the Lucky Dragon on Friday nights in St Kilda. Then she cut through Crossley Street to Bourke Street to end up at the Pellegrini corner and a short walk down to the café Madge had specified that they meet for lunch – Florentino's Bistro – yet another Italian café. Well, why not, as Madge had said she loved this bistro and Italian food. Joyce had eaten at Università Café in Carlton, she'd now just walked past Pellegrini's and soon she'd be dining at Florentino's Bistro: *Perhaps I'm becoming a sophisticate. I might even learn to like those cap a chinos.*

When she got there the restaurant was empty. Empty except for a fat, miserable-looking wine-sipping man. He was seated near the wall-mounted oversized top-end of a wine barrel that served as the café's servery. It appeared that the man was wearing an ill-fitting suit. He was either Oliver Hardy or a bulkier Charlie Chaplin with a hint of a wispy moustache. In fact, the man was Madge Niven. Bizarrely, Madge had chosen to dress in a man's baggy suit, a business shirt and a very wide mustard-coloured tie; the top button of the shirt was undone and the tie was hung raffishly loose. On the spare chair there was a suitcase which Madge placed on the floor so Joyce had somewhere to sit.

'I didn't recognise you sitting at the back.'

'Of course you did.'

'No, not in what you're wearing I didn't.'

'You don't like it? Well I like it. Don't you think it adds a sort of gravitas to me? I think there's a sort of *Je ne sais quoi* about it.'

Joyce, not knowing what gravitas was, let alone what the last bit meant, could only manage, 'Perhaps.'

'Besides, I think dressed like this I command more respect from the waiter.' As if to prove her point, Madge stood up and clicked her fingers at a passing waiter and demonstrated with, '*Cameriere! Cameriere! Cameriere!*' Turning to Joyce, she told her that *cameriere* meant waiter in Italian. Then, pointing at the empty carafe on the table, she said, 'Another carafe, *per favore*. The same again.'

Madge was already well on the way of becoming drunk. To Joyce, without looking away from her empty wine glass, she said, 'First let's start with an antipasto platter to share. Then I recommend the veal with a tuna sauce. It's out of this world. For a side dish let's get a serve of broccoli with flaked almonds and shaved parmesan. We can see how we're going and if we want something else we could order a salad with a garlic and oil dressing. But first things first – for starters we must have their antipasto appetiser platter to share. As for dessert, we can decide later. You'll have some wine when it eventually comes?'

All these dishes were new to Joyce and as such, enough to be happy with, so she said no to the wine.

'Good, all the more of it for little old me. Now, remember it's Christmas time and you're my guest. Ergo it's my shout.'

Joyce thought: *Of course it's your shout. You invited me*, but said, 'That's very generous. Thanks, Madge.'

During the antipasto dish both women ate in an awkward silence until Joyce said, 'This is absolutely fantastic.'

Madge, on the other hand, had begun to look, if that was possible, more miserable than when Joyce had entered Florentino's. After the waiter had cleared the finished platter, she started crying.

'Joyce, I'm not happy. I'm tired. I'm frightened of the future and I'm old. Worse than all that, I'm lonely. Very lonely.'

Joyce thought: *Oh hell. Here we go* – and once again, as on the Friday outing to Carlton, Madge had caught Joyce unprepared. Although she was not wired to do feelings, she tried.

'No, no, no. You're a really lovely person who's got a lot of things going for you. Things I wish I had. You're educated, knowledgeable and you've got a good job. It's not that bad really.'

'I worry that you haven't forgiven me about last time. I didn't mean to scare you. I just misread about how you felt about things.'

'Pish tish make a wish. Ancient history. Forgiven and forgotten. Now tell me more about their veal and tuna.'

Madge reached out to grab Joyce's hand just as the waiter brought the next dish.

'Ladies. Your vitella tonnato. *Buon appetito!*'

In the meantime Joyce had pulled her hand away and disguised the fact by taking a plate from the waiter.

The meal continued with slabs of silence wedged between Madge's intermittent sobs and nose blowing and Joyce's insincere: 'Please don't cry,' and sincere lip-smacking: 'This dish is wonderful. I can see why you like Italian food.'

Now quite tearful, and having poured her heart out to Joyce, Madge poured what was left of the wine in the carafe into her glass and emptied it in one swig, She said, 'Do you remember we met near here on the Moratorium March? That was a day to remember, wasn't it? People power and all that. We all thought we could change the world. Well, I'm here to let you know that I've changed something. I'm moving to Sydney. Leaving tonight. Ergo the suitcase.'

'Just like that you're leaving for Sydney? Tonight?'

'Yes, by train. Tonight from Spencer Street. I wangled another job in Sydney. It's a university job and what's more, it's better paid than the one I'm leaving. Sydney's the place for me. I've been told that more than once. It's said they cater for girls like me up there.'

Madge picked up the menu, did a mental calculation of the additional price of a dessert and a coffee and added, 'Now promise me to have one of their desserts. I suggest, as it's Christmas, you must try the panettone with a coffee.'

'Yes, of course.'

'Well, I'm off now. On the *Spirit of Progress*. Eh! Spirit of bloody progress indeed! Just my sort of train, all spirit and all progress.'

'Why don't I go to the station with you?'

Sobbing some more. Madge said, 'I'd rather go alone from here but all the same, thank you for the offer.'

Madge then went to the cashier with her suitcase, deposited a bundle of notes and left the restaurant.

Joyce ordered her dessert and coffee, relieved that she had avoided being seen out in the open with a sobbing Madge dressed like a man. What would Clarrie have thought?

Joyce had hoped that was the end of Madge, and so it was but for three postcards that arrived over the next couple of months.

Postcard #1: A scene of Bondi Beach packed with people

My dear, dear and dearest Joyce,

Have arrived in Sydney safely. Sorry for my display at Florentino's. Chianti does that to me every time. I must admit I was more than a tad tipsy when I boarded the train and I cried all the way to Albury. Tired, emotional and chiantified?

MOST IMPORTANT: Once again I hope you can forgive me for my stupid behaviour at our farewell lunch.

Flat in Newtown (near the university) is smaller than my Carlton flat. And it's more expensive! The people at work at the uni are okay and I'm starting to settle into the job at hand. Please write to me. My address is …

Much love (with kisses and hugs) from little fat old me,

Madge

xxx

PS: I hope those other Nixons of yours aren't getting you down. And once again, please write to me.

Postcard #2: Night photograph Sydney Harbour Bridge lit up

Dear Joyce,

Although I haven't heard from you, I trust all is well with you (& your Nixonian brood).

Are you still attending party meetings? I suppose those bastards have already forgotten me. I hope you haven't forgotten me. As I said in my previous card, I'm adapting to life here. I suppose it doesn't matter where I am, I'm destined to be miserable. I pray you've forgiven me. I would like to hear from you so please write to me. In case you've lost it (ha ha ha) here's my address (again!) …

Much love,

Madge

x

PS: Still waiting for my fruit boxes of books to arrive. I feel naked (a dreadful sight at any time I'm sure!) without them.

Postcard #3: The Three Sisters in the Blue Mountains

Hello Joyce,

It's me again. I went to Katoomba (ergo this postcard) last weekend with some girls I've been meeting up with. We meet regularly in a café near the university. Café's okay but coffee's not as good as in Melbourne. The girls are postgrad students. Lots of fun and frolics, a real hoot. One of them, Germaine, is particularly nice. I rather like her. Can you believe it she prefers to be called Germs to Germaine? It was Germs who suggested the group getaway to the Blue Mountains (she has an aunt there). I think I'll be happy in Sydney after all.

All the best to you. I had better tootle off as there's cleaning work to be done around the flat. Imagine – me cleaning the flat! Can you believe it? Well that's a big change, isn't it? By the way, Germs is coming over for drinkies. She comes over every Tuesday evening. Sometimes she stays overnight.

Regards,

Madge

AFTER THE THIRD POSTCARD AND JOYCE'S THIRD NON-REPLY, NO MORE POSTCARDS ARRIVED FROM MADGE AND JOYCE BREATHED A SIGH OF RELIEF AND THANKED ME (AND BY NOW YOU KNOW WHO I AM) THAT IT WAS OVER.

The case of the disappearing husband

WHEN GYPSY WAS IN the seventh month of her pregnancy, Paddy O'Sullivan disappeared. I don't know what it was about the Nixons, but husbands of each generation vanished. Mr Nixon's father had gone out to the corner shop to buy tobacco and cigarette papers in 1933. He didn't reappear until 1962 and even then, it was without tobacco and cigarette papers. Well, I suppose by then he had no need for that paraphernalia as he was gasping with full-blown emphysema.

Now if, as I considered then, Paddy O'Sullivan was almost part of Mr Nixon's generation and neither Cliffy's nor mine, then he was the disappearing husband of a generation just ahead of Cliffy and me. I suppose without giving much away I can tell you that Cliffy became the Nixon family's disappearing husband of our generation. But more of that later, I promise.

When Paddy O'Sullivan disappeared, a near full-term Gypsy thought: *What the hell am I going to do now?* As it turned out, his leaving was the best thing that could have happened to her. Mr Nixon thought: *That bastard still owes me so much money!* – but the good part for him was that Paddy O'Sullivan's disappearance had given him a new someone to hate with a vengeance. Mrs Nixon thought, well, to be honest nobody really knew what she thought.

I thought: *Good riddance; he was far too old for you, Gypsy.* Cliffy on the other hand thought: *The disappearance of a Mr Paddy O'Sullivan is a mystery worth solving.* You see, Cliffy had always thought of himself not only as an alien hunter but also a cross between a detective and a spy.

Paddy disappeared not only owing Mr Nixon money but also owing lots of other people money – apparently owing money to some very dangerous people. We didn't know it at the time, but he had been cooking the books where he worked as the bookkeeper – cooking the books to his advantage. If that wasn't bad enough, he had a gambling problem. At the time of his disappearance he owed some of the seediest illegal gambling places in town a small fortune.

Now a question of his disappearance was whether he had disappeared by choice or whether the shady people from whom he had borrowed gambling money had organised his disappearance. Whatever the answer to this question, Cliffy said he would get to the bottom of it.

Looking back, I can see that Cliffy approached the mystery of Paddy's disappearance with a teenager's eye and teenager's limitations. For example, Cliffy was not in a position to follow up anything that led to the shady money-lending people. You see that no matter how important clues from that milieu might have been, Cliffy had no entrée into that world. Cliffy, however, being Cliffy, was not going to be stopped by such limitations. On the other hand, his obsession with aliens did not exclude for him the serious possibility that Paddy had been abducted by them: *Who knows? The bastard has probably returned to his people. And by that I mean his outer space people and not his supposedly Western District ones.*

'I'm going to find the bastard.'

'And then what, Cliffy? What then?'

'I haven't thought that far. I just want to find out where he's gone.'

And so began Cliffy's search for the missing Paddy O'Sullivan. With only a kid's resources, Cliffy was stuck for what he could do. He could look at newspapers, and so for weeks he scanned the newspapers to see if there were any clues – news of underworld hits, personal notices and obituary pages.

'Look, Cliffy he might not even be in the state. If it was me and I wanted to disappear, I'd try to get as far away from here as possible.'

'Point well made. I suppose I've got to expand my search. I'll get hold of back issues of interstate papers. They're at the library.'

'Ever thought he could be out of the country?'

'No way. I know he didn't have a passport because I heard Gypsy say he was too stingy to get one. And even if he did have a passport, he'd be too tight-fisted to buy tickets to go overseas. So he must still be in the country. But the question is – where?'

Cliffy's next approach was to try to think the way he thought Paddy might have thought, but being a kid he could only think like a kid.

'You know what I would have done?'

'What would you have done?'

'Well, as he doesn't have a car, and I don't even know if he has a licence, I would have hitched a lift to some place far from here.'

'Good thinking, Cliffy, but he could have taken a train, a bus or even a plane to get out of here.'

'No, all of those cost money and he would have been too mean to take any of those. He's too cheap. I'm sure he would have hitched out of here. Stands to reason. It's what I would've done.'

As Cliffy didn't have any money of his own, one night over dinner he tried to convince Mr and Mrs Nixon and Gypsy that they should place a notice in the papers asking if anyone had picked up a hitchhiker matching Paddy's particulars on the relevant date. He went as far as showing a crumpled scrap of paper where he had drafted the wording of a suitable notice. Needless to say, each in their own way thought it was a stupid idea.

'I am not spending any more money on that bloody sod!' yelled Mr Nixon.

'I don't know about a notice in the papers,' said Gypsy who was secretly warming to the identity of being the aggrieved and abandoned pregnant wife. On top of that she had taken to think of herself as a crossword puzzle that was still waiting to be solved. She had given Paddy all the clues – across and down – and he hadn't been able to complete her. She knew there was more to her than Paddy could ever discover. She had told him once in schoolgirl French

Je suis tres tres exotique. That last word she pronounced with an emphasis on the *teak* sounding part. To which Paddy had shrugged his shoulders and turned away, wondering why in God's name she was talking about teak. So if truth be known, then the truth was she would be happy if he never came back.

Mrs Nixon just opened and closed her mouth but whether she said or thought anything about it was unknown as she made no sound.

You would have thought their reactions might have dampened Cliffy's enthusiasm for the newspaper notice but no. He was never one to be daunted by negative feedback to what he believed was an excellent idea. Not having any money to pay for his newspaper notice was no impediment to him. Certainly not an obstacle while his mother persisted in leaving her purse lying around. *She's so careless, she deserves to have money taken from it.* So with the money he stole from his mother's purse, he placed a notice in *The Sun.*

Personally I had little confidence that people read those notices in the newspapers, let alone responded to them. So I was expecting it all to come to nothing. Well, I was wrong. The notice attracted the attention of a conman and attracted a grounding for Cliffy.

Mr Nixon took a call from a stranger calling about the notice. 'Is that the Nixon household?'

'What's it to you if it is or isn't and how did you get this number?'

'The notice. In *The Sun.* Mr Patrick O'Sullivan. His whereabouts and the like.'

'What about it?'

'Not so fast. I know where he is but it'll cost you some.'

'The turd has cost me enough money already so you, whoever you are, can bugger off!'

Mr Nixon then slammed down the receiver and went on the hunt for Cliffy.

So the notice didn't yield the desired result.

Cliffy, having excluded trains, buses and planes in favour of his hitchhiking theory, decided he would go to all the truck stops he knew. *I reckon he left by truck. You know, he did the books for a trucking company. He'd know the trucking world.*

The truck stops exercise yielded no results. To tell you the truth, I didn't think it would, but as I hinted before, once Cliffy decided on something you couldn't talk him out of it. You know, people used to call Cliffy an optimist and me a pessimist. I prefer to think that Cliffy was starry-eyed and I was a realist. Be that as it may, despite all Cliffy's theories and efforts, no Paddy O'Sullivan was found by Cliffy, or by anyone else for that matter. And so it rested.

Interestingly, the case of the missing Paddy O'Sullivan was sort of solved eventually by Cliffy. It happened by chance many years later when the adult Cliffy was planning a holiday up north. He was flicking through a travel brochure, and you know how those brochures have photos of hotels and their features. Well, this one was for a hotel casino complex in Queensland and who should be featured in a photo? A beaming Paddy O'Sullivan working as a croupier! Of course, it could have been a look-alike but we were all sure it was him, despite some of his face being hidden by an eyeshade croupiers wear. *That's him all right. Look at that snubby nose and podgy face. That's him all right!* The funny thing, though, was that by that time, it didn't matter where Paddy had disappeared to. Gypsy had remarried and was expecting her third child with her now not-so-new husband. Cliffy had other life mysteries to solve. I didn't care one way or another.

As for the senior Nixons? Well, by then Mrs Nixon had forgotten who Paddy had been. It only mattered to Mr Nixon. He still hated Paddy O'Sullivan with a vengeance and as he had started to swear more colourfully in his later years, all he said was, 'That cunt still owes me a lot of money. A lot of money indeed!'

Clifford Nixon aka Cliffy

APART FROM TELLING YOU a few small things about Clifford, Cliffy Nixon, I haven't told you much about Cliffy and me. Yes, I've told you about our time together when Melvin Marx was around and some other things, but do you know that for a long time we were like brothers. No, you wouldn't have got that yet. Well, let me tell you we were in each other's pockets from when we were five until we were just over thirty-five: thirty formative years. That's a long time. To tell you about Cliffy and me, I could work backwards from the time I heard he was dead. There, I've said what I didn't want to say. Now that wasn't as hard to say as I thought it would be. Come on let's hear it. Cliffy's dead. Cliffy's dead. Cliffy's dead! He's dead, dead, dead!!!

I could go forward from the time before we were introduced – from before we ever met and someone had mentioned a potential playmate called Cliffy. That day to me he was nothing other than an imagined Cliffy. That's one way to go but my memory of him doesn't work that way. My memories of him are all over the place, our times together now summed up by a jumble of scattered photos.

At the end, the very end … the very end is not a memory but a fact, so I can tell you that Cliffy died of the same disease that had killed his mother. I saw nothing of Cliffy's decline because by the time he died, we had not seen nor spoken with each other for over thirty years. Sorry, but once again I'm getting ahead of myself so let me back up a bit to before Cliffy died.

You might think it weird, given today's technology, despite all my searches after he had disappeared I could never find him; he had zero presence on any platform. For all I knew he might have been abducted by the aliens he was always looking for. Another upfront bit of information, although I hinted about this before, he was another of those Nixon family's disappearing husband.

As I said, we were like brothers of the same age but who aren't twins. I mean, in our times together we sometimes slept in the same bed. There were times when we had baths together. We'd sit on the toilet and talk to each other with the door open. We even had jerking-off races, ironically the winner being the one who came last; it was like the bible said: *So the last shall be first, and the first last: for many be called, but few chosen* – well, if that doesn't make you brothers, then what does?

The last time I saw Cliffy he was painting window frames at his house in Malvern Road. It was a house he had bought after he'd married and over time, he had painstakingly restored it. He was the one who taught me to use masking tape: *That way you won't get paint on the glass.*

In the past he would have scraped off the window frame's flaking old paint. He would have sanded back loose paint and used filler in the cracks: *If you want a good finish you've got to prepare it right.* That day there was no preparation, just dips of the brush into the tin and then straight on to the unprepared frame. He was in a hurry to get the job finished.

Two days after he had finished the windows, he left his wife, Zoe, and the kids. Two weeks after that he put the house up for sale. It was an exit strategy he had planned well. He'd masked his intention to leave. You'd have thought he would have told me, his almost-brother, what was going on. It caught me off-guard but most of all, it caught Zoe off-guard. He had prepared it all well in advance. Probably as far as he was concerned, he had finished off well.

After he left, he cut off all contact with anyone who had known him. He was uncontactable and all I could find out from Zoe was that he was living with a younger woman.

Once, many months after the Malvern Road house had been sold, I spoke to him. It was by accident. He answered the phone when I had called to see how Zoe was managing. I did that from time to time. He told me that he was there to take his kids out for the afternoon. No more was said. Maybe it was too awkward for both of us and anyhow, I was now part of everything he had left behind.

I went on, as anyone does. In time I lost contact with Zoe and the children. It was a slow drift away from each other. Not by intention; it just happened ever so slowly that we didn't notice. As for Cliffy? For years I wondered what had happened with him. Those who had been mutual friends knew as much or less than I did about the why and the where of his disappearance. Eventually I had my life to get on with, and anything to do with him was pushed into the background. That's not to say that from time to time I didn't do web searches for information about him. I searched for aliases I knew he had used in the past; I used variations of his name. I tried reversing the order of his names but in each case, the search came up with people who were not him.

One day many years later, I drove past the old Nixon house and there was Mr Nixon working his front garden. Old Clarrie Nixon, still alive and living at home. I had to stop and speak with him. He recognised me. He told me that he was ninety-seven and he was proudly fit as ever. He told me, 'As you can see, I haven't joined the slipper brigade of old shufflers yet and I don't intend to for a long time. I don't need anyone bothering me. Do my own looking after yours truly … all by myself … cleaning the house and the gardening.'

I learnt from him that Mrs Nixon had died years earlier and he had later remarried.

As for Mr Nixon's second wife? According to him, 'The slut turned out to be a real bitch. She tried to kill me. In the end I had to kick her out.'

Then, and I must admit it threw me, this ninety-seven year old man, said, 'Though to tell you the truth, I do miss the sex. Jeez, I miss that with a passion.' I recalled what Cliffy had told me years ago about a summer's evening when he had overheard a conversation between his father and Paddy about sex. This latest revelation did not gel with what Mr Nixon had said then. I suppose Mr Nixon must have got hornier in his old age, or perhaps he was lying then, now or on both occasions.

I asked if Mr Nixon knew anything about Cliffy. He replied, 'That shit. He's crazy just like his mother. She croaked with the Alzheimer's, you know, and I reckon he's got it too. And as for that spineless sister of his, Gypsy, she's a piece of work. No, nowadays I don't have anything to do with either of them. They tried to have me put away in an old people's home, you know. They were just after this house. With the market being as it is, this house is worth a packet now. You see, they wanted to get their grubby hands on this house. Get their hands on it even before I've carked it. The cunts. They're not getting it before I'm dead … or after. I convinced the powers that be that I'm okay looking after myself here and here I'll stay until I die. Do you know I do everything here myself and I'm ninety-seven. Ninety-seven! You wouldn't credit it. Bet you couldn't tell that just by looking at me, could you? If Gypsy and Cliffy think that they're getting the house after I'm dead, they're got a big surprise coming. They're getting nothing. Not this house, not even a brass razoo. I've gone and changed my will and left the house to my niece Meg and to that fat half-wit Asparagus – you know, Joyce's sister Lizzie's boy. I've left it to them in equal shares with the proviso that they can't sell it for at least fifteen years after I'm dead. I put in that proviso to get up Gypsy's and Cliffy's noses every day for at least fifteen years. Fifteen years will probably see Cliffy out, maybe even fewer years in his case.' Mr Nixon then broke out in a laugh.

CAULFIELD HOSPITAL

Assessment suitability to return and remain at home

Draft Report

Patient: Mr Clarence Nixon, Ward 3 North

Assessment Panel:

Social Workers: Dr Maxine Jones, Jenny Wong, Sanjay Ghosal

Gerontologists: Dr Sam Horowitz, Dr Amanda Clarke

Aged Care Nurses: Bronwyn Sutton, Allison Doyle

The patient, Mr Clarence Nixon, was interviewed and assessed prior to discharge following a fall at his home. Mr Nixon is a widower and not long separated from his much younger second wife. He reported that there was no possibility of reconciliation with his wife.

At the time of this assessment Mr Nixon was aged ninety-three and living alone at his home. His two adult children, from his first marriage, have expressed concern about him living alone at the home he has occupied for the last sixty years. His children have also raised questions regarding his mental capacity and level of insight about his age and physical condition. It should be noted that nursing staff reported that Mr Nixon has been a vexatious patient while in hospital.

At the interview Mr Nixon appeared as a 'feisty and bristly' elderly man who was well aware of his situation. He presented as alert and cognitively capable. He was able to coherently converse with the panel and was able to answer the standard test questions satisfactorily.

As for the fall that resulted in his hospitalisation, he angrily maintained that it was caused by tripping over the small companion dog his separated wife had abandoned when she left. He has since surrendered the dog to an animal rescue centre. Mr Nixon claimed that his fall had nothing to do with his age and physical state.

Mr Nixon presents as being in exceptionally good physical condition for a man of his age. Indeed, hospital records of his vital indices suggest the physical condition of a man in his mid to late sixties.

Up to the time of his fall, Mr Nixon had taken care of himself. Evidently he cooked all his meals, showered himself and did his own house cleaning; by all accounts his house is well maintained. He has had, and continues to have, many recreational passions, his current passion being oriental lilies. He told the panel that he spends a great proportion of his day working in his garden and apart from lawn mowing, of which he reported there is very little, he does his own gardening. To quote him using our recollection of his own words, 'Listen to me, you geniuses. Just listen to me. What's with all this questionising (sic)? I'll tell you this and listen well. I refuse to be a bench warmer in some old people's home. So I'm telling you clearly that I'll be going home as soon as possible if you don't bloody well mind.'

The panel concluded that Mr Nixon was capable of living at home and he should be permitted to continue at home, but it is recommended that periodic visits from the visiting aged care team should occur.

Additional Information

Mr Nixon's adult children (Mrs Noelene Davis and Mr Clifford Nixon) were interviewed previously. At their interview they voiced concern about Mr Nixon's physical abilities and especially his mental state. Initially they were adamant that he should be placed in the care of a nursing home. They changed their minds, however, when it was explained that such a move would require the sale of Mr Nixon's family home to fund his placement in care. They were both adamant that under no circumstances should Mr Nixon's family home be sold to finance any nursing home accommodation for Mr Nixon.

I had believed everything Mr Nixon had said when we talked in his front garden. Everything except Cliffy having Alzheimer's. After all, it was something a vindictive, hate-harbouring, hate-loving old bastard like Mr Nixon would say, wouldn't it? Just look at how he structured his will just to get at his children. Perhaps, along with his former second wife and Paddy O'Sullivan, Cliffy and Gypsy had joined the ranks of people Mr Nixon loved to hate with a relished vengeance. It left me wondering whether the passionate hating had allowed Mr Nixon to live so long. Perhaps WC Fields was thinking of someone like Mr Nixon when he said: *I am free of all prejudices. I hate everyone equally.*

Not long ago a tragic thing happened. A young man was killed in a spectacular car accident. The evening news reported how a speeding car had, without any obvious reason, swerved into a lamppost and burst into flames. The next day the newspapers ran with the story. It turned out that the young man had been Cliffy's oldest son. Almost as a postscript it was noted that the son had been close to his father and had not recovered emotionally from his father's death six months earlier. As it turned out, Cliffy had spent his last few years in a nursing home in Western Australia where he died of Alzheimer's. So Mr Nixon had been telling the truth.

On the morning of the day Clifford Owen Nixon died, he looked at his face in the mirror and though there was a touch of familiarity about it, he didn't recognise the face looking back at him. Mean eyes and thin lips. Who was that man? Maybe it was that bastard, his father, then again, maybe not. No matter, he thought, sooner or later someone would be coming around with the lunch tray so there's time for a small nap.

Epilogue

Well, there it is. The Nixons and others. I suppose I've been a cannibal. I've fed off their lives. Dined on all of them – the Nixons, Paddy O'Sullivan, Melvin Marx, Asparagus and Madge – but I had to tell you about the sweetness of being young with them. It was a time when so many exciting possibilities lay ahead for Cliffy and me and everything good seemed within grasp.